D0261622

Motherland

Motherland

JO McMILLAN

JOHN MURRAY

First published in Great Britain in 2015 by John Murray (Publishers)
An Hachette UK Company

1

© Joanna McMillan 2015

The right of Joanna McMillan to be identified as the Author of the Work has been asserted
by her in accordance with the Copyright, Designs and Patents Act 1988.

All rights reserved. Apart from any use permitted under UK copyright law
no part of this publication may be reproduced, stored in a retrieval system, or
transmitted, in any form or by any means without the prior written permission
of the publisher, nor be otherwise circulated in any form of binding or cover
other than that in which it is published and without a similar condition
being imposed on the subsequent purchaser.

Motherland is a work of fiction. Characters, events and place names are products of the
author's imagination, or, if real, not necessarily portrayed with geographical and historical
accuracy.

A CIP catalogue record for this title is available from the British Library

Hardback ISBN 978-1-47361-199-3
Trade paperback ISBN 978-1-47361-200-6
Ebook ISBN 978-1-47361-201-3

Typeset in Bembo 12.25/15 pt by Palimpsest Book Production Limited,
Falkirk, Stirlingshire

Printed and bound by CPI Group (UK) Ltd, Croydon, CR0 4YY

John Murray policy is to use papers that are natural, renewable and recyclable products and
made from wood grown in sustainable forests. The logging and manufacturing processes
are expected to conform to the environmental regulations of the country of origin.

John Murray (Publishers)
Carmelite House
50 Victoria Embankment
London EC4Y 0DZ

www.johnmurray.co.uk

For Guy

TOWER HAMLETS LIBRARIES	
91000004688552	
Bertrams	08/07/2015
GEN	£16.99
THISCA	TH15000295

Ach, wir
Die wir den Boden bereiten wollten für Freundlichkeit
Konnten selber nicht freundlich sein.

Bertolt Brecht
'*An die Nachgeborenen*'

Oh, we
Who wanted to prepare the ground for friendliness
Could not ourselves be friendly.

Bertolt Brecht
'To Those Born Later'

I

Selling the *Morning Star*

It was never going to be easy selling socialism to a town like
Tamworth. But here we were again pulling Saturday *Morning
Stars* from our Co-op carrier bags. My mum filled her lungs
with shopping precinct air – hot, sour and bloody from the
butchers. She hauled her breath so hard you could hear it. It
was the kind of last gasp you took as your ship went down.

'The truth, the whole truth and nothing but the truth! *Morning
Star!*'

Middle Entry precinct rang with shoppers shopping, with
the click-clack of round bodies on sharp heels. I knew these
women from every Saturday with their orange perms feathered
at the neck, the sheen and clash of rayon, and glasses that made
marbles of their eyes.

'All right, bab.'

'All right.'

'How's the babby?'

'The babby's doing all right, bab, ta very much.' Which was
the update on the new great-grandchild. They tipped round
shoulders and beaked at each other's trolleys, clawed at the
multi-pack nappies and milk formula and now, just after Easter,
at the half-price eggs which, with a bit of luck, should still be
good for next year. And the babby'll have teeth by then.

'*Morning Star!* Twelve pence and cheap at the price.'

Tamworth loved a bargain. Shop windows fluoresced with

offers, spelt as they sounded, the lettering unplanned. And Tamworth bought in bulk. People with a car drove to the industrial estate and filled the boot at the Cash & Carry. Everyone else wheeled a trolley round the market, laying up supplies for a rainy day. My mum and I did too, except we shopped for Armageddon, for the day the Americans pressed the button and started World War Three. Our kitchen cupboards were full of the packets and tins that would see us through the End of the World and ever having to cook.

Now the church struck noon. St Editha's counted out every quarter-hour of Tamworth time. There'd been four hundred and forty thousand of them so far – rounding down for the sake of morale. But we had three clocks on our living-room wall set to Havana, Moscow and Hanoi time. At home, I lived in any zone I wanted of the Eastern Bloc.

'On sale for one hour only! *Morning Star!*'

Most weeks, someone with a strut and a smirk winked at us and called 'Morning!' back. Or they made a show of checking their watch and told us it was the afternoon.

'Only ten copies left! Hurry, hurry!'

There was no rush, even though the whole town was in town. Or nearly. The posh Tammies were in Lichfield and Ashby sniffing antiques and plants for the patio. But the old Tammies were here, the ones who lived in red-brick terraces with dangerous wiring and wallpaper their grandfathers had hung. And the new Tammies, the Birmingham Overspill, who lived in cul-de-sacs with spillage in the name: Redlake, Seaton, Waveney, Purbrook.

Now my mum spotted a pupil. 'Mandi-with-an-i. Ex, but only just.' She waved so wide the whole precinct thought she knew them. My mum was primed for pupils. She spotted them a mile off and knew all their names. She taught in a school in the Warwickshire coalfields where hundreds of children came from a handful of families, dishing out maps of the world to pupils who never left the village. Or if they did, it was to take the bus all the way to Tamworth for a shopping expedition. Mandi came over with a baby in a buggy, and a toddler trailing Smarties on the floor.

'I didn't know!' my mum said to the pale lump squashed into the pushchair. The chewing gum was called Darren. Four months old.

'This your daughter, Miss? Looks like you, don't she, Miss.'

My mum did chit-chat about babies and breastfeeding. She nudged me in the ribs. She'd never have been milked to nothing at the hospital if I'd been able to keep up with production. Her chest size was all my fault. She made Mandi laugh and made an easy sale. She was good at hearts-and-minds, my mum. 'Hearts, anyway,' she always said. Sometimes, when she was feeling maudlin, she said, 'I'm the queen of hearts,' because according to the song, 'To the queen of hearts is the ace of sorrow, he's here today, he's gone tomorrow.' Which was true. My dad didn't die the day after they'd met, but he wasn't around for long. And anyone who'd come after had only ever stayed one night.

My mum called out, 'Only nine left! Hurry or you'll miss it! *Morning Star!*' Our voices swelled under the Perspex roof. It was why we chose the pitch – to sound mass, my mum said, because that was the point, the masses, and to be here every week regardless of the weather. She checked the front page. 'Carter shelves neutron bomb! No modernising Lance!' Whoever he was. The neutron bomb wasn't actually today's headline, but it was catchier than 'Tory brew stinks of apartheid'. And my mum was big on peace, and she was big on people. And on people being peaceful. On being nice. Not killing each other, if possible.

But there was no rush to ban the bomb.

Maybe Tamworth didn't mind. After the neutron bomb, the town would still look like its picture postcards: St Editha's, the Riverside Flats, the Castle, the Castle Pleasure Grounds where geese padded about near the crazy golf, hoping for crusts from the crazy golfers. My mum puffed with the effort and the heat.

3

She blew air down her front. It was baking for April, the first hot day for as long as I could remember. She pulled off her sweater and tied it round her waist. Underneath, what she had on yesterday: a *Sixty Years of Socialism* T-shirt, the red turned pink, the hammer and sickle flaking because of Co-op own-brand powder. The T-shirt clung to her chest. You couldn't help noticing how flat it was, and skinny enough to count the ribs.

Sometimes, in front of the bathroom mirror, when my mum did a demi-plié for a dibble with her colour-coded flannels, she said she had a ballet dancer's body. When she was eight, my mum wanted to be a ballet dancer. It was just after the war, and in 1945 anything seemed possible – even for a girl from Bermondsey who spent the first years of her life sleeping in the bottom drawer of the bedroom chest. Even for the daughter of a cabbie and a cook. And later, she wanted to be a diplomat and tour the world for peace. But she didn't have a chance, not with a Saturday job in Woolies, schoolgirl French and no idea of cunning.

Now she tugged the T-shirt from her trousers and flapped air up at the waist. She looked at her belly. It was white and empty. We hadn't had anything since breakfast. We'd been up since seven, which was two in the afternoon on Hanoi time and how we put it to give ourselves a lie-in. We'd eaten the usual as usual – boiled eggs and soldiers, three-and-a-half minutes, Soviet soldiers. All morning, we'd sat in our pyjamas at the living-room table and ploughed through TODOs. Today, it was minutes: Campaign for Nuclear Disarmament, National Union of Teachers, Communist Party. I'd dictated from my mum's jumbo pad, the pages dug deep with her oversized blackboard hand. My mum didn't actually need me. She could touch-type. She could even type and talk – have one sentence coming out of her fingers and another out of her mouth. But it was quicker if I read her notes back to her, just short of speaking speed and dropped a few tones, like a 45 set to 33. And being quick mattered because there was always the question of Time. "'Man's dearest possession",' my mum said. Which wasn't true. And she knew she was misquoting. *Life* was actually man's dearest possession. But Life was measured by Time, and there was never enough of it. So I read, and my mum's hands flew across the keyboard, and our house filled with the sound of the alphabet punching paper – landing softer blows since we'd got an electric. And in the background, *Tiswas* murmured through the wall from Ron and Reg's.

Now I nudged my mum. The butcher was throwing us dirty glances across his polished glass – which he did every week, but these looks were especially lethal. He'd probably spotted her hammer and sickle. He had a Union Jack in his window, and sold English meat to English people who cooked English food. Today he had an offer on Lichfield lamb. In this town, they killed and ate their own. He shook his head at us, dipping bloody fingers into a tray fringed with fake green lawn. He tossed a joint into the air, onto the scales, and stared at us as he sharpened his knife. I tugged my mum's T-shirt. She knew what I meant. She'd have loved to head to the Co-op café for a sit-down and some fuel. At our elbows, speechless parents and boys who'd make genital sculptures from their sausage and mash. But, 'quarter of an hour yet, Jess'. My mum never gave up early. My mum never gave up. Sometimes towards the end of the hour, she wound down like a gramophone and let the vowels slide, aiming her pitch at the butcher's as the 'Moan 'n Stare'. Most weeks, though, she tailed off with a song, sung in a half-voice because of the boom of the roof, taking her cue from the news. Now I heard her run through a first verse, checking she had all the words: '"Don't you hear the H-bomb's thunder, echo like the crack of doom? While they rend the skies asunder, fallout makes the earth a tomb . . ."'

But that was as far as she got because a man came out of the butcher's and lumbered over to us, see-sawing his weight between wide-set legs, his dead meat swinging in a carrier bag. He was neckless, pointy-headed, monumental, and tall

5

and close enough to cut out all our light. 'I'll buy one of them off you.'

'Pardon?' My mum hadn't expected it. Neither had I. He didn't look like a *Morning Star* reader. But then not many people did.

'I'll have one of them papers.' His face was engraved with politeness, but I didn't like the look of him – the beige shirt blotched black with sweat, the pock-marked skin that fifty years ago must have weathered acne. But my mum didn't notice. She did maracas. 'Here we go, Jess! Two down! Good-oh!'

The man took a copy and held it at arm's length, leafing through it, showing us his knuckles mossy with hair. I thought he looked familiar, but then everyone in Tamworth did. Everyone knew everyone and everyone was related. Even though the town was famous for its railway junction. Lines ran north–south and east–west, which meant you could leave Tamworth in any direction you wanted, but hardly anyone did. You were born here, married here, and you died here. And that's when I placed him. This man worked at the Co-op Funeral Service, the one with the sign that said *Our Limousines Are Available For Weddings*. I'd see him on the way to school. Some mornings he swung an arm around the window, hanging a sign for a bargain burial, or replacing the flowers – fresh lilies for dead ones, when dead was surely the point.

Now he reached the back page and skimmed Cayton's tips for Newbury and the winners at Kempton. He rolled up his *Star* and tucked it under an arm. 'It must be hard for you trying to flog this.' Actually, every Saturday we cleared all ten because we put the unsolds around the Co-op Furniture Department – on nests of tables and bedside cabinets, on three-seater suites, sideboards, pouffes and garden-loungers, as if every modern home took the paper. Sometimes we went back at the end of the day to see if the *Stars* were still there. They never were, which my mum took as proof. 'The paper needs the money,' she said. 'It doesn't matter who pays for them as long as we get the message out. As long as it's read.'

The man toppled his weight towards us, his stubby feet in socks and sandals. 'You know, I pity you. Here you are every week and no one's the least bit interested. Everyone's against you.'

'Not *no one*. Not *everyone*.'

'In this town, all people want is the *Herald*.'

We took the *Tamworth Herald* too to see if they'd published our letters. We wrote every week to the editor – about peace, unemployment, racism. And because we've got to stay in touch, my mum said, with how real people live. Sometimes she said 'real', sometimes 'working class'. What she meant was: we have to know who they are, these people who should be on our side, but aren't yet.

The man said, 'All you need's the *Herald* and a hobby. Them's enough to fill your time.' Because that's what you did with Time in this town: filled it. Because you weren't born with a life, but a giant hole. Though actually what the man said was: 'the *Erald* and an obby'. Everyone in Tamworth had a hobby-without-an-h: ome-brewing, up-olstery, istory. And especially istory. The town loved itself for it. We went back to Offa and his dyke and right back to the Romans. Watling Street ran through the town. My mum took it to work, which was handy because she was often under-slept and the A5 was straight and didn't need steering.

Now the man looked us up and down. He flicked his eyes between us and found the likeness – the same face, the same build. We were the same person except for twenty-eight years and half an inch. 'Runs in the family, I take it.' Which was true. We came from a long line of dead communists: my grandparents, great-uncles and aunts. Even my dad, who joined the Communist Party before he was old enough – they let him in early he was so keen. And he died before he was old enough too, and they let him in early there. Wherever that was: heaven, hell, limbo, in a tin in my mum's knicker drawer. Our whole family was Jewish or Scottish, on the run from Hitler or the midges. One branch ended up in the East End, near Cable

7

Street. They sent their children to the International Brigades and lost them all in Spain. Some of my family were locked up in Franco's prison camps and had their skulls measured for the fascists. My nan spent the Second World War making jumpers for the Red Army. The whole country had knitted for Stalin. Then after the war, my mum joined the Young Communist League and sold *Challenge* down the docks. She had a long history of flogging unpopular papers.

The man reached round and felt in his back pocket. 'How much do I owe you?'

'Just have it,' my mum said. 'Present. I'm just glad if it's read.'

When he brought back his hand, it held a lighter. He ran a thick thumb over the flint, the nail cloudy and probably dead. It took a few goes. Then the cough of ignition and the tip of the flame tonguing the air. He held it against the paper. A corner crept from yellow to brown to black. But the fire wouldn't take. He had to fan the *Star* and force the flames to chew their way through the news. Then he fanned it under our nose. The air above the paper wavered with the heat. I looked across to the butcher's, where phantom figures jeered. He said, 'That's what we did in them olden days when there were trouble. Burned it.'

By now a crowd had gathered. People wondered at a distance if it was bad enough for 999. They repeated the telly safety ad: *get down, roll over, call help*. A story drifted over about a neighbour who'd died after home-made doughnuts. He put water on a chip pan and could only be identified from his teeth. I glanced at my mum. Her mouth was clamped shut, her eyes closed and tears forming. I wasn't sure what kind they were – chemical ones or sadness. My mum was full of water, even more than they said in the biology book. Just the *Nine O'Clock News* could bring it on – tears flicked onto the living-room tiles where they took a long time to dry. And all the while her hands tore at each other, leaving white flecks in her lap.

Now my mum felt for my hand. She wove our fingers together,

8

fixing us to the spot. Through closed lips so as not to inhale, 'Just think of the guerrillas. Think of the Vietnamese.' So I shut my eyes and thought: whole villages turned to smoke and the air sucked from the sky. Tarred bodies, the water boiled out of them, and a girl, naked, full of ribs, skin falling off, her arms like broken wings.

When I opened my eyes, the man was gone. White flakes had settled on my shoes. It was Tamworth and hot and April, but that could have been snow. My mum picked the paper from her hair and dusted down her Soviet chest. On the floor, what remained of the news – the neutron bomb, the Tory brew – fingered the air as if it were alive. I turned to my mum and looked up half an inch to a face full of ash and angles, to her insurmountable bones. The sun poured down, taking away her colours, turning her black and white – her complicated face made simple.

'Can we go home now?'

'Or the Co-op? You hungry?'

I felt sick. 'What we going to do?'

My mum slipped an arm around my waist and pulled me to her, joining us at the hip. 'We're going to soldier on, Jess. You know that. We'll. Just. Soldier. On.'

2

In Loco Parentis

Tamworth, April 1978

My mum forgot all about The Burning. She didn't mention it again. It was as if it had never happened. But the smell had stayed with me all weekend, and it was still here now as I waited outside the headmistress's office, watching Miss Downing struggle for keys under her gown. Things like that took a while when you only had one arm. Over her head, the gold-lettered memorial to the Grammar School boys who'd died twice for King and Country. I stood in the smell of burnt *Star* and leftover sponge and custard while silent women with hairnets and no names flitted about between banks of steam and giant tubs of steel. *For what we are about to receive, may the Lord make us truly thankful.* Even the dinner ladies stopped work to pray for that.

The headmistress had just careened into History, ignored the teacher, and steered over to the map of Anglo-Saxon Tamworth. She'd held out her arm and tracked the purple line that encircled the town. 'Offa's Rampart has protected us from all the people who have ever wanted to destroy our way of life. And who are they?'

Hands had shot into the air.

'The Danes.'

'The Vikings.'

'The Jutes.'

'The Normans.'

'The Russians.' That got a laugh.

'Jessica.'

I'd looked blankly at the headmistress. I wondered why she was telling me my name. '*You*, Jessica Mitchell, are to come with me.'

Now Miss Downing threw open her door. She made straight for an easy chair and tipped her bulk into it. She fell the last few inches, her feet leaving the floor. Her shoes had a deep tread that had made tracks in the pile of the carpet. I'd never seen the headmistress from this angle, the top of her head a skein of gunmetal grey. Usually, she was several feet above us, addressing the school as if extracts from *The Christian Assembly* were oratory, compensating for the missing arm with wide arcs of the other one.

She invited me down to the opposite chair. I propped myself on the edge and resisted the tilt that was intended to put me at ease.

'Are you sitting comfortably?' Which made me uncomfortable because I knew this wouldn't be *Listen with Mother*. 'So, Jessica. Why do you think I've called you here?'

And that sounded like a trap.

'I don't know, Miss.'

'No idea at all?'

'Is it good or bad?'

'I'd say it's good. It's good, and timely, that we're going to have a talk.'

Which still sounded like a trap.

There were two glasses and a jug of water on the coffee table. Miss Downing filled them both, re-settled herself, and placed her arm on an armrest. No one knew what had happened to the other one except it'd been lost honourably – rumour had it in the war. She would never have lost it carelessly. And certainly not genetically.

'Tell me about your mother.'

'My *mum?*'

Silence. Through the door came the muted version of *The Planets*. The music teacher beat phrases from Mars on the piano. The school orchestra hammered them back. Miss Downing waited. She arranged her gown. Underneath, a black suit – the headmistress was always in shades of black – the large matt buttons riveting her chest.

'She works, doesn't she?'

'She's a teacher.'

She gave the kind of nod which meant she knew that already. 'Which means she's out all day.'

There was something in her tone that made me say, 'Not *all* day. She comes home at night.' Which didn't sound how I meant it to. So I added, 'She's there when I get home.'

Miss Downing's face was blank in a way that said that wasn't true. 'There are, of course, extenuating circumstances.'

I didn't know what that meant. 'What are they?'

'Your father.'

'He's dead.'

'I'm aware of that. I know there's no father at home.'

It was a strange way to put it: not *at home*. As if my dad might come back one day. I'd dash in from school, raid the kitchen, grab the Wagon Wheels, and there he'd be, resurrected on the sofa, an arm along the back of the cushions, just like the picture my mum kept with the ashes. Miss Downing waited for more about my father. I looked away. I checked the kit on her desk – the bells, keys, whistles, Bibles, the ruler that meas-ured her blotting pad, but only imperially. In the end, she said, 'Cancer, wasn't it?'

Everyone knew. It was on my file. School secretaries held it in their fingertips as if cancer were contagious. I caught them sometimes thinking things behind their eyes because no good ever came of no father.

The way my mum told it, my dad woke up one morning, put a hand on her belly and felt the bump. Then he went to the bathroom, combed his hair in the mirror and found a bump there too. A month later, he was dead. I went to the funeral inside my mum. 'You were inches apart,' she liked to say. 'One in a coffin, one in a womb. Each just the other side of life.'

Miss Downing said, 'It must have been hard for your mother.'

'Yes, Miss. It was.' Which wasn't true. I said it for sympathy. To make up for the fact that my mum was a teacher and out all day. But, actually, according to my mum, it wasn't that bad. She was convinced my dad would get better till the day he died. She sat by his bed and made plans for the future till a nurse took her hand and told her he'd stopped breathing. It meant she never said goodbye. Not to his face. Which was probably a good thing, because for my mum, 'goodbye' wasn't a word. It was a drama – a hug and a kiss on the cheek, your hand cupped between hers, squeezed, shaken, given back finger by finger. My mum's long goodbye might have been more than my dad could take.

'And she's never remarried, has she? Your mother's alone.'

'She's not *alone*. *I* live with her. She lives with me.'

'I mean a stepfather. Or similar.'

No, my mum didn't have a similar. No time to look. And anyway, no point. Not in Tamworth.

'And other family?'

'They're dead too.'

'That's untrue, Jessica. And unkind. Your grandmother is still alive.'

How did Miss Downing know about the Granma?

'But I gather she's not terribly close.'

'Weymouth.'

'I mean family ties.'

The Granma prayed for us. When my dad suddenly died, she converted to dieting, then to a low-draw, high-intensity church with a synthesised religion and its own upbeat hymns that she tapped out on the organ. She lived in a pebble-dashed house

13

with a mahogany crucifix and a vase of yellow roses she'd somehow proofed against wilting.

'So to all intents and purposes, the only family you have is Mother.' Miss Downing manoeuvred for her glass and took a sip. 'And I'm aware of her leanings.' Which made me lean forward because I wasn't sure what she meant. 'Her communist beliefs. Card-carrying. Chronic.' As if they were a medical condition. 'You know, you have a mind of your own. You don't have to do what your mother does. You're old enough to think for yourself.'

'I *do* think. And I like it. It's what we do. It's what we do, and I like it.' Which didn't sound as convincing as I'd hoped. So I added, 'It's important to get the message out.'

'Which is?'

I thought there were probably lots of messages, so I said, 'Whatever's on the front of the *Morning Star*.'

Miss Downing slid fingers inside her gown and stroked the empty sleeve that was stitched into a pocket. I watched the turn of the wrist – thick with campanology. Handbells had got her into the *Herald*. 'You see, I'm concerned, Jessica. Your mother's politics are not very . . . *English*. Who knows where things like that fracas might lead.'

It took a moment to link 'that fracas' with The Burning. 'I didn't see you in Middle Entry.'

'That's because I wasn't there. But you live rather large – you and your mother – in a town that talks. I was informed. And fracas are to be expected if one peddles subversion in a town like Tamworth.'

'But it was Saturday. I'm free on Saturdays.'

'You represent this school every day of the week. You are *never* free of the Grammar School.' Miss Downing tipped her nostrils at me, the fine down metering her breath. 'This school is, in every case, in loco parentis. And we've established that in your case even more so.' What she meant was: with a dead father and a communist mother, I was as good as orphaned.

Then she turned to my friends. 'I imagine you find it harder than most to make them.'

From time to time, I found someone trying to tag along – the school's Jehovah's Witness, who skulked around the cloak-room, slipping *The Watchtower* into blazer pockets; the girl whose mum had run off with a lover and whose dad had taken to drink; the prefect exposed in the *Herald* and expelled from school for running round the Castle Pleasure Grounds in his sister's underwear. It was only the unloved, unwashed and unac-countable who ever tried to make friends with me. But it was like my mum said: 'Friends are hard to come by in a town like this. There's just no *basis*.' And anyway no point. They took up time. You had to maintain them. We liked people, my mum and I, but we just couldn't fit them in. Apart, maybe, from Rosie.

'There's my mum's friend, Rosie.' She taught Drama, supply, to the Overspill. It meant she mostly stayed at home and made candles for The Movement, or swung in her hammock folding CND newsletters, or reading broken-backed books, the smoke from Cuban cigars curling blue against the ceiling. She was bored of Tamworth – she'd told me often enough – but instead of getting on a train, she dreamt her way out of town – onto any old country road in *Waiting for Godot*, or into the asylum in *One Flew Over the Cuckoo's Nest*.

Miss Downing said, 'And Rosemary's a good friend, I take it.'

'My mum says she's a brick.' Actually, she said: There might be a lack of analysis, but there's no doubting she's a brick.

'And *your* friends?'

'Rosie's also my friend.'

'Among your peers.'

My peers thought 'the class system' had something to do with school timetables. They thought Lenin was a member of the Beatles.

'Your peers, such as . . .'

I glanced at the floor. The carpet was flattened by the feet of other interviews. I slid my shoes about, trying to rustle up the pile.

'. . . such as Rebecca Caldor. You sit next to her in class, don't you?'

Sitting next to her, I'd had time to study her sideways-on. I knew her hands so well I could draw them from memory: the neat hem of the nails, the fall of the freckles across the knuckles. I'd have known her in the dark just from her shampoo – over-laid lately by some kind of quiet perfume. Because I sat next to her, I didn't often fall into her line of sight, but when I did, I got that distant look. I was so out of focus I might as well not have been there.

'She's invited you home, I believe. For a birthday party. And how was that?'

I'd eaten cakes. Made from scratch. Till then, they'd always come from Greggs the Bakers or a Co-op packet. The front door had opened to Mrs Caldor waving a floury hand at me. From the other side of the house I caught the babble of girls excited to be on the brink of teenage. 'Shoes, please,' Rebecca had said. Which meant: take them off. I waited in the hall for the smell to die down. On the wall, antique engravings of Tamworth, Staffordshire dogs, a pistol that a Frances Caldor had taken to the Crimea. There was even a visitors' book. All the girls in my class had signed it. Rebecca was the first to turn thirteen. She said I had to come to the party because *everyone* would be there, and the idea of everyone-except-me meant I went.

Afterwards, Rebecca had said, 'My mother wants to know if you ever look in the mirror.'

'Our mirror's bent.' We'd guessed where to drill the holes, filled the mistakes with toilet paper and run out of places to put the screws.

'Which would explain why you're so unkempt.'

'What's unkempt?'

'It means you're dirty.'

I didn't know what to say. I knew I was sometimes dirty. But you had to be dirty in order to clean yourself. That was the point.

Rebecca said, 'You know what cleanliness is next to, don't you?'

Which was another good reason not to wash.

Now Miss Downing lurched as if her seat had hit uneven ground. She propelled herself upright and chevroned a path round the back of my chair, trailing Coal Tar Soap. I remembered it from my nan, years and years ago. I hadn't expected the headmistress to smell of a kind old lady in Streatham who'd fed me rice pudding with the skin on and knitted for the Soviets. For a moment, it almost made me like her. She stopped by the wall of photos. There was one for every year she'd led the school. We were all there, panorama-ed in the playground, regiments of us in Anglo-Saxon tunics. 'Your peers, Jessica.' She signalled me over. Her finger moved from face to face. She named the girls in my class and told me how every Saturday they did something improving – led the town's wind band, breast-stroked their way to local glory, Guided Girls.

'And there's me, look, selling the *Morning Star*. Making a spectacle of myself. Shaming the school.'

It just came out. For completeness.

There was a pause, long enough to make me turn to her. I took in the neck wired with veins, the rustle of her gown, the flash of insignia on her lapel. Then I felt something sharp slam into the back of my hand. For a moment, my body was baffled. And then the pain hit. It rolled across my knuckles and drove up my arm. I cradled my hand to keep the pieces together. I was afraid the headmistress had broken my bones.

'Just what that *milieu* encourages. Promise you will never talk back like that again.'

I couldn't speak. I dug teeth into my lip, willing myself not to cry. The pain ebbed from my hand and lodged behind my eyes. I felt the pressure build. Miss Downing's edges blurred.

'Answer me.'

'No, Miss.'

'Pardon?'

'Yes, Miss.'

And she put the ruler down. 'I am in loco parentis. Doing my job. One day you'll look back on this and thank me.' She held out her arm, already reaching for gratitude. I couldn't move my right hand, so I gave her the left and made an awkward jab of a handshake. Her skin was cold, the fingers unbending. 'I took you out of History.' She glanced at her clock. 'In this half-hour you will have missed decades.'

Which was the trouble with history. Sometimes whole chunks of it just passed you by.

At the end of the afternoon, when the school-bell sounded, I was first out of the gate. Running went straight to my hand, so I speed-walked home. Next door, Mr Howard sat at his front-room window, his shiny head trophied on the sill. I tried not to see him. He'd come out and talk – about the heat, the hosepipes, the colour of his bowling-club green. But he must have seen my failed duck because he just nodded and mouthed through the glass, 'All right, Jess.'

I found a warm cup of tea on the living-room table and a half-eaten piece of toast. My mum had left me a note: *In and then out again. Back . . . depends. Find something in the fridge.* In the fridge, I found another note: *This?* on top of a still-frozen pizza. But that meant lighting the grill and waiting. Or else, there was a jar of pickled eggs, which I'd liked for a while, but had been there since I'd changed my mind. Or the last slice of haslet, stuck to its own tracing paper, cut by the man in the shower cap at the Co-op deli counter, who my mum used to teach. He always asked for news of the school. 'Same old, same old,' she said, every single week.

The fridge sighed shut. I took my mum's toast and finished it on the way upstairs. My hand was purple now. I went to the bathroom and held it up to the mirror because even though it was bent, you sometimes saw reflections clearer – as if bits of your body weren't your own. But the toothpaste constellations got in the way, and it was hard to tell if it was me that was buckled or the mirror. I checked the medicine cabinet and found paras, senna, TCP, fluff. I tried to think what my mum would think. She'd say: Remember the guerrillas. Hand-smashing happens. It's combat training. So I pressed my fingers against the sink, ignoring the pain, and focused on the silverfish that cleaned the plughole, till the tips turned white and I thought I heard something click. On a scale from one to ten, it was a seven – worse than not blinking and Chinese burns, but not as bad as water torture. That had become known as The Drowning. My mum had hauled me half-conscious from the bath, screamed loud enough to scare the neighbours, and pounded my back till I brought up lungfuls of scum. When I'd recovered, I made a will. I left my Nationwide savings to the *Morning Star* and a tin of my ashes to my mum. She was spooked and told me I had to stop trying to die. But I wasn't afraid. Not really. If I died, it'd be heroically. I was never going to be killed by cleanliness.

From the bathroom, I could see across the landing into my mum's room. On the floor, all the signs of the dash to the meeting – the schoolbag spewing papers, the lightning change of clothes lobbed towards a corner. I twisted myself one-handed out of my uniform and added it to the rope of laundry. I sat on her bed. It was April and her room reeked of Christmas, which was actually Rosie's candles. Despite Christmas, I could smell my mum in the sheets, the Oil of Ulay, the rosewater. I mapped the yellow archipelago where she'd lain on her front and dribbled in her sleep. Last night's tea stood on the bedside table, half-drunk, the mug skin-ringed, the crumbs from the digestive swept onto the carpet. There were the earplugs for when the alarm clock ticked too loud, and the second alarm because of the earplugs.

When I got to my room, I took out the Black Book – actually a class register – and leafed through all the people who'd be shot Come the Revolution: James Callaghan, Jimmy Carter, Bob Monkhouse, the Granma, Pinochet, Benny Hill, Rebecca Caldor, her mum, the Osmonds – proposed by my mum. Which was a problem because, at the time, I'd secretly liked the Osmonds. Or at least, the B-side of 'Long Haired Lover from Liverpool'. I couldn't veto them, not when they were Mormon and American, but sometimes at night, when I felt moody, or maybe just hungry, I sang along under the blanket to 'Mother of Mine'.

Now I took out my italic pen, the one with the gold nib in the black velveteen box, and my Quink ink, because a death sentence demanded ceremony. Or at least stationery. I topped the pen up and wiped it dry, all one-handed, and it made me wonder how the Christmas-card people painted whole scenes with no hands at all. There was a slow turquoise leak into the side of my finger. I got bored watching the ink dry and blotted the excess out, lifting fragments of *MISS DOWNING* away from the page in mirror-writing.

There.

Done.

As good as dead.

I must have fallen asleep because the next thing I knew I was flat on my bedroom floor, my back hairy from the carpet, my skin covered in goosebumps. It was dark outside. I listened for sounds from downstairs. I tilted my head towards the door and called down to my mum, pressing an ear to the floor.

Nothing.

My hand was heavy, the ache turned solid. I lifted it to the window. It was orange from the street light, the fingers stamped with blood as if they'd been checked out of the library. I flicked the door with a foot and shouted louder.

Silence.

Which meant my mum really wasn't home.

I didn't know what time it was, but her meeting must have been over. Which meant she'd gone to the service station café for late-night liver and chips. She'd have sat on a stool at the window and watched the A5 traffic to the flicker of a one-armed bandit and the fried-over burble of Radio 1. And on her way home, she'd have popped into Hamlets for a nightcap. Just the one. And it would be – she was good like that. That was where my mum would be. Bryan would have reached for the glass before she'd got to the bar, and said: 'Double whisky. No ice. No water. No nothing. Neat. Double,' which he said every time, a repeat of the first time he took the order. Then my mum would gaze over to the Tesco Precinct, where the pet shop had a chained-up parrot that'd learnt to say hello. She'd mull over the meeting, fingering the *FUCK OFF* carved into the wooden seat. And when it seemed the meeting hadn't gone so badly, not *so* badly, not *really*, she'd get into the minivan and hope not to be breathalysed in the fifty yards from the wine bar to Church Lane.

Or if she didn't want to risk it, she'd walk home. She'd take Little Church Lane and pause at the newsagent's, her face swimming in the glass. She'd drink in the jars of sweets: sherbet lemons, rhubarb and custards, pear drops. My mum loved pear drops.

I got into bed and kicked the ruckles out of the sheets. I pulled them over my head and blew till I was dizzy and had warmed myself up. Through the wall, the sound of knocking pipes, which was Mr Howard doing his teeth and splashing his face before he went to bed. And that meant it was getting on for ten-thirty. He'd be up at six, 'on the dot, no alarm, because you can't change the habits of a lifetime'. Mr Howard used to be a miner. At the end of each day, he came home to Nancy who had pie-and-mash ready and Mr Kipling cakes, and in the winter, a fire in the grate with coal they got for free. Once, I said to Mr Howard, 'If you could press a lump of coal hard enough, you'd have diamonds.'

'And what would I be doing with diamonds?' as if he had everything he wanted, as if he were content.

And then Nancy died.

She was sitting at the front-room window watching the home-time crowds, her tin-can ankles full of fluid no pills could shift, when 'she just collapsed, felled by a stroke', Mr Howard said. Though she didn't topple over like a tree. She sat in the chair, arms on the armrests, eyes open, looking exactly as she did when she was alive, only breathless. He didn't notice until she'd already started to harden. She was fitted with hearing aids and sometimes switched them off so she often didn't answer the chit-chat he offered to keep her company from the living room.

That's what he told me.

He buried Nancy in Wigginton cemetery, in a plot close to fields with elderflower, comfrey and burdock, and with room at her side for him. When he came back from the funeral, damp patches under his arms, dabbing at his face with a hankie and blaming the heat, he said, 'Jess, she's in good earth.' And he'd know about that kind of thing. He'd spent a life underground. When I told my mum, she said, 'I didn't think a miner would know the name of so many flowers.'

I listened again to the sounds from next door. Mr Howard had gone quiet now. He'd be getting into his paisley pyjamas, the ones that appeared on the line every Thursday. He'd say something to the photo he kept on his bedside table – you'd think it was Thora Hird with that perm and those glasses – then he'd climb into his side of the bed, which it always would be, even so, and he'd be out like a light. I knew this because Mr Howard liked to talk, and sometimes I didn't mind listening – when I was home and I'd done my homework, and my mum was still out, and it was a warm evening, and we both happened to be out the back.

I heard a bus fret into place in the garage. I slid out of bed and went over to the window. I looked north, which was the direction the minivan might come from. I fixed my eyes on the bend in the road, willing the minivan round the corner – the sight of mustard-yellow, the throaty catch of the engine, my mum's face soft at the wheel. Then I looked south, to where my mum might walk from – through the graveyard, singing to herself – to where the bells of St Editha's had just gone quiet and left the hour hanging.

3

An Invitation

When I woke up next morning, my mum was home. Over boiled eggs and soldiers, I told her what had happened and let her inspect the damage.

'That Miss Downing is not "in loco" me. You don't hit people.'

But you sometimes killed them – if they'd deserved it. That was what the Black Book was for. But my mum didn't want to wait for the revolution and the executions. She was going to make an immediate complaint to the school. My heart sank. I had to be a pupil for another five years. I said, 'Víctor Jara had his hands smashed.'

'And he died.'

'That's because he was shot.'

And I saw the clouds descend. Chile did that to her. But I knew Víctor Jara was a good tack. My mum lifted my hand and held it to the light of the kitchen window, turning it at the wrist like a trophy. I watched concern unwind into pride. Then she found a song. Not a Víctor Jara one – she could only mumble along in made-up Spanish to the records. But she knew 'One Man's Hands'. It was a Pete Seeger and Alex Comfort song about all the things you couldn't do with just one pair of hands – you couldn't even manage if there were two of you. It took a group. And I always wondered about that song because wasn't Alex Comfort the man who wrote *More Joy of Sex*? I'd seen it on a trip to Birmingham and that was full of

24

groups. But the song scuppered the formal complaint, and instead of going into battle with her, Miss Downing remained the daily apparition at assembly. Once or twice, I passed her in the corridor and she held me in her sights with a look full of meaning, scanning for signs of thankfulness. I looked away and sniffed for Coal Tar Soap.

It was a mistake to mention 'in loco parentis' to my mum, though, because it seemed to trouble her. She didn't like the idea of someone else standing in for her, so she started standing in for herself – acting like my mother, pulling rank. She bulk-bought bananas and told me I needed vitamins. She checked her own armpits and told me I needed a bath. And then she told me some James-or-other-from-the-Party would be calling round and it was best if I wasn't at the meeting.

'What's so secret?'

'You know I don't do secrets.'

'Will he be staying over?'

'I'm not answering that. But no.'

Because very occasionally someone did: Neil the guitarist, Trevor the panel beater, Eamonn the Labour councillor. And this James seemed to qualify better than most, being in the Party. I entertained the overnight guest as well as I could, then slipped away for the rest of the evening. When I gave them a wave and wished them goodnight, I knew it was actually goodbye. Everything was always back to normal in the morning.

'So why can't I come? I *always* come to meetings.'

'That's because you live here.'

'And to help with numbers.'

'That too.'

'So why not this time? I'll take the minutes.'

'Because he doesn't expect a daughter. Because he invited *me*,' and she tapped herself hard on the breastbone, the way doctors do when they're checking for infection. The word 'me' came out sounding hollow. 'Afterwards, Jess. I'll tell you every-thing after. But it could be something good. For both of us.'

But maternal distance meant effort, and my mum didn't have any to spare. She couldn't resist the pull of thirteen years, the draw of an entire life. The evening James was due, I asked if I could listen from behind the stairwell door. It was plywood, a sheet of opaque air, and you could hear everything through it. My mum said, 'You know I don't do subterfuge. But as long as I don't know if you're there or not. As long as it's not me doing the subterfuging.'

James must have been waiting at the Pay and Display, biding his time round the corner, because it was exactly six when I heard a car in the lane – the slow cut of wheels through rainwater, then the silence of the engine. I trained my binoculars on the street. I didn't know much about cars and couldn't name any of them, but this one didn't look like a Party car. I'd expected a cloud of exhaust and bad driving knocked into the bodywork. This was the kind of car that took important people places on the news: smoky windows, black lacquer, looking fast even when it was parked.

I pinned the binoculars on the car door and watched magnified polished feet swing out. They were placed with care to avoid the puddles. I scanned the target: a middle-aged man with a briefcase and a mac folded over his arm. He put a hand to the car door and it shut with a muted click. He checked the house fronts for our number, and hurried to the gate, ducking from the weather. He rang the bell and waited.

I waited.

Our bell was out of battery.

James was getting wet. He brushed a hand over his hair. He flicked the rain from his mac and squinted up at the sky. I tipped the binoculars away from the window. They landed on the Territorial Army offices. They were shut because it was Sunday, but several times a week, boys from the Secondary Modern came out of the building dressed as bushes. They climbed into the back of a truck and were driven to Cannock Chase where they spiked the air with bayonets as if they were seeing Russians.

James tried the bell again. He held his finger against it long enough to be annoying if it'd worked. Then he checked his watch and rapped a gloved hand on the door, then took off his glove to rap harder. 'El-ea-nor!'

I shouted down the stairs, 'Target at twelve o'clock.'

'What o'clock?'

'Your meeting's arrived.'

There was a pause, then the light over the front door went on, a bright beam that switched on his colours: white hair, thick and sharply sliced, a mauve scarf crossed on his chest like a vicar. I heard my mum undo the lock and invite him in, then the turn of the key in the door.

There in the yard, my bike thrown into a corner, petals from Mr Howard's baskets brought over the wall by the wind, the tubs of mud my mum had forgotten to plant and now it was already spring.

Then the light went out.

I took off my shoes and crept halfway down, my feet wedged against the walls to stop the stairs from sounding. I heard the scrape of chairs and burble about our three clocks. It was a loud burble, more of a boom, which meant James was probably a teacher too. I sat on a step and fingered the carpet – cut-price green nylon, 'because it's greener on the other side,' my mum had told the man who laid it. I played with the patch that had melted when she tried to iron lettering onto a banner and turned a strip of Paradise into hard black pearls.

My mum's voice grew louder over the heating kettle. 'And what's this course, exactly?'

'Run by their Ministry of Education. In Potsdam. Gorgeous place.'

I edged further down and took up my listening post, perched just the other side of the stairwell door.

'Every summer. In-service training. Very competitive. They all want to go. Only a hundred get on. A hundred English teachers. A hundred French.' He was broadcasting snippets as if talking over the radio, which meant my mum had probably gone into the kitchen. 'Our Party sends tutors. The French Party likewise. They can't come to us, obviously, so we go there.'

Can't they? I thought.

'No!' my mum said. But it wasn't surprise. She was yelling over the kettle. And then it must have boiled because a few seconds later I heard her say, 'No, that's right,' and through the door, without seeing her face, I couldn't tell if she was confirming the fact or commending it. 'And who is it dropped out?'

'Not so much dropped *out* as dropped.'

'Because he's a gangster?'

'His politics weren't the problem. No, it's not entirely clear why. The GDR side let it be known they weren't happy. He must have got on the wrong side of them somehow. And it's their prerogative. *They*, after all, invite *us*. It's Gavin Barber. I'm sure you'll have come across him. Whisky-breath disguised as Parma violets – which can't have helped. Rather full of himself too. Comes across as archive footage from the BBC.'

And that was when I was sure something was wrong. It was exactly what this man sounded like. People in the Communist Party didn't talk like that. We didn't have vowels like those.

'So I'm looking for a replacement. I've already mentioned you. More than mentioned, actually. And they're all for you.'

'*For* me? Really? But I haven't done anything.'

'I told them how good you are. A real gem. How much I like you.'

There was a hoot from my mum, which was pleasure smothered by embarrassment.

'The people who decide are really keen: Peter Roth, head of the English course. Saskia Wolf, head of the whole operation. They want you there.'

My mum started the denials, but they were just embarrassment too.

'It's for solidarity, Eleanor. A chance to give practical support.
And unlike Tamworth, your political work is recognised. *And*
paid. Ostmarks. Not convertible, of course, and not many. But
a goodly honorarium.'

My mum liked the sound of honour. She made noises like
the Clangers.

James said it was hard for GDR teachers to get on the course.
They could wait years for a place. If they were one tutor short,
ten people would be very disappointed. 'Stepping in like this,
you'll save the day. You'll be a hero.'

My mum laughed at the idea of being a hero. But she loved
it too, I could tell.

'Think about it,' James said.

And so I did.

Germany. It was double lessons on Mondays and Thursdays
with Mr Long and the Frank family and their dog, Max. It was
simple tasks in the present tense with complicated adjective
endings. It was modal verbs and a long wait till the end of the
sentence to find out what, in the infinitive, was actually going
on. Germany was *The World at War*. It was *Colditz*. It was Pat
Reid in a balaclava, hanging from a bed-sheet rope, creeping
across the kitchen roofs to the *Kommandantur* and making it all
the way to Switzerland. It was the library book on the Nazis
with piles of scrambled bodies and women tied to trees with
their breasts sliced off.

My mum said, 'So no gangsters on the team?'

'They did their damnedest, of course. But the GDR knows
what's going on. The Ministry would have none of it. Guaranteed
Euro-free. Potsdam is ours.' Then they talked about The Split.
Alphabetti spaghetti poured out about the NCP and the CPGB
and EFT and staying inside to fight. It was the kind of thing
I heard in my mum's telephone calls, the late-night calls she sat
on the floor for with a cup of tea and the biscuit tin. She made

a knuckle-duster of the telephone cable, then coiled it off again, jiggling towards the end because she was desperate for the loo, and saying, 'But the point is, the point *is* . . .', but never getting to the point because the person at the other end had a better one.

James listed names I vaguely knew: Cynthia Lukov, Don Palethorpe, Dorothy Hill, Mark Johnson . . .

'Not the Mark who went to South Africa?'

'I think he might have.'

'For the ANC?'

'Quite possibly.'

'Underground?'

Something I couldn't catch.

'Armed resistance?'

Silence, which was probably a nod.

'Bombs?'

'*That* I honestly couldn't say.'

There was a pause. I imagined my mum letting that sink in, sipping at her tea, taking stock behind the rim of the mug. So, she might spend the summer with a bomber and a snob. I leant back on my good hand, fingers falling on the black beads of our carpet rosary.

'And Jess?'

'She's most welcome. They've given her the nod.'

And that meant so might I.

I heard the scrape of a chair, the legs catching on our uneven tiles. Then the door opened. My mum cocked her head round, her face an inch from mine, and she yelled to the top of the stairs for me to join them. I backed away on tiptoe and made sure to clatter down. When I got to the living room, James was out of his seat. His handshake was long and tighter than it should have been. And two weeks on, a grip still hurt.

'James Clancy,' he said.

I didn't say anything. He knew who I was.

My mum felt the gap. 'My daughter, Jess.'

'I've heard a lot about you.' He said it with a smile and meant it as a compliment, but I didn't like the asymmetry. I knew nothing about this man except he didn't sound right. I waited for his grip to loosen, then took a step back. A cardigan, buttoned. Shirt, ironed. Cuffs, linked. Tie pressed against his neck. Why was a Party member dressed like a banker? And why did my mum not notice?

'You're tall,' he said. 'Strapping, even.'

I was just thirteen and could see straight down the pink line of his parting. You're short, I thought. And old. I slid my legs under the dining table and took the seat opposite. It was hard to tell exactly how old he was, and he aged the longer I looked. I counted the creases of his concertina neck. His cheeks were flushed with thread veins, or alcohol – though there was no hint of drink. Instead, I got wafts of those wedding-day men outside St Editha's with their Brylcreemed hair and awkward suits, who'd sprayed themselves with something from Marmion Motors. I linked my hands on the table and interviewed James with my eyes: *And how long, Mr Clancy, have you been on Her Majesty's Secret Service?*

My mum bustled in the kitchen. She came back with a new packet of biscuits and poured us all tea. She didn't, for once, put the cosy on her head. She toyed with her pen as she listened to James, rolling it over the lump on her finger. Every so often she made notes, filling the space between the lines of her jumbo pad as if still learning to write. I slunk low in my chair and glanced under the table. James's trouser legs had risen and he wore long socks. His shoes were shiny black and looked as mean as his car. Then I saw the wedge of his heels. James wasn't even straight about his height.

With one ear on their conversation, I checked the documents he'd brought. There were letters in German typed hard on thin yellow paper, the full-stops hammered holes. Copies of *Education for Today and Tomorrow*, a motoring map of Europe. The summer course programme was upside down, but still I could read it. There'd be an Opening Ceremony with someone from the Ministry of Education, a tour of Berlin – to the Brandenburg Gate and the TV Tower – and a bazaar to raise money for the *Morning Star*. Every day, there'd be language classes and lectures on British politics: working-class traditions, the position of women, the economic crisis, British schools.

James said, 'Jess, you and your mother have been invited to the German Democratic Republic.'

I reached for a Jammie Dodger and wondered if in company like this I was still allowed to dunk it.

'*East* Germany,' he said, as if I might not know. '*Our* Germany.'

I didn't know much about our Germany except Progressive Tours arranged coach holidays there. Sometimes, children from East Germany wrote letters to the *Morning Star* listing stamp collecting and making friends as hobbies, and asking for pen pals from capitalist countries. East Germany was a long way from where the textbook Franks lived in the shadow of Cologne cathedral. They never, ever mentioned it. It would have been easy to forget it even existed.

I reached for the map of Europe and slid it towards me. I placed Jammie Dodgers on the capital cities and ran a finger along the borders. So that was East Germany. Over there by Poland.

'See the GDR?' James said. 'See Berlin? To the west is West Berlin. Potsdam knocks up against West Berlin.'

'From where you're sitting, James, east is west.'

'Don't be daft,' my mum said. 'East is east and west is west wherever you are. It's left and right that swap over.' She raised her mug to her lips and said through ceramic, 'And that's why compasses are more reliable than people.' There was a pause, because none of us really followed that, not even my mum, judging by her face.

'It's a chance to see Actually Existing Socialism,' James said. 'You've seen it, Eleanor. Poland, wasn't it?'

It was the World Festival of Youth, 1955. My mum leant back in her chair and remembered Poland out loud. She'd stayed in a local school and made friends with the dormitory cleaner. They'd had sandwiches on the banks of the Vistula and smiled at each other over the language barrier. She'd met dancers from Kraków and musicians from Zakopane. Her contingent from the Young Communist League went by train from London to Warsaw. The food and water ran out, and there were delays at every border. Everyone slept sitting up. My mum arrived aching with hunger and clammy from broken toilets. But it didn't matter. This was the People's Republic of Poland and there were 30,000 youngsters gathered *For Peace and Friendship – Against the Aggressive Imperialist Pacts*.

'There you have it, Jess. So, what do you say to a summer of German socialism?'

I kept a hold of James's bright blue eyes. 'I say we can't go.'

My mum gasped.

'We can't go because we've already made plans for the summer. We've booked Rosie.'

'*Rosie?*' as if my mum barely recognised the name. 'It's only camping. On Silbury Hill. We'll cancel her. She won't mind. Rosie's a brick.'

'Also,' and still I held his gaze, 'I don't have a passport.'

'Passport!' My mum threw her hands in the air as if to say what kind of objection is that. 'We can fix a passport, can't we, James. Easily. And then you can leave England, Jess. Any time you like.'

I picked up the course programme and flipped through it. There was my summer, a timetable mimeographed in purple ink. I made a loud slap of the pages, got to the end, turned it over and started again, protesting in paper-rattle. My mum put a hand on my wrist.

'But I wanted a holiday.'

'We get a holiday. They give us a holiday,' and she took the programme and showed me where. At the end of the course, there'd be a four-day educational trip to Thuringia. 'We'll visit a cattle-rearing station, a kindergarten, an agricultural museum, Buchenwald concentration camp.' The words 'concentration camp' came out loud and with too much enthusiasm. My mum ducked into her tea, one of Rosie's gaping home-made mugs, smeared in blues and fired into that faint wobble. James took a deep breath. It could have been the start of a sigh. Instead it was another tack. 'How many people from Tamworth, Jess, will *ever* get to see the GDR?'

I took the Jammie Dodger off Berlin, dunked it and scraped the biscuit away with my teeth.

'It'll be cracking. I promise. A whole month of sunshine. Living in Sanssouci Park.'

'Sanssouci?' I said. 'Isn't that in France?'

When James left, he shook my hand again, only with less claim on it this time. He told my mum he'd be in touch. On the wall behind him, there was our Oxfam calendar. It was April 1978, and all this month I'd looked into the muddy eyes of a rake-thin girl who'd swum out of a flood. She'd looked back at me from China, from under debris and striped tarpaulin. Soon, it'd be August, and the Oxfam calendar would have a new disaster. It might be somewhere with civil war or a military dictator, or somewhere the rains failed, the crops withered and children with big bellies took away your appetite. But I wouldn't have to look at that disaster because I'd be away. I'd be in East Germany with my mum and a man who just had to be a spy.

We stood at the front-room window and watched James walk back to his car. It was the kind of gait you saw on an army parade ground, straight-legged, chin up.

'Is that the goose-step?'

'It's arthritis.'

He made an elegant three-point turn at the end of the lane, avoiding the lamp post and the first of the graves. As he passed our window, he held up a gloved hand and doffed his head at the windscreen, which was his way of nodding without crashing the car. My mum raised a clenched fist. I picked at my fingers. My mum's face followed James till he disappeared around the bend at the Pay and Display. Then she turned to me and waited.

I knew that when I said yes, she'd shout 'Good-oh!' and do maracas, then wrap herself around me and press us till it hurt. If something came to mind, she'd sing. *Hold the fort for we are coming . . .* started up in my head. But if I said no before I said yes, we'd have meetings. We'd discuss the pros and cons of a summer of German socialism. We'd draw up tables of advantages and disadvantages, to her and to me, weighted equally.

I looked across my mum's shoulder to the hardback books lying flat on their stomachs, too tall for any of our shelves. They were unread, barely opened, Book Club books from the back of a Sunday magazine, from a subscription she'd never managed to cancel. She broke the silence with a sigh so meant it was voiced. She scanned my face, reading it line by line, looking for signs I hadn't meant the things I'd said, that all those objections were really just strop. 'Don't you *want* to go to Potsdam?'

'I want to know who James is.'

'He's James. James Clancy. He told you that.'

But I meant the cardigan. The socks. The cufflinks. Communists didn't wear cufflinks. 'And the accent. Where did he get that?'

'In an orphanage, actually. James is a foundling.'

That made me snort. We didn't have foundlings. Not this century. Then I saw my mum was serious. She said James was abandoned. An orphanage gave him 'class and a clarinet'. That's how he put it. Then the war started. He joined the army band and was shipped off to India. He saw what the British did when they went abroad and stayed. The war changed his mind about everything.

But even if James was a foundling, would he really have turned into a soldier who turned into a communist who turned into a spy who doubled as a teacher and looked like they worked in a bank? How many people could you be in a life-time?

My mum took my good hand, weighing it in hers. 'I've known James longer than I've known you.'

Which was forever.

That and the foundling thing changed the mood. I turned my face to the floor. There we were, toe-to-toe in our Start-rite sandals, our cords with the elastic waistband, which were the only kind it was safe to buy from a catalogue, our fisher-man's sweaters from the Co-op. My mum had pushed her sleeves up to the elbow, her arms freckled except under the watch that she never took off. There were the whiskers on her lip that she'd missed with the scissors. Sometime soon she'd feel them and ask me to trim them, and as I did it, she'd check the lip where I'd get mine.

And that's when I saw that something had changed. Her face – a face that could be so suddenly tired, so paper-thin with things to do and tearable – had softened.

'They're *for* me, Jess. That's what he said. *For* me.'

James had offered an end to hostilities. My mum, the soldier who was never off duty, had the chance, for a summer, to put her lists away.

4

Actually Existing Socialism

Potsdam, August 1978

By August, I'd been certified as a subject of Her Majesty the
Queen, and a national of the United Kingdom of Great Britain
and Northern Ireland. I had a passport now. On the cover, *Honi
soit qui mal y pense*, which had come up once in a general
knowledge quiz and I still couldn't remember the right answer.
And the Lion and Unicorn embossed in gold, as if the UK
weren't a country in the atlas but a made-up land you'd find
in a children's book. My mum presented the passport to me.
'Your path out of Tamworth.' I listened to the clack of the pages
and fingered the stamp for the German Democratic Republic.
Whoever it was at the embassy had processed me in a hurry
and shut the passport too soon. They'd smudged the inks so
that instead of looking like special permission, it was more of
a ripening bruise.

We flew to Berlin with Czechoslovakian Airlines. The hostess
came round twice handing out silver sachets of salted peanuts
and miniature bottles of schnapps. She looked like a nurse in
her stiff blue uniform and dispensed snacks as if they were
medicine. I watched faces turn to her – men in middle-age
wearing white cotton shirts and metal-rimmed spectacles and
an expression that was still in their newspaper. I was offered
prune juice. My mum loved prune juice, but took the alcohol.
This was the first time she had ever flown.

She was excited and nervous, offset by lack of sleep. Last

night, she'd tried not to nod off in case she overslept. She'd left the bedside light on and the radio chatting low, and went to bed in her clothes to save time in the morning. It was an early start. We drove from Tamworth to Heathrow and were on the road before it was light in case there were hold-ups on the motorway, in case the minivan broke down, in case of in case, 'and I just don't know how long airports take, Jess, how long you need to get out of the country'.

For an age, I pressed my nose to the aeroplane window and looked down on the broken edges of Europe, hoping for a sign of where the West ended and the East began: flags, fortifications, something that might look like an iron curtain. But instead, we flew over a veil of cloud. Above the weather, needle-sharp planes pulled fine white threads across the sky. My mum nodded at them and said how strange it was that not so long ago German planes were in these skies, about to drop bombs on Bermondsey. One house in her street took a direct hit. It was flattened into a tatty-papered wall for playing ball and a stage for dancing on. My mum had danced in cotton dresses her mother had made and hand-me-down shoes from the dead Mrs Hogan. She was the neighbour who lived in a wheelchair and her cast-off footwear was as good as new. My mum said she could still remember the day, somewhere towards the end of the war, when things had gone quiet and she'd decided that, actually, it was all over. She'd been to Beckenham Place Park with Dolly Cheeseman, Pat Wormley and her brother Billy. They'd gone to the POW camp and taken toffees from the stringy man behind the wire, and eaten them even though they couldn't be trusted because they weren't Sharps or Quality Street. When they didn't die, they took it as a good sign. The Germans hadn't poisoned the sweets and it meant they'd given up on the war. 'That's when we heard the engines. We looked up and could see their machine guns. Then they dived at us: rat-tat-tat-tat-tat.' My mum clenched her fists and poured imaginary bullets into the man in front of her. He turned the pages of his *Neues Deutschland* as if nothing had happened. I lifted myself from my seat, checking the heads, trying to work out from the bald patches and grey if any of these men could have flown those planes. My mum said she and her friends had taken cover in the privet, but by the time the Germans had gone back to Germany, Billy had bled to death.

Now my mum took a large swig of schnapps straight from the bottle and gasped as it went down. She tapped three fingers against a leg, doing arithmetic on her thigh. 'It wasn't that long ago. Only thirty-three years. That's all.' But thirty-three years was forever. In thirty-three years' time it would be 2011, which was a date that didn't exist. It was further away than a space odyssey. I would be forty-six. Which I wouldn't, in fact, because I'd be long since dead, filled with bullets at the barricades. In 2011, my mum would be drawing a pension, a hero of the revolution and living in a flat with her mementoes and arthritis, her hands thick, her freckles pooled into liver spots. She'd sit in an armchair, her arms on the rests, the skin falling over the edges, and she'd talk to the photo of me – the portrait she'd have made for my funeral. She'd chat to me, and I'd look back in sepia, eyes cast towards the top corner of the frame, and listen to my mum say, 'The point is, Jess, the point is . . .' because even after the revolution, there'd still be points.

The next bottle of schnapps sent my mum to sleep. Her head sank, pressing out a second chin. Her breath lengthened until it turned into a snore. After a while, she was in tune with the hum of the engine. I checked the contents of the seat pouch. I found a bullet of chewing gum wrapped in a napkin, a receipt for airport coffee and a sick bag. I studied the safety card and learnt to write 'emergency' in Russian. When my mum woke up, the hostess was holding a bag of boiled sweets under her nose and making sure her seat belt was fastened. Then she worked her way down the aisle trailing a dustbin bag, and told us all to prepare for landing.

We dropped towards Schönefeld airport and hovered over

yellow-chevroned fields, over matchbox tractors and pin-head farmers who no longer noticed planes. We hit the runway hard and bounced up and down on the GDR. It was solid proof, my mum said, that Actually Existing Socialism did actually exist. Then we lost speed till the engine choked and died. The door opened and the hostess thanked us. She said goodbye in German, Probably-Czech, Maybe-Russian and English, and we stepped onto bright concrete under a hot blue sky. We followed the men, who knew where they were going. They wore brown jackets now, and swung briefcases. They acted as if the war were forgotten, that killing Billy in the privet was nothing to do with them, as if it were easy to be German.

We joined the end of a long queue. Behind us, the corridor telescoped the length of the terminal building. Folk dances pattered through vents in the ceiling. Fans set to maximum wrestled with their mounts and whisked the scent of new polish into the trail of smells from the plane: sweat, schnapps, hot leatherette. We shuffled towards the open arms of a stuffed bear – a real one, you could tell by the teeth. It reached out to new arrivals, a sign round its neck: *Welcome to Berlin! Capital of the GDR!*

My mum wanted to do maracas. She wanted to snap this moment on her Kodak Instamatic. But she couldn't. There were signs saying no photography, no smoking, no guns. So instead, she fiddled with her passport, reading all the pages, even though they were mostly blank. It said she was five foot six and had no peculiarities. I studied my passport photo, taken in a hurry in the Anglo-Saxon tunic, grabbed after school from the booth in the post office. I looked grim and dark under the eyes, my chin just reaching over the bottom edge of the picture from a swivel seat jammed too low.

At border control, a heavy-headed man sat in an aluminium kiosk and faced us across a dim screen. He reached for our documents in slow motion. He took them with a paw and slid them under a bent-necked lamp. He held them there so long

I thought he might have fallen asleep. He kept the letter from the Council of Ministers of the GDR that said we were invited guests and entitled to bring gifts and materials into the country. When finally he looked up, '*Alles in bester Ordnung.*'

'Pardon?'

'*Herzlich Willkommen in der DDR.*' He turned long-lashed eyes on my mum and smiled. She was about to mistake it for interest, start to make small talk, say something about how excited we were to be here. But before she could make friends with the border guard, he rolled a stamp into our passports and nodded us through to the other side.

We emerged into a hall where a giant dove of peace was stuck to the window, heading towards Departures. Groups of young people loosened their neckerchiefs and shifted their weight from foot to foot. They picked scabs and compared badges. I saw faces with more bones than we had in England and heard languages I couldn't name. Most of Eastern Europe seemed to be here. My mum looked around for a face that was looking for us. 'Can you see Peter? Can't see him. Can you, Jess?'

I had no idea what he looked like.

'German. A card with our name on it. Do any of those say us?'

I peered at a line of drum-bellied men holding up names from around the Eastern Bloc. Beside them, a collection box for International Solidarity was a half-made pillar of socialist banknotes. Sunlight struck the Perspex and a column of white light toppled onto the lino floor.

I felt Peter before I saw him, as a ripple on my arm. I turned my head and found a man big enough to create a vacuum and stir a current. I looked into a khaki shirt, the sleeves shoved to the elbow, then up to a black beard and olive skin. Peter wasn't German. He was a guerrilla, straight out of the jungles of Latin America. And a middle-aged guerrilla now I looked more closely, with that rubber that lines the cheeks of the over-forties. He scooped up my mum's hand. 'Eleanor, I am so glad to see you. You are the last ones through. I was beginning to wonder.'

'We wouldn't not come.'

But Peter meant trouble at immigration. Sometimes they wanted very particular wording on the papers. Just the right stamp. 'But they liked you, which is as it should be.' He picked up our luggage and headed out to the car park. We watched as he strode with the cases as if they weighed nothing. At Heathrow we'd used a trolley and had to pay excess, both trunks filled with goods for the *Morning Star* bazaar. James had said to bring things that are typically English, but also have political meaning. We'd packed wall maps of the London Underground in case anyone ever had a chance to visit, even though they couldn't. Tea towels printed with the Rules of Cricket. Co-op 99 tea, Camp coffee, Liquorice Allsorts, Heinz beans, Chivers lime marmalade, Angel Delight. 'Everything's political, isn't it?' my mum said.

We climbed into the *Hochschule* van, into air that smelt of hard-boiled eggs and heavy industry. The front seat took three and we filled it. Peter was solid, as big as our Cabinet – a wall-sized piece of carpentry, specially commissioned in beech and brass knobs to house our political files. I couldn't help staring. Men didn't grow that big in Tamworth, not with the Midlands diet and the cloud-cover. I sat between Peter and my mum, thighs touching thighs. Between my legs, grey foam crept out of the seam, held back by gaffer tape. On the dashboard, Bakelite switches and yellowed dials. The floor was strewn with things that'd save us in the event of disaster: a first-aid kit, jump leads, trodden-on maps of Eastern Europe.

Peter turned to my mum. 'You got me out of difficulties, Eleanor. What happened with Gavin . . . It was Saskia's decision. But then we were one tutor too few, and if I could not find a replacement, I would have to explain to the Ministry. And then she wanted the new person to be the opposite of Gavin: under fifty, female, someone who "understands the collective", she said. And does not drink. I cannot believe James found you. Though you do drink, no? At least a little. Because sometime soon, I would like to thank you. Raise a toast.'

My mum had never felt so wanted just for existing. It was a 'Hurrah for you!', the kind of thing other people got on their birthday. But my mum didn't put much store by being alive per se. She kept her birthday quiet. I was the only one who knew when it was, so she didn't expect any cards. Every year, she poured herself a whisky and reread her diary, totting up what she'd managed over the last twelve months and wondering if it was enough. Then I turned out the lights, brought in her chocolate éclair and sang 'Happy Birthday'. She blew the candle out and made an unvoiced wish, which from the shape of her lips, I took to be World Peace.

Now Peter turned the key in the ignition and the sound of a violin spilled from under the seat. A rusty voice talked its way into a tune. He said it was 'Am Fenster', by City, a famous rock band in the GDR. It was his daughter's favourite song, her anthem, even. Martina, apparently, was away at her grand-mother's. She was often away, he said, in her thoughts, her dreams, but right now she was actually away. She was spending the holiday in the far south, putting as much distance as she could between herself and the summer course. Last year she came to one or two classes – she was nearly fifteen and her English was good enough. 'But to have teachers all school year, and then teachers all summer . . . Will you manage, Jess? Will you survive us?'

But the teachers here would be different. They didn't have the right to rank and grade me, to be politely unkind in their termly reports, to decide my future. Unlike Miss Downing, who was already talent-spotting, sending some pupils for extra tuition, arranging mentoring and placements. Even for me. She said she'd encourage my interest in languages if I could prove I wouldn't misuse the opportunity, by insisting, for instance, on learning Russian. Which I couldn't.

43

Peter said, 'I expect you will meet Martina. Eventually.' And that made me frown. *Eventuell* was a false friend, which meant I had no idea how certain the meeting was. Eventually or just possibly? Mr Long had compiled a dictionary of false friends which we had to memorise. Alarm bells should ring, he'd said, whenever we heard one. The whole of German seemed to be a false friend.

Now Peter nodded at the tape deck: 'Did you hear the lyric?' and across the roar of departing planes, he repeated the garbled German. 'It means: I am off, away, in the clouds. You could say it is Martina's motto.'

We drove at a crawl to Potsdam. The roads were mostly empty, but the way was cobbled, which made the van rattle and blurred the outline of my mum's softened face. Her eyelids were heavy, and I knew she could have dozed if it hadn't been the GDR on the other side of the glass and she'd never seen it before. We passed slow-motion villages untouched since the war: brown-dusted cottages with high-pitched roofs and plaster chunks shot from the walls. There were orchards with pears, plums and children strung through the branches. Beside the road, lines of thick-legged women napped in deckchairs, chin on their chest. Baskets of fruit, for sale if you woke them, warmed at their stockinged feet.

But maybe I dozed because the next thing I knew, the van had stopped. We'd arrived at the *Hochschule*, and Peter was nodding at the windscreen. 'That is the welcoming committee. Saskia and Stefan.' Two figures stood in the parking space looking on the edge of impatience.

'Stefan looks official,' my mum said. And he did. He was in casual wear – a polo shirt and sandals – but somehow wore them as civvies, as though he'd mean business, only not today. 'I don't think I know Stefan. He's not the man from the Education Ministry?' She spoke without moving her lips, hushed by rank and the thought that he could lip-read.

'Saskia's brother. He is based in London, actually, at the embassy.

He comes back for holidays. Keeps an eye on the summer course when he is here.' Peter reached behind his seat and groped about for a bag. 'Stefan is a busy man. He has a lot of titles.' He shoved his window shut. 'One day I think he will have a lot of medals.'

Sunlight must have reflected from the windows because it wasn't till my mum opened her door that Saskia's expression switched from irritation to pleasure. But her tone didn't keep up with her face. 'You tutors do not like to do things together in a group!' It came out as one word: *togetherinagroup.* 'Some flew. Some drove. Different border crossings. The French tutors the same. Each your own way. You have kept me busy! But now that you are here, we are all present and correct. Welcome, Eleanor.'

Stefan took my mum's hand in both of his and didn't give it back till he'd finished his speech. 'You have no idea how much you have helped us. And at such short notice. Thank you for sacrificing your original plans.' My mum blushed. She wasn't used to compliments, not with 'sacrifice' in them. And certainly not from an embassy. I saw her about to gabble. Somehow, so did Peter. He put a hand to her elbow and said he should see us to our room.

He led us down a sandy path that widened and fanned, losing its edges till it merged with the ground and turned into a makeshift beach. Sunloungers were lined up with where the sun once was. Towels lay abandoned, and buckets and spades, and castles halfway to being made. Peter threw open the door of our dormitory building to the sound of heated exchanges. Languages muddled in the stairwell. The French lodged on the ground floor and the British on the first.

Peter led us upstairs and stopped in front of a numberless door. 'I hope you do not mind sharing. We all share. We have turned it into an art.' He felt in his pocket and produced a key. 'Please make yourselves at home. I have checked that everything is here, but if there is a lack, do let me know. Now I must ready myself for the Opening Ceremony. I am waiting for you downstairs.'

We were going to spend the summer in Colditz: four bunks with tough white sheets and a square pillow stamped with the college name. Floorboards planed with overuse. Beige woodchip covered the walls like hardened porridge. A sink with cold water, cracked soap, a mirror mottled at the corners. Towels with lilies long since laundered away. Curtains that didn't meet, looped loosely. I opened the windows, old wooden frames, the paint coming away on my hands. Out the back, washing lines curved close to the ground. There were rusty goalposts ringed with wild flowers and round cakes of coal ready for the winter.

My mum found a note: *Dear International Friends! Welcome to our room! Welcome to use whatever you may find here!* It was signed by Brigitte, Barbara, Annaliese and Sonja. I searched the room for things I might want to use. They had shot glasses from Meerane. A typewriter, the T and Z keys locked mid-flight. Under a bed, a beaten volume of Shakespeare's sonnets, obscure words underlined, the translation in miniature in the margin. At the back of the wardrobe, I found a packet of luminous green sweets, and stuffed them in a pocket.

My mum went to the sink and hinged herself at the hips. She studied herself in close-up at the mirror, checking every detail as if she expected to find something had changed now that she was here, her face a puzzle in Spot the Difference. 'Peter's a nice man, isn't he.'

It wasn't a question. All men were nice because men were people and people were nice. Or at least nice until they did something that really upset her, and then they were *horrible*, said with passion. There weren't many of them; most people in the Black Book weren't even horrible. They were just wrong.

Now my mum dragged our trunks into the room and threw them open, rifling through the typical Englishness till she found a clean blouse. It was a new cheesecloth one, the cellophane clinging to her fingers like a see-through flag. She'd bought it on a trip to Birmingham from a market-stall man who'd said, as she pinned it with her chin to her chest, 'You don't know how gorgeous you'll look in that, bab.'

My mum liked the idea of gorgeous.

'You changing, Jess? We're all changing. Peter's changing.'

'I like what I've got on.'

'But washing, though.'

I checked my armpits. They'd done well, considering. I searched the cases and found fresh socks, then skated up and down the corridor. I tried the doors to the Bathroom, Drying Room, Broom Cupboard, Private. All were open, and Private was empty. Loud English voices broke out of the kitchen. I pressed my back to the wall and inched my face around the door. On the windowsill, bottles of beer, rhubarb juice and a slab of rubber cheese. Chocolate from somewhere Cyrillic. The eggs were muddy and hadn't come far. In the window, I watched a film of a meeting. Fingers jabbed the air as if the kitchen were Speakers' Corner, but when I listened, the tutors weren't trying to change the world. The campus shop had sold out of bread and they were having a vote on how best to revive old rolls.

When I got back to our room, my mum was poring over her grey parting, wondering if they had henna here and what GDR people did about their roots. Then she did the detritus check: 'Clean, clean – clean, clean – clean.' Sleeper, bogies, food. When we heard movement in the corridor, the clatter of the end of the meeting, 'Time, Jess. Here we go!' But my mum didn't move. She hovered at the window, the sun lighting up her greys. She took stock, memorising our new home, filling her lungs with heat and soap and coal dust.

She stood there so long, Peter came to find us. He'd gone from the jungle to the asylum. He looked straight-jacketed in a grey flannel shirt buttoned up to the neck and grey flannel trousers, belted. His lace-up shoes creaked down the stairs. Outside, we joined a throng of bright faces – young women, mostly, in children's clothes: polka dots and flowers, puff-sleeves and flounces, spangles and bangles and slippers. My mum was right. Everyone had changed for the Opening Ceremony. But why had the teachers of East Germany all come as Snow White?

'They're just being happy, Jess.'

We shuffled in the hum of excitement and the scent of fresh toothpaste across to the Audimax. 'This is why Martina could not be here,' Peter said. 'En masse is not her thing. It is sometimes a problem in our GDR. There are not so many of us – the population density is about the same as your Wales – but we tend to do everything in a group. For her, two is company, but three is already a meeting.'

Inside the hall, Peter gestured to the front, to where the English tutors were still bickering about old bread, but in an undertone now. My mum and I took seats at the end of the row. The podium was set with a long table laid for a tea party not meant to be touched: upturned glasses, unopened bottles of pop, pink-and-brown biscuits arranged like a house of cards. I watched the podium fill. Saskia wasn't in happy clothes. She wore a sharp white suit and towered over the tea party like lightning threatening to strike. Peter sat next to her and drew his legs under his chair, making himself small. He was going to sit out the Opening Ceremony as a grey flannel cloud. I couldn't help noticing the weather.

Then, at a sign from nowhere, a hush fell over us. Everyone stood. There was a clap of folding seats. A figure slipped from the front row onto a piano stool and disappeared behind the flap of a concert grand. Saskia gave the nod. Giant chords filled the hall and the first line of 'The Internationale' blurred with its echo in the ceiling. Saskia sang to the back wall. Peter sang to his feet. It was the first time I'd sung 'The Internationale' with anyone other than my mum. We had a pitch that worked for us – somewhere between the sexes. This time, she opted for the women and I went for the octave down. We both ended up miming and listened instead to starvelings rising from their slumbers in three European languages.

Then a man moved to the lectern. He had the capsized look of the bearded bald. He took metal-rimmed spectacles from his shirt pocket, then the mouth in his forehead said, '*Liebe Genossinnen und Genossen.*' Peter's gaze returned to his shoes. My mum whispered, 'Must be the Man from the Ministry.' I tried to follow what came next, but was lost before he even paused for breath. I had a sense from the flatness of his voice and the thickness of his papers that he might be some time, so I slipped a hand into my pocket and found the packet of luminous sweets. They were rock hard and tasted of lime and factory, but helped pass the time in German.

Then it was Saskia's turn at the lectern. I knew we'd work down the tea party, the length of their speech measuring each person's rank, and my eyes fell to my watch. It was still on Tamworth time. By now, the butcher in Middle Entry would have looked at our empty pitch and cheered. He'd cheer next Saturday too. By the end of the month, he'd think we were dead or had moved. No one left Tamworth that long and also came back. My mum hadn't cancelled the Saturday *Stars* though. There'd be forty for us to collect. But we couldn't put month-old news on the Co-op furniture, so the unsolds would go with the *Herald*s and the freebie-junk, and when the pile was big enough, my mum would take it to the Bells down at Fazeley, old comrades who were stuck inside with their hips, and who made good use of old paper, living with a house full of cats.

It was gone half-two on Tamworth time. People would have bumped into each other in Middle Entry by now and caught up on their bargains and babbies. Men in anoraks would be heading to the Castle Pleasure Grounds to puncture maggots and dip their lines into the river. Everyone else would be going home to do the garden or watch the telly, depending on the weather. I thought of Rosie in her tent on Silbury Hill under English summer weather, in the smell of Calor gas, wet socks and beer, her sleeping bag slurring in nylon. She hadn't minded when we'd cancelled the camping trip. My mum had wrapped her arms around her. 'Oh, Rosie, you're—'

'I know I am, Eleanor. Just bring me something back. Cuban cigars. Russian vodka. They must be drowning in that.'

Then I heard, 'Dear comrades,' and glanced up to see James cropped by the lectern. He still had that accent, but he looked more like one of us now in his Jesus sandals and checked shirt open at the collar. He angled the microphone down and lifted his chin to talk in a big-amped voice about internal battles, which probably meant the gangsters, about the Cold War and crises and critical moments in something-or-other. And my thoughts drifted out of the window, because although James was being stirring in English, it all somehow seemed to be in code.

Outside, the sky was a deep blue. Several suns sat in the windows of King Frederick's palace. Stone figures queued around the rooftop. Golden angels balanced on one foot. I lifted a foot and unstuck my thigh, then slipped a hand underneath and rocked back and forth, tick-tocking away the time till I could run into fresh air and the summer.

Something in James's voice told me he was coming to the end: the sudden drop in pitch, the same words over and over but different each time – the way drunks spoke to no one in the Castle Pleasure Grounds. Then he said, 'We are dreamers of dreams. We are fighters. We are the history makers. Every single person in this hall today,' and he beat a finger over our heads, 'every one of us, is part of a struggle – an unstoppable struggle – that is making history on a global scale.' I tugged my mum's sleeve, releasing the smell of curry. Her new shirt had turned her breastbone purple. I tried to catch her eye, but she was off, gone misty, her face glued to James as she followed the rise and fall of his voice and the promises he made about us and the course of world events.

Then James introduced the English tutors. He started at the other end of the row and worked his way towards us. There were the names I knew from my mum's phone calls, the names I'd heard in April from behind the stairwell door: Cynthia Lukov, Mark Johnson, Don Palethorpe, Dorothy Hill . . . I felt the hoist of my mum's ribs as James drew close, the hand dried on the thigh, the readied smile. Then he said her name. The clap of Peter's palms was loud enough to hear above the patter of applause. My mum stood in her cheesecloth blouse from the Bull Ring, and turned to the hall to mouth a thankyou. I looked round and found two hundred East Germans smiling at my mum. One of them was on his feet. If you didn't know it couldn't be, you'd have taken it for an ovation. Stefan, the man from the embassy, stood at the back of the hall. He wasn't easy to spot in colours that matched the walls. But there he was, clapping my mum, looking proud of her already.

5

A Day Trip into the Cold War

East Berlin, August 1978

'It's hot for a day trip into the Cold War,' James said. 'As the crow flies, it's an easy journey from here to the Brandenburg Gate. But we're not birds. We can't just glide over the facts of history. So we're going round.' He stood at the front of the coach looking older than ever and deathly pale till I worked out it was freshly plastered sun-cream. He spoke across the smell of an egg stolen from breakfast and a bout of hay fever from someone at the front. They'd just mown the lawn of the Communs. 'An extra hour for us. A permanent headache for the GDR. Inconvenient, but there it is. Sometimes West Berlin just gets in the way.'

James did a head count in English. Anton did one in French. Saskia added them up in German. The coach wasn't full, and the tutors had spread out because we didn't like to do things *togetherinagroup*. Saskia and Stefan sat behind the driver and issued instructions over his headrest. She was in white again, looking icy cool despite the heat. Peter sat behind them, his face fixed to the window as he soaked up the view. It was as it always was, except in this light, the New Palace looked like the saturated postcards they sold in the campus bookshop – the walls ultra-pink, sky unbelievably blue, the grass too green to be true.

The seat beside him was empty. My mum had noticed it too. 'Do you think it's reserved?'

'Who for?'

A shrug. 'Anyone.' She paused, glancing up and down the aisle. Then she sat herself back in her seat, as if placed there by unseen hands. She shut her eyes. Her face went soft, but I knew she wasn't asleep by the way her fingers worked. Behind her eyelids, she was thinking about the seat.

A few days after we'd arrived in Potsdam, I'd asked Peter what he'd meant when he said I'd meet Martina 'eventually'. And he'd meant just that – in the end. 'But now, I would say you will meet sooner or later.' He thought Martina would pay a visit to the English course, but he couldn't say when. Putting anything in her diary made her not want to do it. So instead, she gave probabilities, and the chances of calling by were, apparently, over fifty per cent. After that, I was more-than-half expecting that I'd turn a corner and there she'd be. I'd wander through Sanssouci Park, and I'd spot her – talking to the floored cherubs, their chipped faces filled with ancient moss, or listening to the Greeks on pedestals who raised an arm to address the woods.

Now I watched the shadows of Sanssouci trees flick across my mum's face as the coach moved off. I took out my *Stadtplan Berlin* and followed our journey as we headed east towards Güterfelde and Großbeeren. Out of the window, I recognised the journey we'd made with Peter the day we arrived in the GDR. It unfolded quicker in reverse, and we were quicker anyway, the coach able to take the cobbles. According to the map, the road was some way from the border, but on a clear day like today, I might catch sight of the Wall. It depended how big it was. Several times I thought I spotted it, but it turned out to be a factory, a train depot, a housing estate on its way up. I said to my mum, 'It can't be as big as the Great Wall of China because you can see that from outer space. What does the Wall actually look like?'

She shrugged.

'I could always ask Peter.'

She opened her eyes and glanced down the coach. Peter's head dawned above his headrest. 'Will he know? I don't know if he'll know, will he?'

'It's his Wall.'

'Not *his*. It's shared. A collective wall. A party wall.'

But asking Peter meant clambering over my mum, and she was settling in for some quiet now, making a pillow of her cardigan. So I turned back to the map and traced the Wall with a finger. It was a purple line and it ran all the way round West Berlin. It was actually written WESTBERLIN. One word, said quickly, over and done with. It looked just like Anglo-Saxon Tamworth, fenced off behind a rampart. Crossings were marked at Friedrichstraße, Chausseestraße, Bornholmerstraße. There were lots of crossings all round WESTBERLIN, shown with a triangle as if they were youth hostels. WESTBERLIN was mostly white, which meant it was a very high mountain. Or one big industrial estate. Or maybe the mapmakers had never been there and just didn't know. Roads had names while they were in the GDR and lost them on the other side. Thin-nibbed streams wandered into blank space. Half-villages pressed up against the dyke.

Now I heard a murmur from my mum. Behind her eyelids, she'd started to doze. Her words made sense in the language of half-sleep, something about the collective and doing things together.

Last night, we'd gone with our group to the Bolgar restaurant. We'd eaten Bulgarian food and drunk spirits from across the Eastern Bloc. But the Bolgar wasn't Hamlets; my mum didn't just have one double whisky, knocked back alone to help soften the thoughts of a meeting. The whole group had drunk – rakia from Bulgaria, slivovitz from the Czech Republic, Stolichnaya from the Soviet Union. That'd come with a slice of lemon and a spoonful of sugar and coffee. My mum had eyed it closely. 'Really? Is this how the Russians take it? Well, in that case . . .' She didn't flinch. She knocked the vodka back in one and ate the lemon as if she were still hungry.

The group waited for a reaction.

My mum had taken a long time to rise to her feet and steady herself at the head of the table. She'd fixed her eyes on a song-sheet somewhere beyond the restaurant wall: "'Flying higher, and higher, and high-*er*! Our emblem the Soviet star! And every propeller is roar-*ing*, defending the USSR!'"

The group banged the table with their fists. They'd demanded more, then sung the whole song back to her, only in Russian.

Now my mum felt for my hand and held it. She said something too low to hear, but I knew what it was. She said it every time we drank beer in the *Studentenkeller*, or sweet German wine on the steps of palaces: 'Whatever I do, mustn't do a Gavin. Keeping an eye, aren't you, Jess?'

Which I was. The next morning we were always there in the queue that wound up to the *Obere Mensa* for hard-boiled eggs and sour bread, for strawberry jelly served in Petri dishes and burnt coffee from an urn. Then we went to the lecture theatre, in what used to be Frederick the Great's kitchens, and Peter made announcements and handed out the post from home. Then James taught us songs. He stood at the front and brought us in on his clarinet. He conducted with his tough little fore-arms, punching out triangles of air. We sang about struggle, or love, in four-four time. James preferred marches. And then we listened to the tutors lecture. On the walls, portraits of commu-nist heroes and famous physicists. When my mum gave her lecture on British education, she was flanked by Marx and Einstein.

The coach finally came to a halt. The noise of the engine stopped and the silence was filled with the sound of snoring. It was the deep rasp of old bodies that had come loose and rattled when air passed through them. Peter roused James, who leapt straight from sleep into motion, thinking he was the only one. But the whole coach looked like a battlefield. Tutors slumped all over the seats. I didn't know what had done it: the heat, the airlessness, the average age. But my mum's quiet-behind-the-eyelids had worked. She'd recovered and was raring to go. She skipped down the coach: 'Here we go! *Allez-vous! Nous allons! On y va!* Or something.' I had no idea where the tutors had been in their dreams, but they all looked baffled to find themselves here – in Berlin, beside the Brandenburg Gate.

The driver watched in the rear-view mirror as we gathered bags, water, hats. Then he waved us off without looking, a newspaper already open on his lap. His cheese roll was drying against the sports page and a beer warmed on the dashboard. We stepped into skin-pinching heat and onto tarmac that had softened and clung to your shoes. Unter den Linden stretched off, long, wide and plugged with short green trees. The road was quiet. I watched a few small cars drift away from us and shrink and wobble as they headed into the heat haze. Every so often, through grilles in the pavement, I caught the clatter of underground trains and gusts of warmed-up sewage.

A red-and-white barrier marked the end of the public road. There was a knee-high wall here, and a crowd had gathered at it – a holidaying, seaside kind of crowd: mothers in straw hats and big sunglasses, fathers in rolled-up shirtsleeves. Babies hung from arms and backs and breasts. Children were everywhere, whole packs of them, some in fancy dress – a pirate, a sailor, a fairy. Saskia approached the barrier holding out a sheet of paper. A sentry watched her from under his cap, a young man, his skin shiny with sweat, his uniform shiny with ironing. She stopped a few feet away and said something to him. His face didn't move as he took the piece of paper and read. The guard flicked his gaze at the sentry box, at the tutors, at his watch, and he nodded Saskia inside.

My mum said in my ear: 'Jess, Peter's on his own. I asked James. He's alone. Just him and Martina.'

Saskia said, 'Please keep quiet and keep close. Quickly now, quickly. *Un peu plus vite, s'il vous plaît.*' She counted us across the barrier, sculling with her wrist. But we couldn't move fast.

It was single file only over to the other side. And all the while, the muttering from the crowd at the mini-wall swelled. The sentry walked back and forth, underlining the fact of a barrier with the metal-stud click of his heels. Then the miniature fairy pointed a tinfoil wand at us. '*Warum . . .?*', but was silenced with a slap on the shin.

My mum murmured, 'His wife died. And no replacement. No woman around. Apparently.'

Saskia drew us close to address us in a stage whisper: 'I remind you, at all times silence. Remember where you are. Incidents *do* occur.' And she led us into the emptiness of Pariser Platz. On either side, razored lawns, grids of trees and red roses bricked into rectangle beds. The air was still. The GDR flag hung flat against its pole. It was quiet and neat and full of sadness, in the way memorials are. Or crematoriums. Stretching either side of the Brandenburg Gate, a low white wall.

That must be it.

The dyke.

I hadn't expected the Berlin Wall to be clean and white and smooth. It looked more like the edge of the swimming baths than the edge of the Cold War. On the grass of No-man's Land, fat rabbits ate and strolled about as if they'd never been hunted and nothing could disturb them. This was their land and they ruled it, and there were three parts to Berlin: East, West and Rabbit.

We entered a guardhouse at the side of the Brandenburg Gate. Inside, a spiral staircase, and on the wall, all the way up, hung grey, grainy, head-shots of nameless young men. We came face to face with every one of them. We had time, in that slow shuffle, to examine their charcoal lines and the smudge of their heavy eyes. But none of them looked directly back. Their gaze was aimed just over your shoulder, or down the stairs, where something was puzzling, or half-forgotten, or about to make them cry.

At the top, Saskia stood in a doorway and ushered us through:

'*A gauche, s'il vous plaît*, and the British to the right.' We entered a room laid out for a talk – rows of hard wooden chairs, the seats linked together. The curtains were drawn. Somewhere at the back, a projector hummed. A guard stood at the front in knee-high boots and jodhpurs. His jacket was sprinkled with decoration – stripes on his collar, stars on his shoulders, and around one sleeve, a block-capital ribbon said: GRENZTRUPPEN DER DDR. His skin had taken on the tinge of his uniform. But then, in this room, under neon light, we all looked a pale shade of green. When we were settled, '*Liebe Genossinnen und Genossen.*' I knew he'd say that. And then the lights went out.

A map of Europe appeared. The guard ran the tip of a baton around the German Democratic Republic. 'Now where is West Berlin, exactly?' I was about to put my hand up, but he was already answering the question, jabbing at the bullseye in the middle of the country. And then he began to explain. Peter and Saskia translated. I heard names I knew – Stalin, Churchill, Roosevelt, Truman – but it was hard to follow against the oncoming German and the silky turns of Saskia's French. I couldn't make out how they ended up putting WESTBERLIN in the middle of the GDR. Perhaps it was just a mistake. Or they were exhausted and had given up caring about details at the end of six years of war.

'You!' the guard said. He drew a finger around the British side of the room. 'Are here.' Yellow fairy lights flared on his map. 'You!' and he ringed the French, 'are here.' More lights, white this time. 'Also the Americans,' but they were not in this room. As he talked, colours popped and dazzled in what could have been patterns. WESTBERLIN was alight like a one-armed bandit, and from what I could tell, it was all our fault.

'*Faschistisch*,' the guard said. And again. And more '*faschistisch*'. Then on the screen came photographs of trains upended, poisoned milk, exploding sweets, factories on fire and guilty-looking people led away in handcuffs. He made a traffic-warden motion in the direction of the Wall. Skilled workers, he said, had been seduced by the West. I looked at Peter. He was a skilled worker, a university teacher, and he hadn't been seduced. And Saskia. She was a professor and was still here. I glanced at her, at the elegance, how she was poised an inch above every-thing that happened, and thought if she were West German she'd be posh. And yet she'd stayed. Stefan was a skilled worker and he'd only gone to the embassy. I looked along the row to where he sat and realised I didn't know what Stefan was apart from Saskia's brother and a man in line for gongs.

'And so,' the guard said, 'on the thirteenth of August 1961,' the something-to-do-with-the-working-class erected the anti-fascist something-or-other. I couldn't catch Peter's mouthful. But on the screen, photos of old men in flat caps slapping soft cement between breeze-blocks. Spectators, their hands in pockets, followed the work till it was over their heads. Watchful men in crumpled uniforms stood awkward with their rifles. A girl with pigtails roller-skated by.

Then the projector clunked and the lights went up. 'The talk is over,' Peter said. 'And now questions.' He looked to the guard for a cue. He glanced at Saskia, who checked her watch and said we'd rather be moving along. She tapped a palm with the tips of her fingers. It was an inaudible kind of applause, but the people at the front saw the motion and the sound grew as it rippled to the back of the room. Saskia said, 'You saw the photographs on the stairs? Those are *Grenztruppen*, young men who have died defending our border. Some were shot right here in Berlin.' She pointed to the ground as if they'd died at her feet. 'We will now proceed to inspect the border. So I say again: keep close and exercise all due caution.'

We filed down the steps, past the murdered soldiers whose faces were even more serious now, and out into blinding sunlight. Saskia led us through the columns of the Brandenburg Gate and into a wide semicircle of empty concrete that made me think of the airport. She took small, soft steps in shoes you could use for ballet. We tried to follow suit, but were keeping close and didn't have the footwear, and ended up tripping towards the Wall.

A viewing platform stood close to the border – a few precast steps into the air. There was a slow-motion rush, a gentle grind of shoulders as people angled for position. They wanted to be on the front line, to feel the sharp edge of the Cold War. Behind me, someone whispered a protest: 'Have some consideration! Think about it! Tall people at the back. Then we can all see.' But no one took any notice.

My *Stadtplan Berlin* had said WESTBERLIN was blank. But as I took the steps up, and the other side inched into view, I saw woods. Miles of them. And a long, straight road. And a golden angel on top of a column with a bird's-eye view to the east. It could have been waving at us, or showing us its harp, I couldn't tell from here. Then I spotted a viewing platform on the other side too. It was hidden against the darkness of the trees. But there it was – a knot of people in shades and hats who fingered lenses as long as their arm.

I whispered to my mum: 'Are they tourists?'

'Can't be. Not with cameras that big.'

And here we all stood, in their perfect sights. I glanced round. Saskia had slipped on sunglasses. James found shade under a canvas cricket hat. Peter took gulps of the airless air and fiddled with a white hankie in a move that could have been taken for surrender. I imagined the pictures the people on the other side would send back to their office. They'd be cropped for a head-shot, matched with a name, glued to a file and stamped *SUBVERSIVE*. That was how it'd be for each one of us on this platform: marked out for the rest of our lives.

'Us against them,' James murmured. 'Right here in front of us. Couldn't be much clearer than that.'

My mum surveyed the Wall with an expression from the stairwell. Us-against-Them had made her life.

And mine.

Only mine had been shorter, so it counted for less.

My mum felt for my hand and squeezed a finger as if it were a trigger. I watched the way the spies fingered their cameras and wondered if any of them were actually playing with guns. I prepared for a crack that would hit me before I could hear it. I'd seen it on the news. The look of surprise on a face that'd already died. The blood – grey blood on our black-and-white telly – spurting out sideways. And I couldn't help thinking as his knees buckled and he fell off-screen: I had no idea there could be so much pressure inside someone's head.

I waited for something to happen.

I listened to the sounds of the soundless sky. There was no traffic. No planes. Even birds skirted round this part of the fault line where East met West.

I jumped when Saskia spoke. 'You may take photographs now if you wish. But no sudden movements, please. And the use of flash would be most unwise.' My mum found her Kodak Instamatic and held it to an eye. She took snaps of them taking photographs of us taking photographs of them.

We found our driver with the seaside crowd behind the knee-high wall. He looked fed and refreshed, just back from a snooze. We flopped into the suffocating heat of the coach, drained by the drama and the long wait for lunch. There was no air, but still the tutors managed to make a lot of noise about how reckless it was – given our numbers – to expose fraternal comrades to near-death. But you could tell by the way they said it that they were thrilled to have been almost-snipered. The bluster died away when the coach moved and the fans started up.

Peter came down the aisle and took the seat across from us. We were the only ones, he said, who'd never seen Berlin, and he'd point out the sights as we drove up Unter den Linden. He showed us the Ministry of Education. It looked like a comprehensive school, poured in concrete and fronted with tiles. 'It is where you can find Margot Honecker, the Minister for Education and the boss of all of us on this coach. She is also the wife of Erich Honecker.'

The word 'wife' made me turn to him. I checked his face, but the word had come out like any other, as if it no longer weighed on him. Maybe that meant she'd been dead some time. Perhaps he'd been alone for years.

Peter said, 'The Soviet embassy.' I caught sight of a red flag. Fat-faced pink roses leant over the perimeter wall. 'That's still the Soviet embassy.' He waited. 'Now the Aeroflot building.' He held a finger to the glass. I checked his other hand, scanning for where a band once was. But there was no mark from a recent ring. I wondered if there were other signs, how you could tell that someone was on their own. I tried to picture my mum if my dad hadn't died. She'd be fatter, probably, and maybe less tired. Just occasionally – when she'd had enough of the washing-up, or when she'd hung the laundry on the line on a sunny morning and come back from school on a wet evening – she'd say it'd be nice to have someone around. But mostly she'd say: 'What would I do with a man? Where would I put him? And, anyway, can you imagine, Jess, *three* of us at a meeting? We'd never get anywhere. At least you and I agree.'

Peter said, 'The store with the crossed swords is where you can buy Meissen.'

My mum's face hovered as she window-shopped through the glass.

'We don't need crockery,' I said.

'It's *porcelain*. And an investment.'

'But we don't invest.'

'But in the GDR.'

Peter said, 'Or perhaps just a souvenir of the summer. Something to take home with you.'

The coach pulled up at the Rathaus. We followed Peter down a flight of steps into a medieval cellar and the smell of gravy and acid. Iron chandeliers hung from chains and burned electric candles. A few rays of sunlight sliced through the stained-glass windows, spilling kaleidoscopic battle scenes across the tablecloth. Two long tables were reserved for us, the seating prearranged. My mum and I were next to James. Lunch was served by young women in bodices and puff-sleeves. While she waited, my mum played with the knives and forks, making medieval emblems with them. In the end, she leant over to James. 'You know Peter's wife. How did she die?'

'Car crash. Terrible,' said to the tablecloth.

Then the food was lowered in front of us, '*Eisbein*' according to the waitress, but actually severed leg. My mum pulled a face. She took a while to pick up her cutlery, and that was only to make flagstones of her *Bratkartoffeln* and wreaths of her sauerkraut. She watched other people eat. Her eyes settled on the next table, where Peter sat with Stefan and Saskia. They all ate in silence, and slowly too, as if they had a lot to think about. Beside me, James dissected his lunch, peeling back skin and fat and muscle to lay bare the bone. Then he decided against. Even so, the veg was enough to reduce him to helplessness with a downwards rush of blood. Every afternoon he had a nap. All the tutors did, apart from my mum who was too busy ploughing through her TODOs. It was meant to be a summer free of lists: people were *for* her here. That's what she'd said. But my mum didn't seem to mind. Lists to help friends weren't the same as lists to battle Tamworth. And they had different stationery here too. Jobs felt easier on soft, squared paper.

Now my mum watched James sink low in his chair. 'Before you go, James . . . The car crash. How long ago?'

'Two years,' unsurprised, as if he knew the question was coming.

My mum folded her arms and pondered that, sucking on her teeth.

When all the plates were cleared, Stefan ordered Rotkäppchen. He circled the tables, pouring flutes of pink fizz and placing a word in the ear of most of us. I saw faces paused for the punchline, the thrown-back heads, the laughter. Some people made a play of wiping away a tear. When he got to me, 'For the purposes of this round, Jess, you are an adult.'

'You're not the ambassador, are you, Stefan?'

'Do I look like the ambassador?'

'So what do you do?'

'I am a waiter.'

'I mean, really.'

'Really? I am a secretary.'

'No, seriously. What do you do?'

'Seriously?' He reached an arm across to my glass. 'I am a secretary for peace and disarmament at the GDR embassy in London.' I watched the foam rise to the top, bulge as if about to spill over, then sigh back down. 'I deal in peace. And therefore in war.' He leant in close. 'And that is *very* serious.' Then he pulled a face as if to say, 'So there,' and neither of us laughed at that.

They'd arranged dessert in the revolving café of the TV Tower. We trailed across Alexanderplatz where tiers of fountains sprayed patterns on repeat. All the way, my mum murmured, 'Two years, that's all. Not long, is it? Not to get over something like that.' In the tower lobby, urban planners were showing off a maquette of *MARZAHN: Our future.* High-rise blocks towered in miniature over green-felt play spaces. Pregnant women humped over prams. Youths held hands and turned brown under hundred-watt bulbs. My mum took my hand. 'Two years, Jess. Do you think it's long enough?'

We followed Stefan into the lift and were whisked up to the Telecafé. He steered each of us towards a seat: 'Here, perhaps? Do not worry, you will see everything . . . Because it turns . . . Room to stretch your leg?' To me he said, 'Next to Anton? A chance to practise your French.'

But Peter stood beside us. 'Or with Martina? She's back.'

Stefan glanced over his shoulder. 'You said she was away all summer.'

'She was. But is not now.'

Stefan shrugged as if conceding. 'I would catch her while you can, Jess.'

Martina sat next to the window, her back turned, sunbathing through the glass. I'd imagined a female Peter – dark and solid. But Martina was translucent, the light mapping her veins like a figure not yet out of the womb. It caught the down on her cheek and made feathers of the cap of her hair. I saw her narrow shoulders, the first soft, countable bones of her spine. If the window had been open, she could have stepped outside and flown.

Martina didn't notice me standing there, didn't even react when I slid onto the opposite seat. In the end, I broke the silence. 'I didn't know when you were coming.'

She twisted her waist and said over her shoulder, 'Neither did I.'

'I've been waiting,' I said, which didn't sound how I wanted it to, so I added, 'but also not waiting. I hadn't expected to meet you here.'

'That is what my father said. That you were unexpected. It is why I have come.'

Then the waiter appeared. Martina ordered a cup of black coffee. I asked for a three-flavoured ice-cream sundae with extra mango, pineapple, papaya, lychee, banana and whipped cream. When the waiter had scribbled a number on a notepad and gone, she said, 'The international friendship fruits. You have exotic vocabulary. My father said you learn German.'

'A year's worth so far.' And then I added, 'Of West German.'

Martina hooked an eyebrow in my direction. She smirked. One cheek dimpled. Then she shifted in her seat to look directly at me. 'What is the difference?'

'I don't know. I haven't had a chance to learn East German yet.'

'Yet? And how will you? At school in England?'

'I've got a book. From the Foreign Languages Bookstore. I'll teach myself.'

She pulled herself up in her seat. 'And what does your book say about East German?' Martina's face was open, curious, but there was something in her tone that made me uneasy. I felt tested, that I should know already, should have mastered East German just by picking the book off the shelf. I tried to remember what it said. There were chapters on brown coal, Buchenwald and solidarity with the non-aligned countries. There was 'A Glimpse into the Year 2000', which was on the Third World War and human extinction. I'd learn complicated conditionals and subordinate clauses I couldn't follow yet, but which meant the United States was to blame for the End of the World.

'I'll be better at East German when I've read the book. I'll tell you next year.' I paused, wondering if we'd be back. 'If we can come back. If we're invited.'

She shifted her gaze an inch to the side and looked over my shoulder as I said it. I thought it might be to Saskia, or James, because they decided these things. But actually it was just the waiter with Martina's coffee and my ice cream. It came in a goldfish bowl and swam with tropical fruit, the cream spuming over the top. She stared at it, thinking something, I couldn't tell what – that it was as big as my head, would make me fat, was a better idea than a cup of black coffee. I nudged it towards her. 'You share here, don't you. Your dad said you've turned it into an art.' She gave me that thing with the eyebrow. Then she picked up her spoon – the light aluminium kind they had here that floated in your hands – and pinched the end between a thumb and index finger. She stuck an elbow to the table and dangled the spoon over the ice cream, divining with it.

I gripped my spoon in a fist and started to shovel. I didn't care what she thought. And through the ice cream, I said, 'You're learning English.'

'I am learning the English we have here. It is a kind of

English-in-a-can. Like soup. You have oxtail soup in England. Someone put a can in the *Morning Star* bazaar. My father bought it. In the GDR we have Summer Course English, and *English for You* English.'

I looked blank.

'With Tom and Peggy. You must know them. Everyone in the GDR knows them.'

I didn't think anyone in England did.

'The lemon squeezer? You must know that. I squeezed and I squeezed and nothing came out?' Martina frowned, as if I was even more unexpected than expected.

I tried to change the mood and sound breezy. 'One day you won't need *English for You*. You'll come to England and hear the real thing.'

'I do not think so,' said abruptly. 'That is why you come here.' She turned to face the window, narrowing her eyes. I followed her gaze till I found the wide copper glow of the Palace of the Republic. Unter den Linden elbowed down to a full-stop that must have been the Brandenburg Gate. There was the Rabbit Zone and the Wall. It looked like a scratch across Berlin.

'Actually, I am not from here.' Martina reached for the sugar bowl and pulled it towards her. 'I come from a long way away. From Zwickau, in the south of the GDR. We make Trabants in Zwickau.' She pointed at the road. 'It is where those cars are from. It is why we are famous.'

'Tamworth is famous for cars too. Three-wheeled ones.'

'Also for Robert Schumann.'

'We've got a famous Robert. Peel. He invented the police.'

'We also have a river. The Mulde.'

'The Tame.'

'Coal mines.'

'Coal mines.'

'You see? Small towns.' She shrugged. 'They are everywhere the same.' She dipped fingertips into the sugar bowl. I watched her lift packets out and slip them back, playing some kind of draughts with the brown and the white. In the end, she said, 'Only Zwickau is near Karl–Marx–Stadt and the Czech Republic.'

'Birmingham.'

'*Na!*' Which was a German sound that meant something. A half-word. But it wasn't the kind of thing that made it into a pocket dictionary. I couldn't go home and look up what she thought about Birmingham.

Martina said, 'We left Zwickau when my father got this job at the *Hochschule*. And my mother . . .' She tailed off, a packet of sugar in both hands. Then she tore off the top and held it over the cup, but decided against and put it down in the saucer.

Somewhere behind me, my mum's voice boomed. She chatted with Stefan: 'What's the word? *Glücklich*? And adjective endings? You mean I don't have to agree with anything? I can just be happy without any agreements at all?'

But only because she was in the predicative. My mum had no idea how complicated German endings could be.

'And your father?' Martina said. 'Where is he?'

I ran my spoon around the goldfish bowl and took a last mouthful of ice cream. 'He's dead too.'

She pinned me with her eyes, trying to see if I was having her on, if this was some kind of English joke.

'Cancer.'

Martina leant back and took a while to speak. 'It is why I do not like Time. You have it – usually not enough, but sometimes too much – and then suddenly it is gone. It is over.' She crooked her neck against the top of the seat and observed me. 'You know, I have thought about it. And there *is* a way not to die young. Not to die, even. You can have all the time you want. You just live and live and live . . .' She gestured at my wrist. 'No watch.' Which I didn't follow. That wouldn't make you immortal; it'd make you late. But Martina seemed to like the idea and must have liked it for a while. She didn't even have a stripe where a watch once was.

I sat back too. I stopped looking at the meaning of her eyes and focused instead on the mirror of them. There was my reflection. It was pulled out of shape and left to right, but it was me all the same. I rolled my head towards the window. A long, wide avenue headed straight for the vanishing point. Miniature cars took their time. On the horizon, inch-high chimneys pushed small white clouds into the cloudless sky. Trees were green. People lived in white flats with coloured balconies. Red flowers tumbled from them. 'It looks just like the future downstairs in the lobby.'

Martina reached out and wrapped her fingers round her cup. The coffee must have gone cold by now. 'Yes, we have a model future. You look down, and everything you know joins up. It is all planned. Everything is set out for you.' She held the cup to her mouth, the hardness of her soft eyes hovering over the rim. 'They make us a perfect future. They like to have things sure.'

6

The Young Communist League

Walsall, November 1978

The headquarters of the Young Communist League was in suburban disguise – a 1930s mock-Tudor house, four storeys of pebble-dash and peeling paint. Dustbins were missing their lids and off-target litter lay lobbed across the gravel. The autumn rain had turned weeks of give-away papers into papier-mâché news. At the top of the steps, a rack of doorbells and biro-ed names under yellowed sticky tape. I had instructions to ring the only blank bell. I heard the buzz and saw a shadow in the nets in the front-room window.

When I'd told my mum I was joining the YCL, she'd reached out and tugged me to her. She didn't say she was proud. She never used the word. Maybe because she was superstitious and suggestible, and the word 'proud' led in her head to the word 'fall', which was as good as making it happen. Instead she'd said, 'The YCL isn't a mass organisation, you know. Not yet. It's not the FDJ.' She pronounced it 'F-Day Yacht', which is how Martina said it. It sounded as though it took part in the D-Day Landings, but was not, in fact, a boat, as I'd first thought. It was the Free German Youth. 'Only I don't want you to be disappointed. Not after the summer. It's not a League of Martinas.'

But there could never be a league of Martinas. She was a one-off. She was the only person in the world who didn't believe in Time. She'd given up watches and she'd never, ever made a list, but was somehow still alive. And I'd never heard of anyone else who liked company, but preferably one person at a time.

Which meant you had to queue.

Not that I minded, being English.

Over the summer, she'd told me her school wanted her to be more collective-spirited. 'But they are wrong about me being antisocial. And I am for sure not an antisocial *element*' – because that would have made her something on the periodic table.

But it did make me wonder about the FDJ. One at a time made a pair, not a group. Was she actually a member?

'Could you imagine it otherwise? No, I am free. I am a German. And I am a youth. *Ende Gelände.*'

Now I heard, 'You lost?' A bearded man stood on the doorstep, tightening the cord of his tartan dressing gown. He rested his weight on the frame and swung an arm for the pint of milk.

'Ivan?'

He grunted and lumbered round, leaving the front door open. I followed his slippered trudge along the hall. Then, 'Park yourself here,' and he opened a door and disappeared. Hanging from the door handle: *Do Not Distrub.* I turned it over: *Plese Make-up This Room.* I stood in the smell of burnt toast and damp carpet. A reggae bass line dropped through the ceiling. It was dark in the hall, and the light socket empty. On the stairwell, someone was making a call on a payphone. It was full of denials that got louder and more frantic as they ran out of change, and ended without goodbyes. At my ankles, a surf of unclaimed mail. Some of it was personal – Christmas and birthday cards – you could tell by the shape. Someone in Birmingham really liked the Kevin Sinclair who lived here. They'd dotted his 'i's with felt-tip hearts. And they'd liked him for years, and kept on writing, judging by the postmarks.

And that was the trouble with friendships by mail. You never knew what happened to your letters. When we'd got back from Potsdam, I'd asked my mum what to do about Martina, how you kept up friends once you'd made them. She said, 'Put her on your TODO. Write. Keep her posted on what you've been doing.' But I didn't know if Martina would feel the same about letters as she did about people. I didn't want to appear too often and pile up unopened like whoever kept on sending hearts to Kevin. In the end, I put her down for the first of every month – wrote in my diary UPKEEP OF MARTINA, then wondered if it made her sound like a lawn.

Now I heard, 'Order, comrades! Order! Before we start, I've had an application to join the branch. Prospective member in the hall. Comes from an old Party family. I propose we allow her to be present until Membership, which is Item Two.' Whoever it was had hurled his voice at the meeting the way teachers do at broken rules. I heard a murmur, then the man who'd let me in opened the door a few inches and stuck his head into the hallway. He gusted old cigarette and instant coffee across my face. 'I'm actually Education Secretary, not the doorman. I just happen to live here.' He left it ajar and rocked back to his seat.

Inside, I found four people sitting around a table – an ordinary, oval dining table, their papers arranged like placemats. A man stood up and offered me a hand so full of muscle it could have prised my bones apart. 'Bickley.'

'Ivan?'

He pulled up an office chair and tapped for me to sit. Also at the table, a round, dark woman in a poncho, and someone behind black drapes of hair whose sex was hard to tell. Either way, no one here looked remotely like Martina. I glanced around the room. A wall of filing cabinets was labelled from *A* to *TEA, COFFEE & BISCUITS*. A mattress slumped in a corner, and grey sheets coiled across the floor. A jam-jar ashtray lay against the pillow. Footprints patterned the wall.

Ivan saw me look. 'This is YCL HQ and Ted's digs. HQ starts

at the carpet,' and he ran a finger along the line where pine-pattern lino met blue shagpile.

'And what about upstairs?'

'They're the neighbours.'

I glanced at a ceiling treacled with cigarette smoke. 'So the neighbours are in the branch too.'

'We try. We try. But for now, they just live here.'

'So you're the committee.'

'Correct.' Ivan made a salute against his chest. 'I'm Secretary and Chair. Ted-Education. Paula-Membership. Colin-Minutes.'

Ted said, 'This is the committee *and* the branch. We're all on the committee.'

'There are four of you?'

'Four at the heart of operations,' Ivan said. 'Four key players. The Quorum and the Inner Circle. And how many others can we count on, Paula? Who else is on the books?'

She cleared her throat. 'It depends if you count people who are in arrears with the membership. And it depends how long you let them stay in arrears before you decide they are gone, actually. They have left.' She spoke slowly and with an accent I couldn't quite place. Spanish, maybe. Or Greek. She did something with her eyelashes, something fluttery and anxious. 'I am sorry, Ivan. I did not think to bring the papers. I promise next time.'

'*Every* time, Paula. Let's get it right.' Then he turned to me, feeling his fists. 'But in this organisation, we punch above our weight. Why? Because it's not about how *many*, but *where*. Because we take positions of leadership. Vanguard roles. How many isn't the point. How many, after all, stormed the Winter Palace? It's about *where*, and it's about *who*. We pay attention to *who*. Colin.'

Colin jumped. He hadn't expected to be named as one of the Who. Behind his hair, he looked stuck. But it wasn't an invitation to speak. Ivan nodded at his placemat, wanting Item One. Colin gave Ivan his minutes. Ivan handed them out. They

73

weren't typed, and every half-line his writing shifted from leaning forward to leaning back in a seasick kind of hand. Before anyone could begin to read, Ivan said, 'Take it minutes agreed. Minutes agreed *nem con.*'

Colin stirred his hand against the page, then leant across to me. '*Nem con* is Latin for "none against".' But I knew that. All the minutes I'd ever done with my mum had been agreed like that. She said the Romans had such a big empire because they did everything *nem con.*

Ivan called for Item Two, and placed a hand on the back of my chair. 'Jessica Mitchell. Family's active right across the movement. They go back to the twenties. Her grandfather was a founder member. On Hitler's List.'

It was actually my great-uncle, but Ivan wasn't the kind of person you could easily interrupt.

'Mother's a member. Father's a member.'

I couldn't even tell him my dad was dead.

Ivan said things I didn't think he'd know about my mum and her time in the YCL. He said things that even I didn't know about my grandparents and what they did before the war. I didn't sound like me, reported – just as I didn't look like me in the mirror. Then Ivan mentioned 'pedigree', which made me blush and feel like a dog. I didn't know where to look, so I looked down. Under the table, unsold copies of *Challenge* and Ted's toes clawing at the carpet.

'So, Jess. To the formalities. Because we *do* take care of the Who. Please summarise why you want to be admitted to the Walsall branch of the YCL.'

'Because Tamworth doesn't have one. And you're not too far on the bus. And my mum said there aren't any gangsters in Walsall.'

No reaction. I wondered if I was meant to keep going – tell them how I'd written to Ivan and he'd invited me here. He'd sent me a map, hand-drawn with the route marked in arrows from Walsall bus station to a house marked 'HQ'.

Ivan said, 'My question is: why do you want to join *any* branch? Why do you want to join the YCL *at all*?'

And now I was lost. Why would someone in the YCL want to know why I wanted to be in it too? It must be a trick question. So I rolled back and forth in my seat, answering with the creak of unoiled wheels. Ivan tipped his chair, rocking on the front legs. In the end, 'Well, you've seen Actually Existing Socialism, haven't you. Been to the GDR. Been to Potsdam.'

Colin said, 'Potsdam's supposed to be lovely.' He minuted it with a loop on the capital P.

'Not as a *tourist*,' Ivan said. 'Not on holiday. As a guest of the leadership. Working for the Ministry. Making useful contacts. She's got a well-connected mum.'

I hadn't expected that. But maybe she was now. Peter liked her. And Stefan. And James, and . . . 'And I met a girl called Martina, and she taught me German swear words and how to open a beer bottle with a cigarette lighter. And when I got back, I was thinking about Martina, and I was hoping that—'

'We're all friends here, aren't we, comrades. On the same side. Fighting the same fight.' Ivan threw open his arms, as if batting his friends aside.

I glanced round the table. Paula was engrossed in the tin of *All Time Family Favourites*, filing biscuits back into place. Colin was cleaning his fingers, using a nail to hook out grime. Ted stared out of the window and sucked Mellow Birds into his moustache. My eyes dropped to the table, to the blister of something hot in the middle and the extension leaf not quite engaging. Ivan's friends didn't seem that friendly. But then I thought Martina had stared out of the window and played with her coffee too. Maybe that's what friends did when you first met them. It was the over-friendly people you had to be wary of.

And then I heard Paula's voice, muffled through a biscuit. 'We might be a small organisation, Ivan, but it does not mean we take everyone. Revolution is no game. I have felt the bullets.

I have seen the people die on the streets. I have seen the brains on the pavement.'

'I know, Paula. I know about the brains. But there's no danger of that. Not for a while. Not in Walsall.' Ivan checked his watch and checked the agenda. 'So can we move to the vote.'

It wasn't a question.

'All those in favour.'

That wasn't a question either.

And that was it.

Ivan said, '*Nem con*, thank you. You are now, Jess, a candidate member of Walsall YCL.' He splayed his legs, testing the ground with his double-knotted trainers. 'It's how they do it in the GDR. You don't just walk into the Party. You're put on probation. We're not the GDR. Correct. So this is informal. For my own satisfaction.'

'But what do I have to do?'

Ted said into his coffee, 'Whatever Ivan says.'

Ivan put a tick on his agenda, signing me off. Then he announced Item Three: Pol Sit, and my gaze wandered to the window. Political Situations were always long and hard to follow. You were dropped into battles that had been going on for years, and no one bothered to backtrack. You never heard the beginning. Maybe because there was no beginning. Because before every event, there was a previous one. Which was the trouble with history.

I let Ivan's voice drift over me and watched rubbish limp along on gusts of November wind. In the yard opposite, children swiped at conkers and fell in and out of friendship. After a while, I glanced at my wrist. I hadn't worn a watch since Potsdam, but still I felt it. The stripe was white – it would be till next summer – and the skin still flaking. Martina had been right about Time: you could have as much as you wanted. It was her version of Time Dilation, and it was more practical than sitting on a rocket at the speed of light and asking your twin how old they were. I'd read *Einstein for Beginners*, and *Marx*

76

for Beginners, and *Lenin*, and *Cuba*. And even without a watch, I'd not yet been late. But then, there were clocks everywhere: all over our house, in every room at school. St Editha told me the time in my sleep.

Now I became aware of the toll of Ivan's speech, sounding like the trailers for films at the Palace I still wasn't old enough to see. He was issuing doom about Poland and a new Pope called 'Carol', about a CIA coup and a showdown across Eastern Europe. Out of the corner of my eye, I watched Colin scribble. I was glad I wasn't taking the minutes. I couldn't have kept up. I wouldn't have known where the capitals were. Most of the Pol Sit had sounded capitalised.

Ivan reached for his coffee and took a swig, but found it cold and let it run back into the beaker. His face looked swollen. Loose saliva had flecked the dining table. I wondered if he said this kind of thing every meeting, if there was an apocalypse once a month.

Colin used the pause to shake blood back into his wrist. Ivan watched, sucking on his teeth. 'How much you got there? A novel?' He rocked his head from side to side, following Poland and the Pope as they herringboned down the page. 'Here. Give us your pen. Give us your pad.' Ivan took the stationery and gave it to me. 'There you go. Present.'

I blushed. I hadn't expected one of those − out of the blue, in the middle of the meeting. But I could always do with paper and pens and didn't mind second-hand.

'Show us your handwriting, then. Just put the first thing that comes into your head.'

So I picked up the pen and out of the nib came: *Why, man, he doth bestride the narrow world like a Colossus.* We'd just done it in English. Ivan took the pad and turned it round for everyone to see. 'Now *that's* handwriting. That, I would call calligraphy.'

Colin looked anxious. 'What am I now?'

'Promoted too. Industrial Organiser.'

It took a second to realise what he'd said. 'You mean I'm the Minutes Secretary?'

'Your mum's got a typewriter, hasn't she.'

'Am I the Minutes Secretary, Ivan?'

'Can you get her to help?'

'Ivan, have I got to do the minutes?'

'Or can *you* type?'

'Two fingers.'

'*Jess . . .*' offering my name round the table. 'How many words a minute?' And then Ivan suddenly dropped his smile. 'A word of warning.' He tapped the paper. 'This is not paper. This is responsibility. Words are weapons. If you write the minutes, you decide what happened. You make history.'

I'd joined the YCL to make friends, and instead, here I was making history – just as James had said. Not on a global scale yet, but at least on a Walsall one. And I was beginning to think that history might be easier. You couldn't just type friends up, agree them *nem con*, and file them in a cabinet. You had to like friends, and they had to like you back. And then there was all the UPKEEP.

'Next meeting, Jess, we'll have proper minutes. We haven't seen those in a while. Tell your mum, and tell your Martina, you were promoted at your very first meeting. That makes you a branch record.'

Item Four was Humint. I'd read thousands of minutes, and I'd never heard of that. It sounded like sweets. I waited for someone to produce a tin and hand them round. Instead, Colin produced a Collet's carrier bag and emptied a stack of papers onto the table. He listed the meetings he'd been to in the last month and all the things he'd picked up along the way. I was supposed to minute this, but didn't know what was going on. Ivan must have read my face.

'Just put Human Intelligence, Colin, big tick.'

Then Ted reached inside his dressing gown, fiddling with his clothing. 'Unusually sensitive,' he said. He pulled out a sheet of paper and gave it to Ivan warmed. Paula lifted her poncho to hand over blurry passport photos. 'The latest disappeared.' Paula, it turned out, was on the run from Pinochet. My mum would love it that I'd met a real-life Chilean exile. She'd be straight to the Co-op to order two ponchos. 'Think what you can do under those,' she'd say. 'Develop a film, load a gun . . .'

'Jess?' Ivan held out the flat of his hand. 'Pen.' He processed the paperwork, scribbling his initials and the date in a corner. On one or two sheets he drew an asterisk. On one sheet he put two. Then he went to the filing cabinets – listing, full-to-bursting, battleship grey – unlocked them and dropped the papers in, barely needing to look. Then he locked the cabinets up again. Ivan's keys were chained to his trousers. He had to pull in his stomach and rearrange his jeans to fit them in his pocket. 'And something from you next time, Jess. I bet your mum's got Tamworth on file.'

At the end of the meeting, Ivan called for Any Other Business. I put my hand up. 'Can I go now, please? It's getting late. I've got to catch my bus.' It was the Sunday service from Walsall to Tamworth and I'd already have to run. But Ivan didn't react. He seemed not to hear – though he must have because then he asked for any other Any Other Business. I saw Ted stir, then decide against. Ivan said, '*I* have an item: your homework.'

He showed me the branch library – a case of books, their dust jackets missing and spines almost too faint to read. I could make out *One Step Forward Two Steps Back*, which sounded like instructions for a dance. *Left-wing Communism – an Infantile Disorder*, which was odd because I always thought communism *was* left-wing. Ivan pulled out a pamphlet: *The Tasks of the Youth*. 'Joseph Stalin wrote this about the Soviet Union in 1923. But the classics of theory can be applied at all times and in all places. These *Tasks*,' and he clacked its ancient pages, 'apply as much to Stalin's own children as to your mum in the 50s, and to you in Walsall right now, and to your friends in the GDR. And why? Because they're *scientific*. In a hundred years from now, people all over the world will still be reading this. Dialectical and historical materialism are the laws of the universe. They are the essence of everything.' Which made them sound like perfume.

Ivan ran a thumb across the pamphlet, releasing the smell of mothballs and the Granma into my face. Then he found a folded-over corner. 'Now listen to this: "All young workers and the best elements among the poor peasants and the middle peasants must be enlisted in the Young Communist League." Homework: take that sentence and study it. Go home and think about who the young workers and the best peasants of Tamworth are. I want you to apply Stalin to Tamworth.'

Ivan took my hand, claiming it in both of his, and holding on too long considering I was late for my bus. Then he made a gavel of his fist, hit the dining table hard enough to rattle the *Family Favourites*, and declared the meeting closed.

I ran to the station and got there as my bus was swinging out of the stand. I watched the rear lights disappear as it turned the corner. I checked the timetable, but the whole of Sunday had been blotted out with chewing gum. So I sat on the bench and waited. I watched gangs of girls go by with tight skirts and flicky hair, laughing into their fish and chips. The smell of vinegar made me hungry. The pub on the corner served *Apple Pie & Custard* but to *Adults Only* in rained-off chalk. Inside, a Beatles cover band was doing a sound check. The first few bars of 'Yesterday' spilled into the street, amped-up and fuzzy at the edges.

After a while, the cold from the seat seeped into my thighs. I used Colin's minutes as a cushion. At least they were thick. And the *Tasks* would pass the time. Inscribed on the flyleaf: *For Elsa, for being so good* in black ink turned brown. I flipped through the pages. Someone, Elsa probably, had started off making marginal notes, but the paper was shiny and her pen hadn't taken.

Homework: find peasants. The woman on our kitchen wall wore sackcloth and clogs and her wickerwork arms tossed seeds across earth that never gave anything back. She stood ankle-deep in the mud she'd die in. And when she buckled at the knees before she was forty, she'd be buried where she fell. Even dead, she'd carry on working because poor corpses made rich manure.

I knew that in the summer, on the way to Drayton Bassett, there were signs in the hedges for *Pick Your Own Strawberries*. But the people who worked those fields lived in caravans and had hammocks and tyre swings hanging from the trees. And near my mum's school there was Swan Farm, but it had Land Rovers in the yard, and horse trucks, and a sign in the window for two-star B & B.

We had workers in Tamworth, but they didn't clutch spanners and bunches of flowers and chant in Cyrillic, red-cheeked and happy to march in sync from a tangerine dawn. Tammie men assembled three-wheeled cars in the factory at Two Gates. They baked porcelain insulators at the Doulton plant and cut coal in Birch Coppice mine. The women took the bus to the industrial estate and made curtain fittings and three-pin plugs, or they put on a hairnet and took the company coach to the McVitie's factory before it was even light.

I turned back to the *Tasks*. 'What is the League: a reserve or an instrument of the Party? Both. The Young Communist League is a reserve, a reserve of peasants and workers, from which the Party draws reinforcements. But it is at the same time an instrument, an instrument in the hands of the Party, which exercises influence over the masses of the youth.'

And in all that same-but-not-quite-the-same, I was lost. I thought Stalin couldn't actually have written that. Not like *that*. Not in Russian. Someone would have noticed.

'It might be said more concretely that the League is an

81

instrument of the Party, an auxiliary instrument of the Party in the sense that the active membership of the Young Communist League is an instrument whereby the Party influences the youth outside the League . . .'

And in all that same-but-not-quite-the-same, I was back at the Grammar School listening to the coil of Mr Cartwright's voice as he recited over and over, and we murmured along till at some point he'd stopped and we were praying without him: 'Hear, O Israel: The Lord our God is one Lord. And thou shalt love the Lord thy God with all thine heart, and with all thy soul, and with all thy might. And these words, which I command thee this day, shall be in thine heart: And thou shalt teach them diligently unto thy children . . .'

And then I heard, 'Where do you think you're off to?'

A man stood with a boxer dog at the other end of the bus shelter. He was dressed in black waterproofs, the hood up, even though it had stopped raining.

I said, 'Do you know when the next one to Tamworth is?'

'*Tamworth?* What's wrong with Walsall?' Under the neons, the man's moon face beamed second-hand light at me. I looked at his dog, at his dark uniform, at his metal toecaps.

'You're not the police, are you?'

'Security. I'm on patrol, doing the rounds, keeping an eye.' He pointed to the emblem tacked onto his sleeve. I saw a mountain capped with snow, but then he came over and when I looked closer, it was just a holiday badge, a souvenir from Helvellyn. 'I'm a volunteer force of one. Like to make sure no one's going anywhere daft.' He sat next to me, steering his dog by the chain, and settled him between his feet. 'This one's all right, Bugner,' he said. 'At ease.' The dog slumped forward and rested its chin on its paws, its jowls adding wet to the pavement.

The man turned his small, glassy eyes on me. 'Keeps me busy. Lots of fresh air. It's a cold one tonight. Look at that clear sky. You wearing enough?' Then he lifted a hand, the lead tightening, registering in Bugner's neck. 'See that there?' I followed his finger to Orion's Belt. 'That's the Dog Collar, that one is.' He swung his arm across the faint orange glow of Walsall and showed me the Bone, the Paw, the Pedigree Chum. Bugner lay at his feet, listening to his owner rename the stars for him, untroubled by the cold and the sweep of bus headlights and the pull of his master's chain.

7

Election Night

Tamworth, May 1979

After that first YCL meeting, I sent an UPKEEP to Martina
with my minutes as an Enc. She replied with a postcard. It was
of Marzahn – four different views of a housing estate – with
Our future dashed across the back. And then as a P.S.: *How many
young communists do you need to make a revolution?*

And that made me think I should advertise. So I wrote to
the *Herald* with a cheque from my mum, and placed a boxed
ad in the classifieds: *Jessica Mitchell would like to invite all people
under thirty to join her in the Young Communist League with a view
to founding a Tamworth branch and making a better world.*

It appeared between adverts for the Square Pegs Disco and
a Valentine's Day Dominos Competition. I had twelve phone
calls. Nine were on the Friday the paper came out, all from
one man telling me, in ways I knew I'd remember, that I was
a disgrace and had no right to live in the town. After that, I
had two silent calls, just heavy breathing, which was probably
the same man, except he'd run out of ideas for telling me how
to go. The last call was from the prefect who'd been 'asked to
leave the Grammar School' because of his 'taste in clothes', he
said. He was living in Brighton now, but had heard through
the grapevine about my ad. 'Tamworth doesn't care for misfits.
But good for you for shaking up Straightsville.'

A few weeks later, Mr Cartwright, the R.E. teacher, intercepted
me as I came out of lunch. He asked me to follow him to the

sickbay. I ran through my jabs. They were all up to date. I'd had BCG and tetanus and diphtheria. I ran through my under-wear – knickers, socks, bra, vest – all clean because it was a Monday.

In the sickbay, a tall man in a shiny grey suit was waiting for me. He didn't introduce himself. He just made noises about the weather, his gaze focused over my shoulder, on the First Aid poster and the outline figures who'd collapsed with heart failure, asthma, a stroke. Then he handed me a questionnaire and said I had thirty minutes. He gave me a pen – a gold Parker, the kind you use for best.

'Can I have a pencil? In case I make a mistake.'

'There can be no mistakes as there are no right answers.'

'So it's not a test, then.'

'It is not to determine *whether*, but to assess *degree*. We are putting numbers to what we already know.'

There was an armchair beside the sickbed, but the man didn't take it. Instead, he stood against the radiator, adjusting the knob till he realised the heating was off. He went to close the window, but was stopped by the sign from the nurse: *Keep the air within as pure as the air without.*

The title page of the questionnaire said: © *Staffordshire Education Authority, SEH TEST 1979*. I flipped through. It was multiple choice and the questions looked friendly enough. But then I thought they looked over-friendly, and that made me wary. I said, 'In German, a *Sehtest* is a sight test. But this isn't, is it?'

'Because we're not in Germany. We're in England where we speak English. It's the Social and Emotional Health Test.'

I didn't know what he meant.

'To measure how well you function. Gauge your viability.'

Which made me think of the minivan. When my mum had taken it in for an MOT and said she was planning on driving to Germany, the man had told her he didn't think that was viable. But we were still going to do it anyway.

I said, 'Is anyone else having an MOT?'

85

'You are, I believe, the first in the history of the school.'

Which was nearly four hundred years.

I put his Parker down.

'Finished already?' he said.

I'd barely started, but the least he could do was stand in the smell of sick and Dettol till the thirty minutes were up.

If I hadn't made him wait, my scores might have been higher. Instead, when his report came through, I was way below the Staffordshire average for Friendliness, Caring and Respect, Rational Attitudes, Conflict Resolution and Peer Relationships. The report was stamped CONFIDENTIAL, but we took it to the printers anyway and had it enlarged and framed, and hung it on the living-room wall.

I'd been certified Unfit for England.

Alongside my certificate, the headmistress's covering letter to my mum. She'd written: 'You will be aware of the maxim: "Give me the child until he is seven and I will give you the man." The Grammar School did not, unfortunately, have that access in Jessica's case.' But Miss Downing looked forward to the change of heart that was about to transform the country, the return to moderation that would offer me 'a more appropriate moral compass'. What she meant was: the general election was coming up, and Thatcher was going to win.

And she *was* going to win, no question. It was a historic event – you could tell in advance – and we were going to mark it with something special. Rosie wanted a party, 'but a fun one. E.g. sex.'

My mum looked doubtful.

'Drugs?'

'Never have.'

'Rock and roll?'

'Not our thing, Rosie.'

'I know. It's a song.'

Rosie agreed, in the end, to fancy dress.

James was the first to arrive. Now he stood on our doorstep

in a green tabard and knee-high boots and handed my mum a bow and arrow.

'Wat Tyler?'

'Aren't you good.'

My mum leant her bed-sheet shoulders out of the door, smudging wheals of purple lipstick. 'Look what we're up against.' There was a Tory poster in every window, even Mr Howard's. My mum shivered.

'You're cold, Eleanor.'

'No! I am Spartacus!'

'No! *I* am Spartacus!' James said.

'No! *I* am Spartacus!' Actually I was a Free German Youth. Martina had sent me the blue shirt for Christmas. She'd included a note: *I bought you size Small, but now I wonder if you grow out of it already.*

Inside, the election-night coverage was starting on the telly. It filled our living room with doom-laden trumpets, sounding like *The World at War.* The faces of Callaghan, Thatcher and Steele appeared in party-colour code. Then David Dimbleby introduced our old friend the Swingometer, which would tell us whether or not Thatcher had made it. He was in a suit and pink tie, looking neat and keen and way too young to announce the Apocalypse. My mum ladled Bull's Blood punch into Meissen teacups, bought from the shop on Unter den Linden. 'To defeat!' she said, and took a sip. 'And *zum Wohl!*' because my mum was never defeated for long.

'*Santé!*'

'*Salud!*'

'*Na zdorovie!*'

Tamworth library didn't have *Teach Yourself Russian.* The assistant had told me they only stocked holiday languages. So all I could say was '*na zdorovie*', '*pravda*', which meant 'truth' and was the name of a newspaper, and '*mir*', which meant 'world' and 'peace'. Which, according to my mum, was all the Russian I really needed to know.

My mum headed into the kitchen and swung the cupboard doors, happy to hear them slam over the talk of a Conservative win. She searched for sugar to see us through the night. James leant back in his chair and sighed. 'You're a lucky one, Jess. There aren't many mothers like that, you know.'

Which was true.

I didn't know any mothers like mine. James's mum wasn't. She was Catholic and unmarried. She had a diamond voice and had walked all the way from Donegal to London with a knapsack and a baby to try her luck in the theatres. When she got there, she'd handed James over to the orphanage. James was a Coram Foundling, though he wasn't really found because he was never lost. He was, in fact, an Endowment. I looked at him now and wondered how it happened. Did you shrink as you got old, lose your own grip and slip around inside yourself? It was as if he'd come to our party in fancy dress of skin a size too big. He was so old it was hard to imagine he'd ever had a mother.

My mum came back with Angel Delight, cold custard and pineapple rings. She sang, doing her best to drown out the election: '"Every country and nation, filled with youth's inspiration. Young folks are singing, happiness bringing friendship to all the world."'

I conducted James in like he did in Potsdam. '"We-e-e are the youth" – boom, boom – "and the world proclaims our song of truth!"'

But he didn't sing. Instead, he flicked his eyes at my mum. But she couldn't meet his look even if she'd wanted to. She used her gaze as a spirit-level and spooned custard between the bowls, evening the portions up. Then I saw across the flutter of her arms, that James was watching me. He'd gone moody. I pushed a bowl of custard towards him. It usually solved things. He shook his head.

'What's the matter?'

'I'm just thinking back – to when I was your age.'

And that was so long ago, we'd study it in History. He was a teenager in the Great Depression, which was probably why he was looking depressed. When he was my age, the stock market crashed, Hunger Marches wound across the country, and Germans wheelbarrowed money round streets that would soon be full of Nazis. I hoped James wasn't going to tell me that these were the best days of my life, because that's what people said in this town. But instead, his damp eyes slipped over me with a leave-taking kind of look. 'I just hope it works out for you, Jess.'

'What?'

'Life.'

Which was the trouble with old people. They couldn't help being morbid.

Just before midnight, the doorbell rang. It was a long, leant-on ring, kept up till I turned the key in the lock. Rosie was dressed from head to toe in black and pulling hard on the last of a cigarette. I said, 'Provisional IRA?'

'The devil. Have we lost yet?' She took one final suck, making the tip flare. She tilted her chin, releasing a column of smoke, then planted the dog-end in the flower tub. Rosie breezed into the living room, her hair billowing and breath full of recent beer. It was a grand entrance to a room full of people that weren't there.

'I thought I was late. Or is there a queue for the loo?'

'We invited more, didn't we, Jess. But no one else could make it. Who did we invite?'

Mr and Mrs Lily, but they had bad legs. They lived in a bungalow on the Leyfields estate and rarely came to the door. As far as I knew, they never went through it. When you delivered minutes, a smell came out that was warm and sweet and meaty. Opening the letterbox was like puncturing a can of Irish stew. And we'd invited Sam Miller, but then he'd died.

James stood up.

Rosie said, 'Robin Hood!' James's next-door neighbour was in the Medieval Re-enactment Society. At odd times of the year such as not-quite Christmas and not-quite Easter, he appeared in the Nuneaton *Tribune* among the abbey ruins grinding the shine back into blades. Around him, men with plaits played hurdy-gurdies, dogs fought, clowns hammered nails into their nose.

'Offa? Oliver Cromwell? Give us a clue. William Tell? Give up. Who's Wat Tyler?' But she didn't wait for an answer. 'And who are you actually? Not *James*?' She burst into laughter, throwing her head so far back you could see the fillings. 'Not *East German* James? Not *Tankie* James?'

His face flushed. My mum was alarmed. She knew Rosie, and she was in one of those moods where everything was a delight. Rosie saw her look and said, 'All's fair in love and war.'

'Are we at war?' James said.

'We're in love! I've heard so much about you.'

His smile loosened. It hung unhinged for want of what to make of Rosie.

'Rosie's an old friend,' my mum said. She was thirty, which was more than twice my age. It was the age by which you should have done something or you might as well give up. Her birthday was in September, which meant she had four months left. But I knew nothing would happen. Apart from an overland trip from Selly Oak to India between university and her first teaching job, she'd lived in the West Midlands all her life. I always thought it was a bad sign – settling in Tamworth after Rajasthan.

For a while, Rosie's attention stayed with the telly and the election. But beer and the prospect of losing had made her hungry. Her eyes cruised the food on the table, then up to the clocks. 'Could murder a curry. Am I too late for the Light Dragoons?'

It was gone midnight and they only ever stayed open late for an X-certificate at the Palace or the Northern Soul crowd at Susanna's. But my mum gave them a ring anyway, just in case. She knew their number off by heart, and they knew her order. All she had to do was say the name. The takeaway was only round the corner, but we always headed out as soon as we'd phoned. While we waited, my mum could chat about British colonialism and say sorry for all the things we'd done.

Sorry for the Bengal famine. Sorry for the Amritsar Massacre.

'That's all right, Mrs Mitchell. Don't let it worry you.' The white carrier bag swung across the counter. 'Chicken korma, lamb biryani. Please enjoy your meal. It's not your fault.'

My mum did the same in the Mayflower Chinese – chit-chatted to the lady at the counter, who re-tied her ponytail and bounced the end of her biro as my mum apologised for the Opium Wars and stealing Hong Kong.

But the Light Dragoons were shut.

'Just give me anything with fat,' Rosie said.

My mum found a half-eaten slab of Christmas stollen, shreds of silver foil welded to the icing. She scratched them off with a nail, then splayed a palm across the cake as if it had to be tamed when actually it was five months old and as good as dead. But my mum loved to handle food, leaving an imprint if it was soft enough, and pass it to you hallmarked. It was all part of the sharing.

My mum sawed, splintering the icing and throwing white clouds into the air. 'Proper Dresden stollen. From Stefan.'

'Stefan?' James said. 'I didn't get one. He's taken a shine to you.'

'Don't be ridiculous.'

'Is he married?' Rosie said.

'Well, he likes you anyway.'

'*Likes?* That's different. Who doesn't want to be liked?'

Rosie said, '*Who's* taken a shine?'

My mum ignored her and tightened her grip on the cake.

Peter had. He'd sent us stollen too, and we'd eaten his first. It was gone by Boxing Day. He'd taken extra care with the wrapping, folded the paper right first time, cut the sticky tape with scissors and stuck it on straight. My mum had spent ages easing it off so as not to rip the paper, then she'd checked it, hoping for traces of Peter – for hair, lint, fingerprints.

He'd also written a gift tag: *For you sweetness*.

My mum had read it over and over, trying it out with different punctuation. 'What does he *mean*?' And we'd had a long discussion about commas and colons and the difference between 'For you, sweetness' and 'For you: sweetness'. My mum said, 'What do you think's sweet, Jess? Is it me or the cake?'

But she must have known. It'd been clear ever since that dance at the summer course Closing Social. Peter had asked my mum for it, and then he'd pinned her to him, and they'd bounced up and down to the brass of red-faced, crimped-haired men in flamingo-pink waistcoats. It was the final oompah of the evening and the last dance of the summer. Afterwards, my mum had said, 'How did it look to you, Jess? Did it mean anything? Because he danced with all the women tutors, you know.'

But it was only out of politeness. And what he'd done with them wasn't dancing. He'd taken an arm and assisted them to a chair on the other side of the hall.

When we'd got back to Tamworth, Time went from being Man's Dearest Possession to the distance between two summers. We'd spent the first five-and-a-half months looking backwards, and now it was May, and we were looking forward to next time. The low point was halfway through, mid-February – which was, coincidentally, Saint Valentine's Day. The post had come as usual with the freebie-junk and the bills. Neither of us had ever had a card. But I came down for a midnight snack and found my mum not looking in either direction, but poring over a cuppa in one of the Meissens. I think she was reading the leaves.

Now my mum picked up her teacup and took a swig of punch. The television cameras were panning over Margaret Thatcher's house in Chelsea, framing a shot with a foreground bough of cherry blossom. It looked like a picture postcard from the next Prime Minister to the nation. James reached for another slice of Christmas cake. 'Jam today, I say. "He which hath no stomach to this fight . . ."' He took a bite. 'I'll soon be going over to the Other Side.'

There he was being morbid again.

It turned out James meant the GDR. He was going to retire.

'Not from the *struggle*,' my mum said. Because the struggle wasn't something you could retire from. You could only die of it. Different medical conditions were named on death certificates, but they were all just varieties of martyrdom. 'Or is there an OAP shortage? Do they need the experience?'

James had done fifty years of meetings. Half a century of being Chair of this and Secretary of that. 'My attic's so crammed with papers the joists are starting to give.'

'But that's good, isn't it?' my mum said.

It meant he'd get off the plane in Schönefeld and be a Socialist Citizen. No visa this time. No deadline to get back to Nuneaton. But he'd have to give up the Potsdam course. 'I can't bring dispatches from this debacle any more.' He gestured to the walls, to England, Tory Britain, imperialism-the-highest-stage-of-capitalism, which was on my shelves but I hadn't had time to read yet. 'So a new course leader's in the offing. In fact, the conclave's already met. It didn't take them long. And it's *you*, Eleanor.'

My mum slung her eyes at him, knocking the nonsense aside.

'The GDR think you're a marvel. Enthusiastic. Full of energy. The best organiser of the lot of us.'

'They *said* that? *Who* said that?' My mum helped herself to a spoonful of custard, pressing it to her tongue. She loved the taste of Bird's and the feeling of being marvellous. Then she put the spoon down because doubt had already struck. 'But *me? Lead?*'

James said white smoke had never appeared so quickly. Then they'd put the decision to him and he'd endorsed it.

My mum's face dissolved at the compliments and the fait accompli.

'And you've got young Jess here. She'll do her bit.'

But then I was always here. There was nowhere you could go when you were a daughter.

Rosie looked at James with tender eyes, which was part affection and part booze. 'When you go, I'll miss you. Will you send a postcard? Do they let postcards out of the Eastern Bloc?' Then she turned her head to my mum – slowly, careful it didn't fall off. 'And what'll you do, Eleanor, now you're the Pope?'

'Stay here and struggle. We're good at that, aren't we, Jess.'

We didn't do anything else.

My mum said, 'Can I show Rosie your Hopes?' She reached into a back pocket and gave her a bundle of charts. My mum always carried my future with her, always had it to hand.

One meeting, Ivan had announced he wanted a clearer picture of where I was going. He wanted a Five-Year Plan. And that was difficult. I wasn't a tractor factory. And five years was forever. In five years, it'd be 1984, which was an O-level set text I didn't want to read because I'd have to defend the Soviet Union and fail the exam. And, anyway, I couldn't plan that far ahead if I was trying to give up Time. I'd already pruned my diary back to the bare Musts: Christmas, birthdays and UPKEEPS.

'So your plan is,' Ivan said, 'to give up plans. Does that sound logical to you?'

In the end, I'd decided to write down my Hopes. That wasn't planning Time; it was being cheerful about it. And there was nothing wrong with that, my mum said. She was a champion hoper.

After the summer in Potsdam, I'd hoped to join the British Army. I could get hold of information they'd find useful in the GDR. I'd rung Mark Johnson and asked if he could teach me to shoot, and if he had a leftover ANC gun. 'You have not

94

made this phone call,' he said, and the line went dead. Then I thought it was already too late anyway. I was a card-carrying member of the YCL. And since the Brandenburg Gate, I'd been on file. If the army let me in, it would only be to turn me into a double-agent, and I'd die twice, shot by both sides in all the confusion.

Sometimes I had to check my charts to know what I was hoping for. Like now, for instance. Rosie knew more about what I wanted than I did. I watched her read, head bent, hair across her face. I waited for a question, a grunt, a sign she was taking it in. I wondered if beer had put her to sleep. And then a page turned. My mum telegraphed achievements through her fringe: 'Jess's in the YCL now. And Ivan made her Minutes Secretary, just like that. I bought her an Olivetti as a reward. And she's doing her City & Guilds in Typing at the College. And she passed her probation.'

'I heard about that. I can't believe they put people on probation. They're desperate for members. You know Jess tried to get *me* to join.'

But Rosie wouldn't, even though she was just about young enough. All she did was narrow her eyes and say, 'Fail to deliver. It's the best thing you could do. You be careful of this Ivan. I know the type. I bet he's short.'

I still hadn't forgiven her for that.

Now Rosie sighed a parting into her hair. But it wasn't a wistful, wish-it-were-me kind of sigh, the kind my mum made. It was a gust of sadness. When she looked up, her eyes had changed. The tide had turned and the colour left them. Rosie said, 'When I was fourteen, I was showing the world my knickers and screaming at the Beatles. It's not hormones, is it, Eleanor?'

'It's commitment.'

'Oh dear.' She held my Hopes to her face as if to read them again, then her wrist hinged away, her fingers opened and the pages fell to the table. I watched Rosie's eyes crawl to the window and clamber out. After a while, she came back to the room and reached for the Angel Delight. She tipped it towards me. '*This is Hope. One Big Bowl of Pink Hope.*' It was already turning to sludge and a floe eased over the edge. She placed it on my charts. When I retrieved them, they were stamped with an arc of Angel dribble.

Rosie waved a hand as if none of it made any sense and she couldn't get the measure of it – even though that's all it was: Life, measured. She said, 'What if you want to bunk off? What if you're ill? What if something just *happens*?'

'Like what?'

'Like *life*. That's what life is. One thing you hadn't planned after another.'

I pointed to the asterisk, almost too small to see, and the footnote at the bottom of the page. But she didn't look at my Margin of Error. Instead, she leant across the table, across the scatter of plates, sticky knives, the domino-ed slices of cake from Dresden, and put her face so close to mine I breathed her breath. She'd drunk too much to judge distance and brought her lips so close our mouths almost touched. I'd seen that manoeuvre before – on the side of the swimming pool. It was what you did to the nearly drowned for your life-saving badge. That sweet, fuggy, screw-top breath was resuscitation. Rosie was trying to give me the kiss of life.

We jumped at the sound of the doorbell. Only people we didn't want to let in turned up on spec: closing-time drunks, Jehovah's Witnesses, Avon Ladies, neighbours we couldn't name.

'Just ignore it,' my mum said. 'It's no one.'

'It's a human being,' and before my mum could stop her, Rosie was heading for the door. Seconds later, she was back. Through closed lips, 'Error. Ivan.'

'Correct.'

'Soviet athlete?' my mum said. Ivan glowed in a red tracksuit and trainers, bouncing on the balls of his feet.

'I bring good news.' He'd been at the count for Birmingham

Sparkbrook, and the Communist Party candidate had got 715 votes. 'Now what do you say to that?'

James said to himself, 'Are we all *for* elections now, then?'

'Seven hundred and fifteen people voted for *us*. That's getting on for a thousand. And if every one of those got one other person to vote communist, and every one of those got . . .'

My mum handed him a glass of water. Over the rim, Ivan's eyes took us all in. 'Why are you lot dressed like pricks?'

She began to explain, but didn't get far because Rosie had turned to him – tired, slurred and spoiling for something. 'Is that what you do? Collect scalps for a living?'

My mum's face pleaded for peace. But Rosie didn't see it, or wasn't afraid.

Ivan sniffed at her, interested. 'I'm a full-time officer of the Young Communist League. I recruit for the cause.'

'And whose cause might that be?'

Actually, Ivan didn't work full-time for the YCL. Not any more. Not since his girlfriend got pregnant and he had to get married and earn some proper money. Now he had a job as a hospital porter, lifting dead-weight people in and out of bed, and a daughter named after Stalin.

Then Ivan spotted my charts. 'Is that your Plan?'

'No, Ivan, that's your tyranny.'

He didn't respond. He took the seat next to Rosie and leant in close. They were eyeball to eyeball and neither of them blinked. Rosie wore mascara, which meant she was good at not-blinking.

I slid down my chair and let my eyes track a path to the telly without catching sight of either of them. The election results had swollen from a trickle to a stream to a Conservative win whatever happened now. Grey-haired men in suits milled about windowless halls, and earnest women with crunchy perms fingered slips of paper. Every so often, Dimbleby appeared, the gap between his hands measuring the Tory lead.

And then the results for Lichfield and Tamworth: Bruce

Grocott, Labour, 40 per cent. John Heddle, Conservative, 50 per cent. Conservative win from Labour.

We heard the cheer through the window. I put my face around the curtain. There was the whoosh and bang of a firework, then a puff of white like a dandelion clock hung for a second over the Assembly Rooms, which is where they were doing the count. The National Front got 475 votes. We all looked depressed at that – except Ivan, who was rubber-cheeked and pink from the shine of his tracksuit. 'Not depressing. A measure of how much we're needed.'

Rosie said, 'But if every single one of those people got one other person to vote National Front, and every one of those . . .' But she didn't finish. Instead, she turned to Ivan and seemed to memorise his features, as if later on they'd somehow matter. 'Depressing.' Then she counted her cigarettes, took James's bow and arrow, and said she was going out to shoot something.

A gloom settled over us. James rested his hands on his belly and resigned behind his eyelids. My mum picked up the *Star* with the STOP THATCHER headline and buried herself in yesterday's news. Ivan watched her for a while, then jiggled in his trainers, sending vibes across the table till my mum looked up. 'Thank you for your contributions to our files, Eleanor. Your minutes are exemplary. *Concise. Precise.* But I don't know why we haven't heard more about Tamworth. You *are* a busy one.'

And she'd be even busier soon. 'My mum's going to lead the Potsdam course. She's just been anointed.'

'A*ppointed.*'

'Best way.' Ivan asked her to keep him posted. He could widen his scope. Rearrange the filing cabinets and set up a whole GDR drawer. He reached for a pineapple ring and hooked it on a finger. 'Anything for me now by any chance?'

'The GDR's upstairs.' My mum nodded towards the kitchen. 'But I might have left CND by the phone.'

Ivan found the papers. Judging by his expression he'd seen

most of it already. Then he let his big, black eyes linger over our noticeboard, soaking up the telephone numbers jotted on the hoof. He lifted the Light Dragoons menu and the giveaway calendar from the *Herald,* and only gave up when he got to the cork.

Ivan was restless. He wandered to the sitting room, his hands stirring his tracksuit pockets. He stayed in there a while. When he reappeared, it was with an armful of our Book Club books: *The Porcelain Collector, Wild Birds, The Art of Rhetoric.* He flicked through, but didn't read them. He was checking for anything left between the pages. *Decline and Fall of the Roman Empire* seemed to settle him, though. Ivan was finally stilled by full-colour plates of ruin.

I turned my arms into a pillow and watched the TV from the side of my head. The Communist Party had stood thirty-eight candidates in this election. One or two of them would have had their name read out first tonight, but only because results were alphabetical, not because they'd won. 'We will win one day, won't we, Ivan?'

'Win what? Power? An election? Not the same thing. Let's get it right. What are words?'

'Weapons.'

I tried to picture the day we win: Gordon McLennan on the steps of 10 Downing Street in his suit from a tailor in Ho Chi Minh City. He gives an interview into a large foam mic for Soviet telly. Tanks are round the corner, just in case.

I took a slice of Christmas cake, checked it for fingerprints and peeled off the icing. I turned to my mum. 'But will the revolution make it to Tamworth? Will we ever have one here?'

'Of course we will. Productive doo-dahs, Jess. Modes, forces, relatives. Something will happen – something really big and out of the blue – and it'll shake even this little town. And we'll be ready. One hard shove and it'll all come crashing down. The system will collapse at one fell stroke.'

Which was exactly how Nancy had died next door. And

she'd left a stain in the chair that Mr Howard had never got out. Not even with Daz and bleach, which is what she used to get the pit out of his overalls.

'The town's full of workers. It's just that they don't know it yet.' But Birch Coppice will come out, my mum said, and Robin Reliant will secondary picket. The Co-op will feed us all for free, and bury us for nothing too, if it all turns nasty. The TA will come at us with bayonets and bushes, and the *Herald* with banner headlines, but only till they see us winning, then change sides. 'And tonight-in-the-future, Jess . . .' She went to our record collection and pulled out the Soviet anthem.

'But *when*? How *long*?'

'In your lifetime, for definite. Definitely by then.'

I scanned the details of her voice. It'd deepened an octave with custard and staying up all night, but I could read every twist, tug and flight and fall of it. She wasn't making empty promises. She'd delivered 'in your lifetime' as if it were already written, as good as scientific fact.

My mum stroked the anthem with the duster. She squatted to release the needle and turned the volume up as far as it'd go. Then she opened the front door on conservative Britain. *Unbreakable Union of freeborn Republics, Great Russia has welded forever to stand . . . Sing to the Motherland, home of the free . . .* Alarmed sparrows tore themselves from the ivy. The speakers shuddered on their brackets. The front-room walls hummed. That roused us – even James, who'd been asleep for hours. It would rouse the neighbours too. I knew my mum thought of them, of Mr Howard and Ron and Reg, because she thought about people. But this time it didn't matter. Not on a day like this.

When it was over, my mum took command of the top step. She stood in her white sheet that was purple now from the Spartacus lipstick, and opened her arms to address our street. I knew she'd do *How the Steel Was Tempered*. She said it whenever things were complicated and she wanted to be reminded of the

Point. And it *was* complicated – being anointed and defeated in one night: 'Man's dearest possession is life, and since it is given to him to live but once, he must so live as to feel no torturing regrets for years without purpose; so live as not to be seared with the shame of a cowardly and trivial past; so live, that dying he can say: "All my life and all my strength was given to the finest cause in the world – the liberation of mankind".'

And then silence.

I wondered if my mum would really say that on her deathbed, or if she'd be too sick to remember her lines. I thought that what she really wanted was a yearly notice in the *Morning Star* on the anniversary of her death, and for people to read it, and remember, and to say over their first cup of tea in the morning, '*Dear* Eleanor. Dear, *dear* Eleanor.' She wanted to be remembered fondly. My mum just didn't want to disappear.

8

Treptow War Memorial

East Berlin, August 1979

The visit to Treptow war memorial was optional – according to the summer course programme. But nobody had declined. We'd all given up our Saturday Off to make the trip to Berlin: the British tutors, the French, the German leadership. But when we settled on the coach and Saskia did the headcount, we were one person short. Martina was missing.

'But she *has* to be here,' I told Peter. Her probability for turning up was one hundred per cent. For the first time ever, Martina had said for certain we'd meet today.

Saskia said, 'Indeed, she *has* to be here. So where is she?'

Peter mumbled something about stomach problems. They seemed acute, but indefinable.

Saskia pursed her lips, weighing his response.

When my mum and I had arrived in Potsdam, Peter had asked Saskia if Martina could join the summer course. She'd changed her mind about coming along. It was English immersion, as near to being in England as she was ever likely to get. Saskia had taken a while to decide. Teachers waited years for a place, and this would be queue-jumping. But in the end, 'I am unable to turn the clock back, but I can say yes to the course. And if Martina spends time with Jess, perhaps some order will rub off.' But she said she'd be keeping an eye. Martina had to take it seriously. 'No casual dropping in and out.' Peter had murmured guarantees, which he hadn't passed on to Martina.

But so far, she'd appeared every morning anyway, and we'd sat together in the back row. Martina didn't mind crowds so much when there was no one looking over her shoulder or breathing down her neck.

We'd listened to the lectures, and in the lulls played Hangman on the handouts, but with intricate body parts so we never had to die. We'd watched Peter do his turns as postman and MC, and sing the bass line in 'Fairest Isle'. I'd refused to join in, thinking it was about Britain. But Martina had said, 'It is code. The "seat of pleasure and of love". It is the Isle of Mons.'

Which it couldn't be. Mons was a town somewhere over the Channel and a battle in the First World War.

One morning, Martina had said, 'You know, my father gets younger and younger. Working all the summer used to make him old. But I think the course has become no longer work for him.'

Now my mum stood up, pointed down the coach, and said, 'Well, if Martina's place is free . . .' and she slipped past me to sit beside Peter. Stefan saw the move and eased round Saskia to take the seat across from them. It was a stately kind of dance, unhurried, with nods and formal smiles, made to the beat of a loose exhaust. Stefan bowed across the aisle to address my mum. 'So you *are* taking over the Potsdam course, Eleanor.'

'Yes, I *am*,' said with confidence.

Though it hadn't been like that when the news had first sunk in, the morning after the election: 'Me, Jess? Lead? Bollocks! Couldn't do it. Way too busy! And anyway, just couldn't do it.'

I'd told her it was just timetables and lists, and she was a champ at those.

My mum had stared at the living-room table, measuring up the dirties. There was no mess – it'd been a low-key party for a historic event – but still she'd made a tidying-up TODO in her head.

By the time we'd got to the GDR, my mum had decided the Ministry of Education hadn't chosen her by mistake. The conclave had met, the smoke had gone up, and she was The One, just like James had said. So she was ready when the call came to go to the Ministry for the handover. Two officials were at the meeting, kind-looking men, she said, but pale and pasty with the soft bodies of unrisen dough. Saskia was there in something tailored and white, and James, in his cufflinks. Peter was there too. He'd dug out a suit and tie from somewhere, and he'd had a haircut. My mum said he looked quite smart, smart.

They'd had to wait for Herr Whoever-he-was. It was a corner room, two sides glass, and the sun had beaten in, but the windows were closed against whatever might rise from Unter den Linden. Laid out for browsing, dead-weight tomes on pedagogy, but it was way too hot to read. It was too hot even to speak. In the silence, the hum of a mosquito and the turn of a fan that stirred the mothballs from my mum's wedding outfit – a fitted, sage-green two-piece with silver trim. 'Only worn once, and looks ministerial.' Actually, it made her look like a border guard.

Then the door had burst open and a man had come in, burly, too big for the room, too busy for the meeting. He'd asked everyone to confirm agreement with the handover.

Saskia had nodded.

James said, 'Beyond a shadow of a doubt.'

Peter said, 'I do.'

Then the man had delivered a short speech in long German words, opened a folder in front of my mum and handed her a pen. When she'd signed her contract and the meeting had turned into milling, Peter said, 'I can be more in touch, Eleanor, now it is official.'

'I look forward to more intouchability,' she said, because my mum made up words when she was excited, and because she didn't know how to pitch her reply, it being business, strictly speaking.

My mum had left the Ministry with the leadership and a copy of *Die Deutsche Demokratische Republik*. It was a welcome gift and a thankyou. The book would have taken up half our luggage allowance if we'd had to fly back. But we'd driven to the GDR this time, following James's black limousine in our mustard minivan. We drove from Nuneaton to Harwich and onto the ferry, then from Hamburg to the border at Boizenburg. The man in the booth had been expecting us. He hadn't minded what was in our boot and hadn't bothered with the mirror on the pole.

Now my mum said to Stefan, 'You know, the leadership was much sought-after.' She glanced down the coach, to the line-up of tutors' faces. Mark Johnson shielded his brow and squinted through the glass as if that were South Africa, not Berlin, and he might have spotted something – a glint of metal, a hint of the enemy. And there was Cynthia, a hand to her chest, out of breath from winning the argument with whoever was pinned at the window seat. 'And there were some who let it be known they'd done rather more than me to deserve it.' My mum had gone all passive-voice and posh. She did that sometimes – when she wanted to sound acid, but still take out the sting. Stefan leant across to rest a hand on my mum's arm. 'The Ministry chose *you* as leader, Eleanor. They have been most impressed with your energy, flexibility, your willingness.'

'Yes, I *am* willing . . .'

'And your attitude. You *like* people. It is so important to *like* people.'

'Yes, I . . .'

'We admire your organisation, your commitment, your engagement. The whole *you*.' He paused, letting his words sink in. If it hadn't been Stefan, the man from the embassy, my mum would have let herself roar with embarrassment. And she'd have done maracas if we hadn't been about to meet the dead.

We got off the coach, and stepped into silence. A stone gateway was wedged into a crescent of trees. It was the shape of the Arc de Triomphe, but a miniature version, done without fanfare, stacked up three breeze-blocks deep. The Russians had only managed an Arc de Fatigue at the end of the Battle for Berlin. Stefan slipped an arm behind my mum and tillered her towards a grey-stone statue. It was *Mother Russia*, though she could have been taken for *The Thinker*. She sat hunched and head bowed, a fist held tight to her chest. Willows draped their tips to the ground, and red carnations lay strewn at her feet like pick-up-sticks.

'And here lie the dead.' Stefan presented the perfect symmetry of five mass graves – grassed over, the lawn luxurious and edged with calf-high privet. It was well-tended death, regularly watered, minutely trimmed. If it weren't for the slightest curve of the earth, it could have been a bowling green.

'Five thousand of them. One thousand men in every grave. Can you imagine, Jess?'

I tried to imagine, but because he'd put it that way, I found myself doing arithmetic instead, working out how they'd all fit in, doing length by width by depth. I saw my mum gear up, thinking herself into the sum of Soviet losses. She didn't often get the chance to be moved by this much grief, not coming from a town like Tamworth. I knew from her face that her head was already full of mud-brown bodies squeezing into each other, the ones at the bottom pressed so hard they wore each other's uniforms and tried out each other's bones. My mum imagined all the time. She liked to think herself into other people's sorrow. She was addicted to empathy. She loved the feeling of being moved – the shortness of breath, the pressure in the tear ducts. I told her once she could get that from a vindaloo, and she said, 'I don't do drugs. Only korma.'

Now I took her hand and dug my nails into her palm. I meant to say: please don't cry. Not here. Not in front of Stefan. You're Imminent Leader not Mother Russia, and these soldiers aren't your dead. She registered my hand with a squeeze so long and hard my bones hurt. Then she rearranged our fingers, making a knot of them, and she tugged our arms, which could have been to toll her sadness or to flush the pain away.

Stefan stood in front of the graves, red with the heat. A tiara of sweat lay on his brow. His heart beat fast above his collar. 'Do you know how many the Soviets lost in the Great Patriotic War? Twenty-two million.' He took a finger and with a single swipe cleared the tiara. 'Do you know how many foreign powers have invaded? Eighteen. Including by you.'

'As *per*,' my mum said. We'd spent centuries invading – turning the map pinker, making sure the sun never set on us. In the GDR, the first foreign language might have been Russian, but the British tutors were here every summer to fine-tune the skills of their teachers because we might have lost the Empire, but English still ruled the world.

'The Soviet Union needs peace,' Stefan said. 'We *all* need peace. And still they talk of a Soviet threat . . .' He flung impatient arms into the air, making flags of his sweat stains and casting the Soviet threat off into the grass. In the lawn, cabbage butterflies pretended to be daisies. Clover recovered from recent mowing. 'When you get back to England, it is all you must think about. Peace. Peace. Peace. Your CND, Eleanor. Tell me about it.'

So my mum recited all the Crossed-offs of her CND TODOs: the letters to the *Herald*, the petitions, the collections in Middle Entry.

Stefan's eyebrows heaved in sympathy. 'In our GDR, peace is state-funded. We do not need to rattle buckets.' He said the Friedensrat could mobilise the whole country in no time. On the first of November, for instance, they'd circulate a petition on Soviet disarmament proposals, and by the twenty-eighth, when it's handed to the United Nations, almost every adult in the GDR will have signed it. Guaranteed. My mum's shoulders slumped with the effort of Tamworth. She'd love to decree peace to the town. She could do with state funding and a hotline to the UN.

'And what about the bigger picture?' Stefan said. 'Connections to the top. Influences. Structure. How does that work?' I knew from the way he steered her aside that he wanted a dialogue not a cabal. I watched their backs swing-door shut, his arm a crossbar keeping them closed. They walked in step, and all the while my mum drew pictures in the air of committees and subcommittees. It was just enthusiasm, but looked like signing for the deaf and the too-far-away-to-hear. Not that it mattered. Stefan didn't understand how it worked. I was now Imminent Assistant to the Leader, or possibly Imminent Assistant Leader. He didn't know that his tête-a-tête wouldn't stay private, and that tonight my mum and I would lie on our bunks with the windows open and in the heat and the coal dust do a moonlit debrief.

When I caught up with my mum, she was gazing at the jaw of a giant Soviet soldier. He stood on top of a miniature hill, a rescued child in his arms and a crushed swastika under his boot. He looked west, over half-mast granite flags, past *Mother Russia*, to the crystal ball of the TV Tower. Saskia led us up steep stone steps. Stefan waited at the back and followed the slowest up. Saskia wore white plimsolls, but not the toecap kind we had for gym that made your feet flap and smell of rubber. Hers were more like slippers, and she'd brightened them up this morning. But she'd made a mistake with the whitener and left a thread of paint on her ankle. I thought how she'd frown when she found it, and wonder if anyone had noticed, picking at it like a scab with those hard, pearlescent nails.

At the top of the steps, a Red Army guard held the kind of iron key that turned the plot in fairy stories. He unlocked the gate to the pedestal, and we eased ourselves inside. I smelt real flowers past their best and the fake flowers of fresh deodorant. The chamber was too dim-lit to see and it took a while for my eyes to adjust, but slowly, life-size figures grew out of the darkness. There was a grey-bearded man, a young blonde girl, a bent-kneed soldier, a worker in dungarees, someone from every Soviet republic in national dress, and they paraded their grief around the walls. They'd been put together from a million pieces and showed all the ways a face could be sad. We ran our eyes across the chamber and each became a mirror to someone on the wall. My mum's double was the bearded man. In an instant, she took on years, bags, sorrow. I knew she was parched, gasping for a drink in all this pent-up heat, but still water came from somewhere, still her eyes welled.

At a cue I didn't see, Peter laid a wreath from the Germans. But there was no room to bend. He let go before it landed, flicking his wrist and dealing the flowers to the floor. James was half his size, and he squatted in a gap between someone's legs to arrange our flowers. All day, he'd been cradling a bouquet of dark red roses. It could have been a gift between lovers. In fact, it was from the British tutors to the Soviet Union. We'd sat in the dormitory kitchen and argued over the wording on the card – about who the flowers were from and whether we could claim to represent people who knew nothing about the bouquet, or us – the British people, for instance. Whether it made sense, in class terms, to talk about *the* British people. Which conflicts the flowers were for – past ones only or anticipated ones too. Wars in defence of the Soviet Union or the entire Socialist Bloc. Whether we wanted to honour, remember, thank, mourn, or just point-score. Cynthia had lectured and Mark had clicked the bones of a hand, working from finger to finger, taking Cynthia's spit on the face without flinching.

I watched James take his time, tidying the ribbon and straightening up our message. I thought of Poppy Day, how the tray came round the class and everyone felt for a coin. They scanned the flowers and let a hand drift over them, trying to sense the right one, as if it were a tombola and they might be in for a prize. That day, they all hung their heads as they filed in for lunch under the names of the Old Boys who'd died for King and Country. No one told them about the Treptow Five Thousand. No one mentioned the Twenty-Two Million.

My mum and I didn't buy red poppies.

We couldn't.

We were sorry for all the dead, but didn't agree with some of the wars they'd died in.

Now Saskia asked for a minute's silence. Everyone turned their face to the floor – apart from me, who watched Saskia, and Saskia, who watched a second hand that didn't seem to turn. She was the mirror of the blonde girl, her fine face blown to pieces and stuck back together – carefully, but covered even so in fault lines. Saskia's hair had come undone. It was raked on her head and trailed at the ears, which might have been a style, but today, trapped in here, made her look disturbed. She was in white again – like a ghost, or a Miss Havisham. I'd asked her once why she always wore white, and she'd said, 'You make an error. You generalise your experience of the summer. But *in* the summer, I find it the coolest colour. And I find it works. Perhaps because it is no colour. Or perhaps all colours. You would know that, Jess, with your physics.'

When the minute was finally up, Saskia looked to the guard, who was waiting for the nod. I heard the drag of the key on the bolt, then the gate inched open and we stirred towards the rectangle of light. I caught my mum's eye and asked her to hang back for me, but she was carried forward by the swell of bodies, and instead, I found myself filing out with Saskia.

From the top of the steps we looked down on the graves. On each, a huge bronze wreath had greened. The air above the metal wobbled with the heat. Saskia said, 'You see? If you die one by one, you get real flowers, bright flowers with perfume from a garden. But if enough of you die, the flowers come from a foundry.' And the way she said it, so matter-of-fact mournful, I thought it must have happened to her. 'So many men were killed. So many women left alone. And the sad thing is, it is not possible to be sad because it is everyone's story.' Saskia nodded down at foreshortened everyone. I scanned the ground and found my mum. She was with James and Peter, studying stone tablets. Peter held his chin, feeling the bone as if he were punched there once and wanted to test the bruise. My mum ran the tips of her fingers over a rippling scene from the war, reading it in Braille.

Her head was full of the war. She was always talking about it – how she'd been evacuated, taken the train from Paddington to Devon, and on the way eaten blackberry sandwiches picked on The Dumps and turned into jam by her mother. In Teignmouth, Mrs Nicholson-the-Whore was waiting for her. She'd taken in whole gangs of children and stashed them in one room, six to a bed with a single flannel between them and holes in the floorboards and rats.

Later, my mum had been transferred to Mrs Crimp of the Salvation Army. She had a toilet under the stairs with *Daily Mail* squares threaded onto string. My mum was only five and hadn't learnt to read. But she'd kneeled in the gap between the bowl and the sink and tried to jigsaw the pictures back together. She wanted to know who was winning the war and if she'd ever get back home.

My dad had made bombs in a factory on the Thames. I knew his hand-me-down stories of Black Saturday and the Surrey Docks, how the winds from the firestorm had rocked east London and sucked out windows for miles around. I knew how lucky he'd been to escape. There were sky-high flames of Jamaican rum, Indian spices and Malayan rubber. Lots of his friends had died that night, the ashes of Empire stuck to their lungs. Some of his bombs might have landed on Berlin. Saskia might even have seen them.

'That war . . .!' she said. '*This* war . . . It made us. Every single one of us. None of us escaped, did we. Not the living and not the dead.' She tilted her face to the sky as if she thought the dead were up there. 'And that war made this country too. It is at the heart of everything that happens here.' Saskia scanned the ground for my mum and Peter and James. They were deep in conversation and shrunk by distance, but even so I could see my mum making big points with her tiny palms. 'Eleanor will soon be course leader. It is an important position. And you are her daughter. You will come to know our GDR. But if you are to understand this country – I mean, know what it is to be one of us – there is a story I should tell you. The GDR is an anti-fascist state, you know this, Jess. It is our founding principle. And it is why we are making the better Germany. And it is being made by people like me. I am a professor at the *Hochschule*. I have a doctorate. I am a member of the SED, a member of our women's organisation, and of my *Kulturverein*. And when I was young . . .' she paused, looked at me, and seemed to see me, '. . . yes, just like that, just like you now, I was a member of the League of German Girls.'

I didn't know what that was. I'd never heard of it.

'At that time, I also had a fiancé. We met in the theatre in Potsdam. A young man offered me his company home. His family lived in a grand house in Babelsberg. His father was a scholar, an academic. A nice family. A nice theatre. Both destroyed in the war.' She gestured to the graves. '*Ja*, he fell,' which made it sound as though he wasn't shot; he just tripped up and died.

'Here?'

'On the Eastern Front.'

Saskia spoke straight ahead about her war, how her headmaster had come into the classroom with hammers and saws and told the boys to make sickbeds from the desks. The school was now a hospital for injured soldiers. To the girls he'd said, 'Make women of yourselves and mother the Fatherland. *Heil Hitler!* Class dismissed!' Saskia didn't know what he'd meant. Her mother said it meant finding work where she could get her hands on food, so Saskia talked her way, with her long legs and bright blue eyes, into a job at the flour mill. She spent the war working the sifters on the grading machines, white-handed, lungs full of flour dust, and waited for her man to come home.

'We had to hand in our radio, so we had no idea what was going on. But we knew the Red Army was coming when every night we heard the cannons from Berlin. My mother said I should take food to my grandparents to help them through the end. I went by bike through the Drewitz woods, finding my way by the fires. I came to the bridge at Wannsee, and everywhere piles of dead soldiers, everywhere refugees. When I arrived, my grandmother stood in front of the house dressed in just an apron. Everything was hanging. I was there, Jess, when the Russian troops finished with Berlin.' I glanced at Saskia. She had the kind of gaze that could see through anything, but right now, she didn't seem to see. Her gaze hovered over the graves without landing. 'And after the war, came the hunger. Every day, the only thing that mattered was finding something to eat. The GDR was founded around me and I did not notice anything of it. And now, well, here we all are.' A smile glanced her face and was gone again. 'If there is one thing I have learnt, it is your friends can become your enemies and your enemies your friends. Knowing this has helped me to survive.' She pitched her eyes west at the afternoon sun, staring straight into it, and refused to blink, refused to blink, and only turned away when they filled with water.

9

Kulturpark Plänterwald

East Berlin, August 1979

Saskia passed back through the Arc de Fatigue and her reserve returned, her face blank-hewn as ever. She addressed the tutors. 'The rest of the afternoon is freetime.' It came out as one word, said quicker than two, which made me feel I had to hurry, that freetime wouldn't last long. 'It is a free choice what to do. But please tell me your decision. I need to know where you are in case of the many things that could happen if I don't know where you are.'

Mark hadn't had enough of death. He wanted to pay his respects at the Socialists' Cemetery in Friedrichsfelde. I knew the one – I had the postcard: a slab of stone the colour of dried blood and the words *Die Toten Mahnen Uns* – The Dead Remind Us. 'It's personal,' he said before anyone had a chance to ask. James knew he was about to fade. He had to find a beer garden for a Warsteiner and a nap, and there was a general move to follow him. Peter said to my mum, 'Or would you prefer a coffee? In Treptow Park?'

He led us over Puschkinallee. The café was packed, and he took a table that rocked on uneven paving, flashing signals into the trees. My mum was desperate for the loo, and I was too, now that she'd said it. We gave five pfennigs to a woman in a pink housecoat in return for a grey sheet of toilet paper. My mum chatted at me over the dividing wall. I knew she was perched over the seat, knees bent, as if skiing downhill not

114

emptying her bladder. 'Stefan proposed an exchange. Official. Funded. People-to-People, he called it. The Friedensrat to Tamworth CND. Can you believe it?' and all the while, the sound of hot pee fired against ceramic. Then a sigh of relief so deep it was voiced. I heard the kerfuffle of clothing – of zips, keys, money. Then the toll of the toilet chain and the bolt snapped back. My mum went to the sink. She was so focused on People-to-People that she didn't notice she was checking her face in a mirror that wasn't there. Then she turned on the tap, releasing the reek of chlorine. She splashed her face, the cold making her gasp. She didn't bother groping for a towel. 'You don't mind if I use you, Jess?', wiping herself on my sleeve.

When we came out, Peter had swapped table. He was sitting with Martina now. She looked relaxed, softened by the sun, as if she'd been here for hours. Beside her, a four-foot cone listed under scoops of plastic ice cream.

I said, 'I thought you were in bed. With stomach something.' My eyes cruised the empties on her table. Several glasses had been scraped clean of bright desserts. 'I couldn't believe you weren't on the coach. You said today was one hundred per cent.'

I picked up the menu. It was brash and brief, German on one side, Russian on the other. There were lots of Russians here – you could tell by the *da!* and the cheekbones – memorial visitors who'd bid a retreat to refreshment. They were eating purple ice cream, which was probably berries but looked like borscht, and they downed it in a race against the heat.

I said, 'Saskia wasn't happy you weren't there.'

'Saskia is not happy.' Martina picked up a glass and sucked the dregs of Soviet soup through a straw. 'But in the GDR, we have many heroes with many dates, and they all need red carnations. I am always doing memorials.'

I looked at her. Martina was so carefree. Or was it careless? Or perhaps they were the same thing. She was like some kind of animal, full of wants.

She said, 'But I wanted to meet you, so I am here. One

hundred per cent. But you see what certainty does. It worries people. It disappoints them.'

Which was exactly her reaction to my next Five Years. She said it was good, probably, that I had so many Hopes. But best not to be too hopeful about them. Then she'd given me a lesson in verbs, how a 'could' turns into a 'should' – just two letters between hope and duty – and a 'should' soon becomes a 'will'. And 'will' was another false friend.

Martina said, 'I want to show you something.' She stood up. So did Peter. She was looking intent, as near to in a hurry as I'd ever seen her. Martina, who never planned, seemed to have a plan. 'Kulturpark Plänterwald,' and she pointed to the Big Wheel that arced out of the trees. 'There is no Kultur. And it is not a park. But after all that death, I thought perhaps some lightness. I thought we could all go to the funfair.'

In Plänterwald, dazed children swaggered from the roller coaster. They rode bare-back horses with wild eyes and lacquered teeth for a thrill that would last an Ostmark. Over the sound of screaming, the Puhdys fell out of the tannoy.

Martina headed straight to the Big Wheel and asked for two tickets. Just her and me, she said, for the thing she wanted to show me.

My mum was relieved. She was close enough to see the metalwork and had had doubts about going that high up in a gondola that looked like a second-hand sugar bowl. I didn't mind risking death. I'd lived with it all my life. I was genetically half-cancerous, semi-dead already, just waiting for my body to detonate. I kept instructions for my funeral up to date, and my mum had the latest version: speeches that begin '*Liebe Genossinnen und Genossen*'. 'Here, There and Everywhere', and my ashes scattered on a summer breeze from the top of the TV Tower, so long as no one was eating sausages on Alexanderplatz.

Peter said, 'And what about us, Eleanor?'

My mum turned a full circle to see what else there was.

Right round the funfair, banners celebrated the 30th anniversary of the GDR. Fairy lights shone dimly in the daylight. The air roiled with candyfloss. My mum loved candyfloss. In the Bull Ring, there was a shop with pink and orange clouds of it hanging from the ceiling in a gaudy kind of sunset. She always bought a bag, for the nostalgia it brought on, and the maudlin.

My mum's eyes came back to Peter. Her gaze tracked every detail of his face – the cut of his eyes, the curve of his mouth. I knew that kind of examination. She sometimes pored over me like that, sitting on my bed thinking how comfortable I looked when actually she was pinning the blanket down so tight I could hardly breathe, and she felt dreamy and thought back – or maybe forward – and when she spoke, it was wistful, and usually a line from *Casablanca*.

I said, 'How about you shoot something?'

My mum didn't have a clue about guns, but she wasn't opposed to them either. It depended on what they were aiming at. I had a Lone Star twelve-shot cap gun, and I'd once aimed it at the Granma. I'd stood behind the armchair where she was eating breakfast and eased it into her perm till it reached something hard. I'd demanded money for the revolution. The Granma hadn't flinched. She'd raised an arm, removed the barrel, pinched her curls back together, and sighed into the spoonful of soft-boiled egg, timed exactly with a miniature hourglass.

My mum scoured the choice of target. There were plastic ducks, deer, and life-size soldier cut-outs with a bullseye over the heart. She said she didn't want to kill any of them. Not even The Enemy. But she didn't mind training her aim, keeping her nerve, not always thinking she'd miss. And if she was going to practise sangfroid, it'd be easiest on a bathroom accessory. The Duck Man seemed relieved to see us. His cross-wire worry lines faded. I think he was glad of the custom: The Enemy had a long queue. My mum gave him a coin in exchange for a plastic rifle. She sniffed it and peered into the darkness of the barrel.

'It is not army standard, but perhaps I can help,' Peter said. 'They're all just point and pull, aren't they?'

Martina took the gun and spun it in her hands. She did Defence Studies in school now. Preparing for NATO was a compulsory subject. She'd done projectiles in Physics and hand grenades in Sports. She cracked it open, checking for ammunition, then tested the sights and the pull of the trigger. She looked like she knew what to do. Then she pointed at the ducks. 'The target goes from this side to that. Four metres only. My advice is: do not leave it too long.'

Martina and I climbed onto the Big Wheel and jerked into motion. My mum's eyes followed us, watching the drop grow from light injury, to serious, to certain death. She swept an arm over her head and offered all her different versions of 'goodbye'. And then she shouted, 'If it breaks, jump as you hit the ground!' She knew jumping wouldn't work, but it was better than doing nothing. It'd take our mind off dying, and it'd mean the last thing we ever did was *try*. It was my mum's favourite verb.

Up here, the horizon was wide and bent – which proved the earth was round, or our eyes were, I couldn't remember which. Red-and-yellow S-Bahn trains curved from the east and the north into Ostkreuz station. Weisse Flotte cruises ribboned the river. On the other side of the Spree, a factory unfurled white into the sky. Martina somehow gave the slip to the safety bar and pressed herself to the edge of the gondola, not minding that it groaned. She pointed down. 'Volkspark Friedrichshain. You see those hills?'

'Is that what you wanted to show me?'

She shook her head. 'In Zwickau we have the Erzgebirge. In Berlin, the *Bunkerberge*. They are made from the war-rubbish of Berlin. Your bombs made the rubbish and our *Trümmerfrauen* cleared it. You must have them too.'

I supposed we had them, but I couldn't think where. I didn't know what had happened to smashed-up Coventry, London and Liverpool. We must have war-rubbish hills somewhere. Or maybe we just spread the rubble thin and raised the country one inch higher above sea level.

'They have one *drüben*,' she said, and with a finger pointed over the Wall. It was no more than half a mile away and looked like a zip across the city. On the other side, the sun also shone and threads of smoke rose from barbecues. Window-box flowers wrestled for sunlight. A miniature couple browned themselves in matching swimsuits.

'Their hill is way, way over . . . over . . .' and a hand shimmered in the general direction of what she didn't know. 'The Americans use it to listen to everything the GDR is saying. They listen to *everything*. Even us. Right now. It helps them plan for war.' I imagined a GI in battle fatigues in a fuggy bunker below the rubble. Headphones pin back his ears and his jaws spin gum as he twists a dial between thick fingers to tune in to Martina. 'They probably even have the button. Do you know how many minutes we have once the Americans press the button? Eight.'

It wasn't many minutes, for people who counted them. Which Martina didn't. She wouldn't notice the End of the World. Whereas I'd lived through Armageddon hundreds of times. At six in the morning, half asleep, I thought the dustbin men were nuclear war. I thought every thunderstorm was It. Even on Bonfire Night, when I'd seen the Council pyre in the Pleasure Grounds, and I'd watched the ads on telly about keeping your dogs indoors and your children at arm's length, I thought a firecracker over the castle might actually be an A-bomb over Faslane.

And I knew what would happen when The End finally came. I'd seen *The War Game*. You were either turned to a shadow by the firestorm or were flattened by the blast. Or you died of radiation sickness or were shot by the police because your burns were so bad they made a mercy killing. I knew what third-degree burns were like. I'd seen *The Incredible Melting Man*. I wasn't going to spend my last eight minutes sealing the windows and hiding under the table. My aim was not to die a virgin. But it was complicated. Who'd be available at such short notice? Mr Howard? Ron and Reg? They were the nearest, but would they be willing? Would they be able? Would eight minutes be enough? I didn't want to witness the End of the World from under a melting man.

I looked at Martina, at those tightrope eyebrows, at those shoulders that sat like brackets, as a by-the-way to her body. I knew Martina had had her *Jugendweihe*. She'd taken the Pledge, got her copy of *Der Sozialismus – Deine Welt*, a bunch of flowers, the pronoun *Sie* and the right to sleep with men if she wanted to. And I knew, from the Mons Incident and the long discussion after, that Martina wasn't shy. She'd asked me for a glossary of terms with ratings and sample sentences.

I said, 'If they *have* pressed the button, and there's one thing you've never done . . . Are eight minutes enough?'

She narrowed her eyes, timing it in her head.

'And if you don't have long, is it really worth it?' I didn't have much to go on. In Biology, they'd shown us a film – a cartoon of a man and woman who creaked against each other, performing a strange rite in jump cuts, wavy blue lines and church organ music behind them.

Martina nodded down to where Peter was helping my mum with a hands-on lesson. His head was pressed to hers. Their arms were straight and they swung them in an arc. From here it could have been a tango. She said, 'They probably do not have long. And they seem to think so.'

Which didn't make sense. You could see they had all the time in the world. There she was, my mum: Tango Dancer. Duck Hunter. Course Leader. If she stayed Leader long enough and did a good job, she might, in a few years, be called to the Palace of the Republic and be named a Socialist Brick. I said, 'Does the GDR give medals to foreigners?'

'We do not really have foreigners. Only fraternal guests.'

But I meant to foreign communists who helped the country.

'I think we give medals for everything. Sometimes you see the ceremonies on the TV. The broadcast lasts all evening. I think everyone in the country has a medal for something.'

Down on the ground, I saw the jerk of my mum's shoulder, sweat from her palms wiped onto trousers, the stallholder patting her on the back. Maracas. Then a handshake from Peter.

'Was your dad really in the army?'

'Military service. It is where he learnt to drive.'

My mum blew across the end of the barrel because it's what they do in the movies. She reloaded, ready for another go.

'And your mum?'

'Women do not do military service.'

'She did learn though . . .'

Martina leant over the edge of the gondola. In the fairground, children on the dodgems locked their elbows and swung their arms in and out of pile-ups. But the streets were almost empty. Puschkinallee was a green vault of sycamores. Every so often, a car emerged, or a coach, the road more or less its own. On the other side of the river, a lone truck lumbered over waste-land.

She said her mother had waited thirteen years to get a car. And when it had finally come, she wouldn't stop driving it. She'd taken her new Trabbie out every evening after work and was on the road all weekend. She was catching up on lost time and on all the journeys she'd only been able to make in her head. But then the autumn had come and the days had got shorter. She wasn't getting home till well after dark. When they pulled the car out of the lake, she'd had it only four months and there were 20,000 kilometres on the clock.

Martina knew something was wrong when her father had got home before *Aktuelle Kamera*. He never appeared that early. He'd slumped in his armchair, his reflection staring back from the turned-off telly, and given her the news that her mother was dead.

Martina said, 'Have you ever been in a Trabbie? It is very simple. Made from paper and cotton and other throw-away things, pressed into the shape of a car. Which is a good thing, in theory, to reuse things.' But the factory hadn't pressed it hard enough. It'd leaked. When her mother went into the lake, the car had just filled with water.

For a while, we didn't say anything. The Big Wheel turned. In the silence, we listened to a baby tired of a nipple whose crying had set off a dog. Then the Puhdys came back into earshot. It was 'Wenn Träume Sterben'. Martina couldn't help humming along to that.

And then she jolted. 'There! Look! Coming this way. Nearly at the gate. *That* is what I wanted to show you.'

It was Saskia. She was unmistakable in all that white. She looked unhurried, and even from here you could see her smile as thin as a tripwire.

Martina turned to me. She was soaking me up with eyes that didn't blink, with a gaze more forensic than fond.

I said, 'But how did you *know*?'

She shrugged, as if it were simple. 'Some things are one hundred per cent.'

Saskia's eyes were bright, brighter than the fairy lights, which wasn't possible. Light didn't come out of eyes. It went into them in physics books – disembodied, long-lashed eyes that were in just the right place for an arrow of light to bounce off a mirror and show you what was going on behind your back.

10

New Year

Martina was sure there'd be fallout from Saskia, but in fact the last two weeks of the summer course passed off just like the first: the back row of lectures, Hangman, English songs the English never sing. I soon forgot about Saskia and the way Martina's sixth sense had conjured her at Treptow.

But when we got on the train for the end-of-course holiday, Martina wasn't there. Peter said, 'She asked only to be a participant on the course, and it finished at the Closing Ceremony. I was reminded yesterday of this point. And it is, strictly speaking, accurate. Also, perhaps, fair. But I think not very kind.'

My only chance to say goodbye to her was the evening we got back to Potsdam. Early the next morning, we were leaving the GDR. All four of us met in the *Hochschule Mensa*. We gave meal tickets one last time to thick-necked women who ladled food from urns – rough-cut potatoes and tough slabs of meat – and looked tender when I gave them my emptied plate and asked for *Nachschlag*.

Martina said, 'The holiday would not have been a holiday for me anyway.' This year, we'd gone to Zwickau and Karl-Marx-Stadt. 'But you saw the Robert Schumann statue, and the Mulde, and coal coking in August Bebel. And you got to the Czech border but could not cross because no visa.' She'd memorised the holiday programme.

And we'd visited the Trabant factory, too, where the presses sometimes didn't press hard enough, but neither of us mentioned that.

'Dusty little place,' Martina said.

I'd quite liked Zwickau.

She gave me a hug – which I couldn't really take because I hadn't had a chance to change my T-shirt. Martina picked up her tray of dirty crockery and slid it onto the trolley. '*Auf Wiedersehen*, then. Drive safely. Eleanor has passed her test, *oder*?' And before I could answer, she was just the scuff of sandals on the stairs. Martina hadn't waved. She hadn't even turned. But then maybe that's why people said '*Auf Wiedersehen*' – to stop the revolving-door exits my mum liked to make. To keep them brief and meant and painless. Or maybe it would, if I practised.

My mum pulled out her Back-to-Blighty TODOs and recited what we still had to do: check no one had taken souvenir bits of the van, load up with a year's supply of the GDR, make a gap for the rear-view mirror, fill the tank, hard boil eggs, set alarms for five.

Peter glanced at the list. 'And your day will be finished by . . .'

My mum totted the timings up.

'Could you meet me at the Orangerie, say at midnight?'

She liked the sound of that. 'Will I turn into a pumpkin?'

At four in the morning, building work struck up, someone hammering at the end of the corridor. But when I came round, it was actually tapping at the door, and through the keyhole, a hissed, 'Jess! Let me in!'

My mum said she'd been there twenty minutes, but couldn't bang because she'd got to be discreet. And then she whispered what Peter had told her: Saskia had summoned him at the end of the holiday and said, 'Your fraternal relations have been noted. There is a time and a place for everything, and out of place would become extremely difficult.' My mum picked a strand of grass from the back of her head. 'Which means *in* place . . .'

Then I noticed the smell. 'Is that lemons?'

'Citronella. We were outside. There were mosquitoes.' She took my hand and squeezed.

I didn't squeeze back. I didn't know what might be on it.

We didn't bother going to bed. We set out for England early, which was a good thing, because we hit the military convoy from the barracks at Eiche-Golm and spent the first half-hour crawling behind a truck of soldiers, who waved at us and saluted, while we breathed their silver smoke.

There was no James to follow this time and I had the map. It was a long journey – held flat, the entire width of the mini-van. It would take us hours and I wanted to chat. I wanted to know what had happened with the Orangerie and the lemon juice. But through closed lips, 'Can't, Jess. Got to focus. We're on the wrong side of the road.' So we sat in silence all the way to the border at Boizenburg, where we tipped our unspent Ostmarks into the solidarity box.

We waved goodbye to the GDR and shut the windows to drive across West Germany. We reached the ferry at Hamburg and went straight to the All You Can Eat Buffet. Then we tried the on-board *Kino*, but didn't get far because it was a close-quarter screening of *Apocalypse Now*. So my mum called a cabin meeting of the two of us. She was sailing into Leadership, and wanted to make a start on planning her first course. She got in first with Bagsy Chair. Except there were no chairs, so we lay on our bunks and I called down names for next year's tutors. I got sleep-talk back. My mum was already unconscious. I watched her expression relive last night. Or that's what it looked like. Even dead to the world, my mum had an eventful face.

At the UK border, expressionless guards double-checked our passports and placed them on the counter between the tips of two fingers, as if they were soiled and contained a dirty secret. We drove out of Harwich through adverts and noise and hard-pressed people shopping to pop music, and sooner than seemed possible we were back in Tamworth.

My mum pushed open the front door to a mountain of post. She dealt brown envelopes onto the dining-room table. CND, CND, CND . . . It was what Stefan had said: when we get back to England, it's all we must think about: peace, peace, peace.

In fact, all my mum could think about was Peter. Our ordinary life restarted, except it was like the film of our life with 'Peter' as the subtitle to every scene. Term began. Miss Downing held an assembly with prayers for forgiveness for the sins of the summer. When I told my mum she said, 'Roll on more sinning . . .' When I fished for details, all I got was: 'Peter's *mine.*' Not that I wanted her to fill me in on the jump cuts and organ music. What interested me was the run-up. The Biology film didn't mention how you ever got from saying hello to fending off the insects.

In October, it was Speech Day. I shook a hand of Mr Heddle, the new Tory MP, and took *Wie der Stahl gehärtet wurde* from the other. It was compulsory reading in the ninth class, which I was in now, in the GDR-in-my-head. My mum came to the ceremony. A month on, and she was quieter. She turned the book over, pretending to read what it said, and wished Peter had been here to see it.

November was Poppies and selective regret. It brought on Treptow, and sadness, and the first shadows of doubt. Peter's 'intouchability' hadn't been quite what my mum had expected. She'd heard from him, but only two brief phone calls from the *Hochschule* Department, put through by the secretary who'd stayed around for the call. And she'd had one business letter, signed off 'fraternally'. My mum said, 'I don't doubt That One Night . . .' Her doubts were about the future. She asked Rosie, who thought at first my mum was talking about Stefan-the-Stollen-Man. Then she said, 'You mean there's *another* one? You kept him under wraps. You must be serious, Eleanor.' When my mum told her the story, Rosie said, 'It *wasn't* just a one-night stand. The Snow Queen said so. It's officially an all-summer, every summer stand . . . if that's enough.' Rosie made my mum a citronella candle for Christmas. At first, it was the scent of Hope, but by the last inch, it'd become the not-quite lemon smell of public toilets somewhere more exotic than England. But I couldn't ask my mum to blow it out.

And now we'd hit Dead Time, that endless week between Christmas and New Year, and my mum had succumbed to gloom. She took the last of the mince pies, and chewed on it without joy. Her New Year's Resolution was to eat better – three proper meals a day, just like in the *Mensa*. But for now, we were picking at the cold remains of Christmas.

She said, 'You know *That Night* . . .? Peter told me it'd be complicated, no guarantees.'

But then, my mum was used to that.

'He said he'd hung back because he was sure, but also unsure. But surely you're sure if you're sure or not? Do you think it'll last, Jess?'

I had no idea. I'd only ever known men stay one night, but there had to be exceptions. Most of the men in Church Lane had been with their wives a lifetime. Mr Howard married Nancy when she was twenty-one and stayed with her till she collapsed like the capitalist system. On cue, through the kitchen wall, a brass band struck up. It was 'Little Donkey'. Mr Howard liked the sound of miners squeezing stamina out of tubing.

My mum turned on the radio to drown it out, and the man in Broadcasting House told us it was nine o'clock on Friday the 28th of December, and these were the headlines this morning:

President Carter has described the Soviet action in Afghanistan yesterday evening as a threat to world peace.

I glanced at my mum. She frowned, mouth ajar. Pastry had moulded itself into a brace from Mr Kipling. 'Did he say Soviet something? Peace something?' The eight minutes flashed through my head.

She stuck the radio right in front of us so there was nothing between us and the news, and turned the volume to maximum because hearing it louder might make it clearer.

The new ruler of Afghanistan, Mr Babrak Karmal, is a long-standing Communist and is believed to have been smuggled into Kabul before the coup.

'Rubbish,' my mum said. 'Not a coup. The Soviets don't do coups.'

Yesterday, he was reported to have invoked the friendship treaty signed with the Soviet Union twelve months ago under which he requested urgent political and military aid in order to overcome unspecified external aggression.

'Told you. Military aid. *Not* a coup.'

Then an expert on international affairs came on, and spoke through the garrotte of a cold and a bad phone line. He sounded under-slept and over-excited. *The closest parallel we have is the invasion of Czechoslovakia in 1968 – though that was, you might say, an internal skirmish.*

I turned to my mum. 'Is that what it's like? Czechoslovakia? You were there, weren't you.'

'I was in Birmingham.'

'But you were alive.'

'I was busy. Busy with you, with work . . .' It was the beginning of a list. My mum's wrist turned, unspooling all the things that had kept her running around in 1968.

'Because if it *is* like Czechoslovakia, it's all right, isn't it. We know where we stand, don't we.' They weren't questions. My mum had supported the Soviet action, stayed in the Party and taken the flak. The deserters had been crossed off the Christmas card list and forgotten.

My mum put out an arm and switched the radio off. A ghost-voice finished its sentence and we were back to the Little Donkey. She reached a hand to the kitchen window, steamed with breath and kettle, and made a porthole in the condensation. On the other side of the glass, a week of rain had finally thinned to drizzle. She stared for ages at the brown slump of honeysuckle that had never flowered since Ron and Reg creosoted their side of the fence. When the porthole had fogged up again, my mum went to the sink, lifted out the dirties and remade the chaos on the side. She tipped the dregs from the bowl – the round bowl in the rectangular sink – the edge always catching till she hacked a bit off with garden shears. There was a gush of hot water, then she turned the Sunlight upside down, and pumped it till it gasped.

'Where *is* Afghanistan?'

'Dunno, Jess.'

Which wasn't true. It was on those maps she handed out at school. But she was in no mood to tell me, so instead I imagined Afghanistan – somewhere in that blur east of Europe, west of China, where everything was a Stan. Where the mountains looked like meringues and men charged about on wild horses, kicking up clouds of dust, their faces wrapped in tea towels. It was where long-haired hippies got their tangle-haired coats from. It was where blonde hounds with centre partings came from.

'What are we going to do?'

'The washing-up.' She put on gloves, heavy-duty ones, an odd pair, one turned inside-out, and stirred up a meringue.

'What did you do when it *was* Czechoslovakia?'

My mum flattened her Stan with a pile of dishes. Turkey, raisins, stuffing and pips floated to the surface as if the festive season had sunk not far from here. Then she spoke to the dregs of Christmas, and all the while a hand churned. 'I phoned the branch secretary. But he'd gone to an emergency meeting. And when I rang back, he said, "Eleanor, thank God they've gone in."'

I reached for our phone and rummaged in the bits-and-pieces tray for the back of a leaflet and something to write with. I knew Ivan's number off by heart.

'Bickley.'

'Hello, it's Jess.'

'What took you so long? Got pen and paper?' I could see him rocking in his trainers, braced for anything, his pupils big as he stared at me down the phone. 'The Americans are behind it. Blame the fucking CIA.'

'But what I need to . . .'

'No buts about it. The United States *wants* to destabilise the Afghan government. They *want* the Soviets to intervene. They *want* an excuse not to ratify SALT II.'

I knew things came in threes, so that was the last of the wants. Which was good, because my wrist was already starting to hurt.

'It won't come out for years, but the Americans have been secretly funding the . . .' and he said a long word beginning with 'm'. He could even spell it. Ivan knew everything about the place. He'd be top of the class in Afghanistani Studies.

Which made me think of my school report. Mr Cartwright had kept me back after R.E. because he was Head of Pasteurising as well as God. He'd held my report open in his palms the way he held the Bible, as if it floated, as if God's word was hot enough to rise. 'There is a parable here,' he'd said, and he read, sounding like the score draws on a Saturday afternoon:

    Latin: Effort E – Attainment C
    Geography: Effort E – Attainment D
    History: Effort E – Attainment E

'Do you know what this means?'

Relegation? I'd been worried about how things had slipped. I was now in the Danger Zone, twenty-fifth equal with Gayle, whose earnest but defeated eyes blinked through her blonde fringe in an Afghan kind of way. I didn't want to go down to the CSE League where I'd do just as badly but in Sewing, Child Care and Catering. But I didn't know how to improve my ranking. I couldn't make more effort – I didn't have time, not with keeping Ivan happy. And you couldn't do an O-level in Marxism–Leninism. Not in England, anyway.

I said: 'Ivan, what I need to know is: is Afghanistan anything like Czechoslovakia?'

'What's that got to do with it? You weren't even born.'

'I was three.'

'Exactly.'

It was true. My '68 wasn't Prague. It was the moon. Apollo 8. It was when I launched myself into orbit from the top of the garden shed. My mum bought me Milky Ways, which she ate to save my teeth – even though they were milk teeth and I'd get another go. Then she scratched at the wrappers to see if we'd won a Grand Prize from Cadbury's. That was the year the astronauts read a floating Bible in outer space. My mum said it was typical of the bloody Americans to beam religion at the earth as if they owned it.

Ivan called to his wife to put the kettle on. 'Now the background. Got enough paper?' He spoke in his public-meeting voice, booming facts down the line. I hooked a foot around a stool and dragged it underneath me. I signalled to my mum it might take a while, and tilted the phone a fraction from my ear.

I watched her count the Christmas cards. We had more than last year. 'Even more than last year, Jess!' she said every time another arrived. My mum had ranked them on the mantelpiece by how much she liked the card and what she thought of the person who'd sent it. At the back, the flimsy ones that wobbled when you opened the living-room door. They were from her pupils, addressed to 'Miss' and Christmas spelt with an 'X'. Then there were the cards from members of staff with proceeds going to the Rotary Club, Leonard Cheshire, the Spastics Society. They were also near the back because although they were better designed, my mum was broadly opposed to charity. Rosie had sent a card for Winter Solstice instead of Christmas, this year a linocut of a pear, or possibly a penis, wishing us a fruitful rebirth. Filling the front row, our greetings from the GDR. Martina had sent a postcard of the Thüringer Wald under snow. The rest were doves of peace. They circled the earth, flew over rainbows, faked Picasso. I watched my mum shuffle the peace cards like some kind of magic trick. And at the centre was my card – home-made, a Byron quote copied in Gothic script with my italic pen: *They never fail who die in a great cause.*

Ivan had liked it. 'But Byron essentially a romantic. Shelley the real revolutionary.'

'Thank you for the Death card,' Colin had written back. 'Try and have a merry Christmas, Jess.'

Ivan's speech was slowing now and I heard a slurp of tea. He was running out of things to say about the Afghan Revolution and the CIA. Then I heard my name. I checked the leaflet. Since the Three Wants I'd been doodling.

'I hope you got all that. Because I'm not saying it again.'

'Ivan, what I need to know is: what's the basic point? What do we *say*?'

I glanced at my mum. She was fiddling with the Christmas tree now, wrapping the tinsel like a scarf against the cold. But she'd heard the question and looked at me expectant. I put a hand over the mouthpiece and repeated what Ivan said: 'The CIA provoked it and the Afghan government invited the Soviets in.'

She grunted. 'That's what I thought.'

'Thanks, Ivan. And Happy N— ' but I didn't get to wish him one. He'd already hung up.

Then my mum handed me a plug, a screwdriver and a pair of wellington boots. The fairy lights had gone again. She wanted me to fix them because we'd done electricity in Physics and I'd know what to touch without dying.

The next morning was a Saturday, which meant the *Star*. I woke to the prospect of selling tanks to Tamworth. You could palm some things off on this town: the Leyland Princess, porch extensions, built-in wardrobes. But Soviet tanks? I wanted to skip a week. Next Saturday there'd be better news. I flipped back a corner of the curtain and peered outside. Across the graveyard, the Territorial Army was under drifts of spray-on snow. The sky was a sheet of iron. Raindrops clung to the guttering, a line of grey-yellow beads not light enough to evaporate, not heavy enough to fall. I looked at my bed. My shape was still in it and the sheets still warm. I wanted to do what other people did the Saturday after Christmas: lie there disintegrating, colour-coding the *Radio Times*, and stay there till it hurt.

My mum had slept off any leftover doubts. She was up early, guns blazing, ready for a full stint with the paper. She'd finished the Christmas fudge for breakfast and was on her second cup of tea by the time I was down. She watched me drift about the living room, dilly-dallying in my *Volksarmee* tracksuit. 'Are you selling the *Star* in your pyjamas?'

I trudged to the bathroom and ran the tap to make it sound as though something was happening. I did the kind of thing my mum did in the mirror: inspected every inch, looking for signs of decay – or maybe recognition. I probed my navel, the endless spongy folds of it that went deeper and deeper, like potholing in rubber, and wondered how the hospital could have tied such a complicated knot.

We took up our pitch opposite the butcher's. My mum halved the papers. I checked the headline: *Steel strike on, says union as talks fail. 'Let's get it over as quickly as we can': Bill Sirs.*

I was relieved. It was a lot of words for a headline, but not one of them was 'tank'.

My mum held the papers to her chest, then delivered in the lecture boom I knew from Potsdam: 'Support the Soviet action in Afghanistan!'

'What are you *talking* about?' I jabbed a finger at the steel strike and getting it over.

'Afghanistan *is* the headline, even if it's *not* the headline. Blame the CIA!'

The butcher had watched us set up. Now he left his shop and strode over to us looking in for the kill. He'd brought his cleaver with him, clumps of fat stuck to the edge. He stood so close I could smell the blood on his reddened whites – fresh, acid, fought over.

'I have to look at you two every damn Saturday and you ruin my day, you do. Would you mind just shifting, getting out of my line of sight.' He spat the words. They came out wet and landed on my forehead.

My mum spoke straight at him. 'He's being nasty. Just blank it.'

But how could I? There was an angry man who slaughtered things inches away from me, his saliva cooling on my skin. I didn't mind shifting. It was cold, dark and Tamworth. It was the worst possible combination for selling Soviet action in Afghanistan. I put my papers back in the bag.

'Where are you going?' my mum said.

'Anywhere. Away.'

My mum lifted her papers higher. 'The Soviets were invited in!' I tugged her sleeve. Her body rocked, but her feet didn't budge. 'The CIA provoked it!'

The butcher watched us and saw the tussle. 'Got a polite suggestion. Why don't you take your daughter and go back to bloody Russia?'

'It's not Russia. It's the Soviet Union,' my mum said.

He smiled as if charmed. 'I'd kill you if you was in arm's reach.'

Which she was.

'You too,' he said to me, 'if you was old enough.'

He spun the cleaver in his fingers, making the blade flash, then went back to his shop and wiped the cleaver clean.

'I'm off, then,' I said.

My mum checked her watch. 'Not time yet.'

'Not to the Co-op. I'm going back to bloody Russia.'

'You can't go *back* – you've never been. And anyway you don't speak Russian. And it's miles away. And freezing cold. You'd hate it.'

'People do it all the time.'

'They do *not*. Like who?' sounding aggrieved. She rearranged her papers, lining up the edges.

'Like Burgess. Philby. Macleans.'

'That's a toothpaste.'

But, anyway, I didn't mean Russia. Not actually Russia, the country. I meant Martina and Peter. My mum's arms flagged at the sound of their names. Her papers folded. I thought, for a moment, she was putting them away. A smile drifted over her face, landed and lifted off again. Then out of Bejam's came 'Another Brick in the Wall'. It was the Christmas number one. 'But, Jess, we can't just *go*. Not *yet*. Come on . . .' She reached for my hand. I was about to give it to her, but then she said, 'We're triers, you and me,' and my hand landed in my pocket.

'Why is it always *we*? I didn't say we.'

I stared at the ground. Pine needles had crept across from the Christmas tree. It was a present from Bad Laasphe. Tamworth was twinning with the town next year. Someone had taken a saw to it, and the Council had cordoned it off and hung a notice: *It Takes Two To Twin, Thankyou Very Much.*

As I went, I could feel my mum's eyes on my back. I knew she was counting the steps. Then, above Pink Floyd, I heard her shout, 'Just because you *want* something . . .'

I glanced over my shoulder, and my mum had turned into somebody else: a middle-aged woman in an Oxfam anorak, her zigzag parting grey, her face puffed with tiredness. A woman who, every week regardless, found energy she hadn't got to shout big slogans at a very small town.

I waited till Monday for the Nationwide to open. A woman appeared on the dot of nine. She looked crumpled, undervalued

135

and green at the gills, her papery skin worn thin with overuse. She swept the junk mail from the mat and unlocked the door. A few people were hanging around – the broke after Christmas – but I was the first in and nodded straight to the counter. I slid my savings book under the screen. 'I'd like to withdraw the lot.'

The teller took his time. He read every hand-written entry as if it were his money and his right to review the two deposits I'd made every year: birthday, Christmas, birthday, Christmas. Nothing ever withdrawn.

He stamped a smile on his face and closed the book.

Over the years, I'd saved enough for a day like this.

The teller wore a rubber thimble to flick the corners of the notes, counting with his eyes. Then he counted them again out loud, dealing them like playing cards onto the counter. He arranged them by suit: 'Star-crossed Lovers, Lady with the Lamp, Winner of Waterloo.'

It was first thing Monday morning, which was no reason to be cheerful, but it was New Year's Eve and he was probably talking through his first drink of the day.

'And I'd like to close my account.'

He cocked an eyebrow, cod-jovial. 'Let me guess . . . South America?'

When I got back home, my mum was running a bath. She craned into the mirror and sliced at her moustache with nail scissors. It was the 1980s in the morning. She'd be fifty this decade and she wanted to greet it looking as young as possible. She'd bought a dozen cucumbers for our New Year *Mensa* diet and had sliced one for her bags. A packet of hair dye stood at her elbow. This time, she'd gone for something French, permanent and too close to orange. If I were still going to be here, I might have warned her.

I pulled my rucksack from under the bed and checked the contents: knickers, Wagon Wheels, a mohair jumper – Martina had mentioned the winter. My watch, which I had to take because you couldn't defect not knowing the time. A phone number for James. I'd riffled my mum's address books, but Peter and Martina still hadn't got their line.

I clattered downstairs so my mum would hear me, because creeping always sounds louder than making a noise. Over the rush of the bathwater, my mum was singing to the mirror. It was a Ewan MacColl song, 'The First Time Ever I Saw Your Face'.

I'd already written my note: *Gone to bloody Russia. Join me when you can. xxx*

I stuck it by the phone. I wanted my mum to find it, but not straight away. I didn't want her to run after me and be dramatic at Tamworth station. She had to find it when she was out of the bath, had called and got no answer, dripped up and down the stairs checking all the rooms, phoned Mr Howard because she couldn't pop round undressed, then decided I really had gone and rung Rosie to ask what to do.

At Tamworth station, I asked for a single to Harwich, child fare. I expected to have to show proof of age and answer questions about what I was doing on my own on New Year's Eve. But the woman in the ticket office was halfway through a bottle of Baileys and way past caring. She didn't look up from her horoscope. She sold me tickets for a slow train to London and a slower one to Harwich.

I waited in the station café. Christmas still clung to the ceiling, criss-crossing my head in home-made paper chains. That was my last ever Christmas in England. My mum and I had done what we always did: watched *Morecambe and Wise* and *The Great Escape*, pulled crackers and heckled the Queen. And when my mum had fallen asleep, her paper crown on her knees, I'd gone to my bedroom and pieced together my Soviet tank, following a diagram in Russian and German. She'd bought me a T-34-85 in the toy department of the Centrum store in Alexanderplatz, but had made me wait till Christmas Day to open it. A song had played over us as we'd browsed the scaled-down stuff of war: *Unsere Soldaten schützen alle Kinder vor dem Krieg – meinen Vati, meine Mutti, jedes Haus und die Fabrik.*

I unfolded James's number and propped it on top of the payphone. On the wall, the emergency services had been worked away with a patient fingernail. Calling cards offered minicabs and busty massage 24/7. The phone books hung fattened with damp. It was New Year's Eve, but James hadn't gone out. I heard the beginning of a hello, then the fire of pips. I pushed a coin into a half-jammed slot.

'James, I'm defecting.'

'Who's that?' James always knew my voice. But he had his own phone in his own flat now, and maybe I sounded different on an unshared line.

'I'm getting the ferry to Hamburg.'

'Is that *Jess*? Are you all right?'

I was cold, that was all. I jiggled my feet, shoes slapping in a puddle. I put a hand to my lips and blew warmth over the knuckles.

James said, 'How far have you got?'

Through the payphone glass, a discount shoe store had its *XMAS SALE NOW ON!!!* It looked ransacked, the floor strewn with discarded bargains. Someone would spend their first working hours of 1980 matching them back into pairs. Gangs of men in jeans and T-shirts cowboy-strutted between tubs of municipal mud. They acted as if this were Texas, not Harwich, and it wasn't mid-winter and just above freezing.

'Tell Martina: I'll be in Potsdam Thursday.'

'Your mother will be going spare.'

'When I get to the border, I'll claim asylum.'

'It's foolish, Jess. And dangerous.'

'Not when you defect this way round.'

'But you don't just . . . You can't . . . You . . .' But James couldn't decide why not. Then he said, 'You don't know how to *get* there.' His voice was so clear, the GDR could have been

138

just around the corner. And anyway, I did. I had the map. And I'd done it once already. And they knew me at Boizenburg. I was there last summer.

Then pips again, and that was that.

For a while I held the receiver and listened to the hum. Then the crack and thunder of fireworks because someone couldn't wait for midnight. For a moment, the sky was smudged purple and orange like a last-gasp sunset. I leant against the glass and tapped my shoe in the puddle, doing 'Auld Lang Syne' in the English rain. I fingered my ferry ticket. I was defecting on the *Prinz Hamlet*, sailing over to the other side on the last crossing of the seventies.

I made my way to passport control. The man in the booth took a long, bored look at my documents, fiddling with his nostril hairs. He asked me where I was heading.

'The German border.'

'You're an unaccompanied minor.'

'I know. But I'm pretty sure my mum will follow soon.'

He asked me to step to one side, left his booth and led me to a blank door. Inside, a policewoman played a game of patience with a pack of topless women. She was short and wide, and looked put together with Lego, her thighs and chest square with kit. The border guard gave her my passport and told her what he knew. She sighed, put a woman with big blonde hair, who turned out to be the three of hearts, onto the four of clubs. Then she thumbed my passport, clocked the photo and checked I was me. She reached into a pocket, took out a notepad and spoke through tar. She wanted to know my name, address, phone number, who my parents were and where.

Silence. It was all part of the training. Name no names. Reveal nothing. I focused my attention on the walls. They were plastered with ways to keep England safe: mugshots of criminals on the run, bans on explosives, radiation, mad dogs.

The policewoman pressed her chin to her chest and addressed

her left breast. 'We have a lone female minor, located quayside, in possession of personal possessions only. Over.'

A mouthful of static back.

'ID established through ID carried about person in question. Over. Mike, India, Tango, Charlie, Hotel, Echo, Lima, Lima. Over. Attempting to leave the country for East Germany. Over. East. Over. I know, Sir. Over.'

Just before midnight, the policewoman pulled keys from a pocket, opened a cabinet and brought out a column of plastic cups. She filled one from the sink and handed it to me. The tap hadn't been run in ages, but at least it wasn't the usual: a tot of Teacher's; a list on my mum's fingers of all the good things, 'because there *have* been good things too, Jess'; a Resolution because my mum started every year trying to improve.

I watched the hands of the clock reach midnight and toasted 1980 with police supervision and water that tasted of pipe. The *Prinz Hamlet* had long since gone. I pictured the ferry spot-lit at the dock in beams that spun with mist. It belched black smoke and moved into the water. The lettering *Harwich-Hamburg* turned askew and shrank. Tail-lights winked and dimmed. Seagulls tracked it into the darkness.

Then I must have dozed because the next thing I knew, the policewoman had turned into a policeman, and Ronald McDonald was standing in the doorway. My mum was pale, her nose red from crying, the New Year hair dye dazzling orange. Her eyes scanned me as if they didn't dare look, braced for something awful. Then she whispered to the policeman, 'Thank you *very*, very much.'

Which you never, ever said, as a matter of principle.

Because the police were Instruments of Division and Rule, like the geometry sets we had in maths.

It was also why Tamworth invented them.

My mum came over and squatted by my chair. I let her pull me to her and put her lips to my ear. I narrowed my eyes against the chemical reek and the gush of what she might say.

Instead, she just made me listen to her breathe. She squatted for ages, longer than was good for her knees. I think she wanted to tell me that I'd killed her, but now we were here again, it was safe to come back to life.

She pressed her cheek to mine, putting our warmth back into circulation. Her skin was blazing. My mum said, 'You've gone cold, Jess . . . It's cold in here. Are you cold?' and she took off her anorak and draped it round my shoulders, the way they do in films to the survivors of bad news.

She said she'd known something was wrong when she'd called from the bathroom for the kettle. She'd wanted a hand rinsing out her hair. When she got no response, she'd looked all over the house, and then she'd found my note. She didn't think it was serious at first, but then she'd begun to wonder, and then to worry. And then she'd rung Rosie and Rosie had said to wait because teenagers just sometimes disappear. She'd waited all afternoon and evening, picking lumps of dried L'Oréal out of her hair. Then she'd got a call from James.

My mum said that all the way to Harwich, she'd talked things over with herself, and she'd realised she hadn't realised how much I wanted to go to the GDR, how important Martina had become. She put a hand on my arm and worked her way down, pressing inch by inch, hard enough to feel the bone. Under her touch, the mohair jumper. 'Such softness, Jess. I'd forgotten how soft, you know.'

Then she reached into a carrier bag. 'I've got something for us. Something GDR.' She pulled out a bottle of Timms Saurer. We'd brought a crate back in the minivan to see us through to next summer. My mum wanted to toast the New Year. 'Let's try again, Jess. Do it better this time. Let's make Tamworth as GDR as we can.' She raised a plastic beaker and tapped it to mine, making the clink with her tongue, releasing the scent of vodka and lemons, of Potsdam and bitter-sweetness.

11

At the GDR Embassy

London, April 1980

The year began very GDR. My mum's Resolution came good without us even trying. First, Stefan rang out of the blue. It was time to get going with People-to-People, he said. Friedensrat to Tamworth CND. GDR to us. And he invited us to the embassy. He wanted a dossier on how People-to-People might work, and we could give it to him when we were down with the summer course admin. For days, my mum hummed the theme tune for *Opportunity Knocks*.

Soon after Stefan's call, a letter arrived from the GDR. It was addressed to both of us, but my mum knew instantly it was Peter's handwriting. She must have pored over samples. She gave me the envelope to read. I recognised the stamps: the Karl Marx bust we'd seen for real in the summer. A Zwickau postmark, sent just before Christmas.

My mum turned her back to read the letter because she didn't want me reading it via her face. When she was done, 'Do you want the good news or the bad?'

I didn't want the good news, because that would be the Bible.

She gave it to me anyway. 'Peter's written to me, Jess.' Her voice was fairy-tale soft. What she could have said was: 'Happily Ever After'.

'To you and me. He's written to *us*.'

'And it's all OK.' Peter had apologised for the *Hochschule* letterhead and the fraternallys, but this was the first chance he'd

142

had to be away from Potsdam and put anything personal on paper. His letter was a licence for my mum to long – to let her eyes drift to the window and glaze over, to ebb in and out of sentences, to be unsure if that ache in the stomach was missing him or meals. My mum loved longing. It brought her closer to Chileans and their disappeared, to the Vietnamese and their dead. 'And in this struggle, there's a lorra lorra longing,' which meant she was delirious. My mum hated Cilla Black.

Peter's bad news was more fallout from Treptow. Martina had told Saskia she shouldn't have been barred from the holiday, and somehow it'd all got out of hand. Now Martina wasn't allowed on this year's summer course.

'How can Saskia ban her? There's no fence.'

'She's not *banned*. It doesn't say that. Martina's just . . .' and my mum found the exact words, 'discouraged from being seen on campus.' But there was a way round. Peter said I could meet Martina at their summerhouse. We could go sailing on Schwielowsee. I was invited to stay all of August if I wanted, and I was welcome to stay all winter too if I ever had the chance. I could try out things you didn't do in a country where the water falls as rain. Peter had enclosed a photo of what looked like a lifeguard hut, clinker-built and sinking under snow. In the garden, a boat was beached up on drifts. The sky was deep blue, the sun brilliant. 'Looks picture postcard,' my mum said.

I thought it looked cold.

Martina squinted at me against the glare. She wore a parka and raised a gloved hand to greet me, or to stop me, I wasn't sure which.

In April, we went to London with our dossier for Stefan. According to the *A to Z*, the embassy was just around the corner from Buckingham Palace. I thought it would be against the GDR's principles to own a mansion in Belgrave Square and have the Queen for a neighbour. I thought an outpost of the GDR would be somewhere cheap and full of workers – maybe Tooting because that also had Wolfie and the Popular Front.

Number seventeen had a wide door, wide enough for embassy people with world peace in their diplomatic bags. We'd brought Co-op carriers, handfuls each. The door opened before we'd even rung, and a woman was waiting on the doormat for the summer course papers. She stacked them against her chest – a black-and-red striped blouse that looked like an Olivetti ribbon – and all the while kept her eyes fixed on my mum as if I wasn't with her. Then she typed a one-line smile on her lips and headed for a door. She wound through backwards, which might have been politeness, but was probably just a balancing act with the handle and the paperwork.

I didn't see Stefan coming and I didn't hear him, his tread silent on the thick pile carpet. Then, 'Did you bring a book, Jess? Or else Hyde Park?' He forgot for a moment to shake our hands. He said something over his shoulder to the man at reception who fretted through his visitor lists, and mumbled apologies.

'Or feed the ducks, perhaps? Such a nice day.'

It was still drizzling. My anorak was wet from the walk from Victoria station. I tried to read Stefan's expression and gauge how serious he was about the wildlife, but it was blank in ways I hadn't seen in Potsdam. My mum's face puckered with disappointment, and that was a good sign. So I stood, hands in pockets, and waited. I fingered the tube ticket from Euston. I found an Opal Fruit, an orange one, it had to be.

My mum said, 'Jess'll just listen, won't you?'

I nodded. I would have said yes, but I was already just listening.

'And we prepared for today together. Joint effort – you'll see in a minute. I couldn't have done it without her.'

Stefan flicked his eyes from my mum to me and back again, his gaze tying us with some kind of knot. Then he stepped aside and gestured us both upstairs. He followed on behind.

'Can I help you with your bags? They look heavy, but I must say, also full of promise.' We'd come laden, filling carriers with everything we could think of. Stefan thanked my mum for the Potsdam materials. For the first time ever, he said, no passports were close to expiry. All the lectures had been typed. He'd somehow been through her paperwork already. My mum didn't notice, though. All she heard was the compliments. She blushed and gabbled to herself about pulling out all the stopperoos and making her first course splendiferous.

'And you will introduce the GDR to the traditional British sport of netball.'

My mum had been in the YCL netball team and hadn't played for years. But since Peter's letter, she'd been dying to put on a gymslip and show her legs again.

Stefan motioned us to his desk. It was empty except for a nylon flag and the Brandenburg Gate locked in Perspex. He found an extra seat. Then he slid into a black leather swivel chair and dangled his wrists over the armrests. Behind his head, a photo of Erich Honecker – the official one I knew from all over the place with the blue background and sun-lamped skin. Stefan was hard to recognise, though, in his shiny suit and tasselled shoes. He'd done something to his hair too – put a parting in it and slicked it flat. He could have stepped out of a Burton's catalogue and into an edition of *Mastermind*.

'Is it as you thought, Eleanor? You look surprised.'

She probably thought what I thought: that there'd be more Battle-of-Britain action – flashing phones, barked orders, tabletop battlefields and armies you directed with croupier sticks. But Stefan's office looked like all the GDR sitting rooms I'd ever been in: a swirly carpet in the shades of his brown tie. Orange chairs. A display cabinet with sets of crystal glasses. Shelves of floor-to-ceiling books.

Stefan said, 'It is homely here. I find it peaceful. And yet the Cold War is right outside the window.' He said the British finally stopped pretending the GDR didn't exist and then they arrived in the very same square as the West Germans. 'We are neighbours here also.' The Federal Republic was at number twenty-two.

I watched my mum slip into GDR mode, filling her lungs with familiar air, glad to be back. She shifted her seat for a direct hit of the sun. Her face glowed with Alberna. It was her favourite lotion now. She'd brought bottles of it back to Tamworth and had used it all winter – sat by the gas fire, eyes closed, and there she was in Potsdam reliving her August.

Stefan fired off a spiel about the status of the embassy and extraterrestriality, and it occurred to me I could defect right now. I could sit here opposite the *Mastermind* chair and refuse to answer questions till the paperwork was done. My mum must have had the same thought because she said, 'Jess tried to leave England at New Year.' And because it hadn't worked, my mum could be proud of it. 'She tried to defect.'

'Not to the GDR?'

'She nearly made it. She got to Harwich ferry terminal.'

'They let a child on the ferry?' Stefan drained the last of a tumbler of water, then rocked back and forth in his chair, fanning the smell of dry cleaning across the desk. 'You know, Jess, even if you had got to the border, our guards would have turned you back. There are proper methods.' That made me sigh. 'Methods' were what you had in Cookery – folding in and basting and baking blind – which were just ways of wasting time on things you could buy from a shop. I looked away and tried to find patterns in the swirls of the carpet, but there were no repeats, at least not around our feet. I didn't think there could be proper methods for defecting. That was the point. They were one-offs, surprise exits over to the other side.

'And, anyway, Jess, you are needed here.'

Which is exactly what Ivan had said. Though, what he actually said was, 'What the fuck were you thinking of? My investments don't go AWOL.' Then he'd made me Assistant Secretary and handed me keys to the filing cabinets.

'I thought you were angry.'

'I am. But flattery and promotion work better in the long run.'

When I'd told Martina, she'd replied with a postcard from Altenburg: *Wait till you hold trumps.* Which was very Martina, nothing said straight. And then another card had come with a photo of the tractor works at Nordhausen. On the back: *Wish you were here . . .*

Stefan wanted to get straight down to business. 'Why have I asked you here?'

My mum rattled her carrier bags.

'Because things have changed. Now is the time we all must know a friend from an enemy.'

Which was a line from a song. I glanced at my mum, willing her not to sing.

'E-N-D,' Stefan said. He spelt it with gaps between the letters as if it were an awkward combination, bit of a hard word. European Nuclear Disarmament was going to be launched on Monday, at a press conference in the Houses of Parliament. Stefan reached into a desk drawer and gave my mum the text they'd use. He'd highlighted the bits he didn't like. It glowed in her hands and turned the tips of her fingers pink.

'You know their tactic: appear even-handed . . . *Both* sides are responsible for the arms race . . . Dissolve *both* power alliances . . . It all sounds just fine, does it not?'

My mum's head circled, unsure if that needed a yes or a no.

Then she read what hadn't been released yet and Stefan told her what it meant: 'They will link peace with civil rights. Muddy the issue. Find our dissidents. Give negative-hostile forces a lifeline. No good will come from it. I know. I can feel it in my bones.'

Stefan had fewer bones than last summer. He'd put on weight, or his skin had thickened against the turn of recent events. He rolled on his chair, untroubled by the grate of metal on metal. Then he picked up his crystal tumbler, but found it empty. He turned it, refracting sunlight and spilling O-level physics problems across his desk.

'The problem people are Einhorn . . . Kaldor . . . Coates . . . Benn.'

'Surely not Tony?'

'You know him?'

'Everyone knows Tony.'

Which wasn't true. My mum didn't know him either. What she meant was, she recognised him on demonstrations, and when she gave him a wave, he waved back.

'Edward Palmer Thompson.'

He sounded too posh for my mum to know, but it turned out she did. '*The Making of the English Working Class*. Bit of a classic. Got it. Read it.'

Which must have been ages ago. My mum hadn't finished a book for as long as I could remember. She'd been on *War and Peace* for years.

'And now he works on another classic project: "The End of Socialism".'

Which was a bit hasty. Socialism had hardly got going. But I knew my mum would buy it whenever it came out – because you had to know what the other side was saying – and it would lie face down on her bedside table, gathering tea rings and broken digestives.

'This so-called E-N-D.' Stefan's tongue tried not to taste the letters. 'My job is to counter it. I must build other networks, link different people, get the right message out. People-to-People. Friedensrat to reliable groups on the ground. And that is where you come in, Eleanor.'

My mum sat to attention at the sound of her name.

'You have the dossier?'

She reached into a carrier and handed Stefan a wad of clippings from the *Tamworth Herald*. There was the report on our trip to Rugby market when we'd told shoppers they were sitting on a Polaris transmitter, and watched them duck for cover. The editor had thanked my mum for that story. He said he had no idea there was real news just down the road.

She showed Stefan photographs of us collecting signatures in Middle Entry. This was the Hard Core, she said. She'd ruled lines from faces to names, like one of her Geography handouts. 'Forty on paper. Twenty reliables. Ten dead certs. No one *pro-*Soviet, most not *entirely* anti.'

She handed him our letters to the *Herald* about the latest Soviet peace proposals. My mum said the paper wasn't usually so willing, but they gave us space in return for Polaris. Party members had kept that going for months, the ones too old to leave the house and help with anything else. Sam Miller had had his heart attack writing to the *Herald* about Brezhnev.

Stefan responded with his diplomatic face. He didn't gasp or squawk, which is what my mum would have done. She took it as a bad sign and gave me a thumbs-down kind of look. 'I hope not too run-of-the-mill. When you said details of the workings of a local group . . . I wasn't sure if . . . Did you want . . .' But her sentences died before they were out. Then she pitched herself on the edge of her chair. '. . . Or else we've got this,' and she gave him a handful of sheets, densely typed, badly photocopied. 'Higher-up stuff. From district committees. Minutes. Reports. Everyday running – subs, staffing, the usual.' She said the West Midlands district was a battlefield. The Antis were there in force and in league with the Euros. Unscrupulous lot. Unkind. And against them, there was Us. She drew clashes in the air, furious battles for peace, as they raged in front of her eyes.

Stefan watched the drama, then he turned to the papers, reading fast, his face unmoved. We listened to the sound of pages turn. All was quiet on the Cold War front. The silence drove my mum to speak. 'Or is *this* more like it?' and she handed over the last papers and put the empty folder back in the carrier bag. 'National committee. Policy stuff. Resolutions to CND conference. Including one on the Soviet Union.'

Stefan didn't react and he didn't meet her gaze, even though her eyes dug, trying to unearth a response. Her frown deepened. It was as if she wasn't there, perched right in front of him, and my mum couldn't bear not being there. It was one of the reasons she resented Tamworth. Half the town pretended she didn't exist.

'Or is that not very helpful either . . .?'

Stefan leant back in his chair, extracted his tie from his trousers and flipped it over his belt. When he looked up, he ran his eyes along his bookshelves, doing an inventory of the almanacs, yearbooks, the technical dictionaries. In the end, 'Oh, but it *is*.'

'Is what?' My mum had forgotten the question.

'All of it. Who's who. How the movement functions. Where it is going. What it is thinking. That is *exactly* what I must understand.' Stefan looked her in the eye as he spoke, delivering his thanks in the form of full attention. 'But how did you get hold of it, Eleanor?'

'I didn't. Jess did.'

'*Jess?*'

'She just borrowed it, didn't you, from the YCL. You know Jess is in the YCL now. Ivan made her Assistant Secretary, and gave her keys to the cabinets. They've got a whole library in there, and Jess can just dip in.'

Now I had access, I knew what Ivan had collected: years of material on groups we belonged to and groups who wouldn't have us. Meetings we'd been to and meetings we should have been to, but weren't invited.

I said, 'On a Need-to-Know basis.' It was the first time I'd spoken all meeting. 'And *you* need to know, Stefan.'

His face registered that. He gave himself up to his chair and folded his hands on his belly. His eyes had gone moist and glinty. They'd turned into crystal tumblers.

'*And* we've got a file on END. In fact, I set it up.'

'Aaah, *Jess*.' Stefan sighed my name as if it were Aaah, *Bisto*. 'And to think you were going to defect.'

There was a knock at the door and the ribbon woman was back with our Potsdam paperwork. She stood beside Stefan and fed it to him open at the right page. He ran his fountain pen across it, his signature losing shape and letters as he worked through the pile.

Stefan held up the last one to show us. 'Your crew for the summer. All aboard!'

I thought: all summer, Martina would be stuck on a boat on a lake. Couldn't Stefan have a word with his sister? Get Saskia to change her mind? I glanced at our dossier. What would a diplomat call it? Trading favours, mutual benefit?

I turned to my mum and tried to beam the thought at her. She caught the look and said, 'There she blows! Weigh anchor! All hands on deck!'

Stefan stood up to raise a toast.

My mum fumbled in a carrier bag, then swung a bottle at him as if to launch a ship. Stefan caught it in both hands and made a play of struggling to lift it. He read the label and gave a frown of mock disapproval. 'You are too, *too* generous.' My mum had bought the biggest bottle of own-brand bubbly the Co-op had. In fact, she'd bought two. There was an offer on, and she'd got the second half-price. The woman at the till had said, 'You know it's just nasty Asti, Miss' because my mum used to teach her.

My mum said to Stefan, 'It's Tamworth Rotkäppchen.'

He came to our side of the desk. He put a hand on the top of my arm and wrapped it round like a swimming float. 'What do you say, Jess? Shall we, Eleanor? To People-to-People?' He pulled the plastic stopper, buckling at the waist to avoid the spray. He let it spill over his hand and onto the brown-swirl carpet, which was what brown swirls were for. He poured three glasses, inch by inch, waiting for the head to die down.

'You know I'm underage, Stefan.'

'Not any more.' Then he raised his tumbler. There we were, all three of us, lit in miniature in its cut-glass mirrors. The Tamworth bubbly was warm and gassy. It caught in my mum's throat, the way tea did sometimes when she was chatting on the phone and forgot she only had one mouth. When she'd recovered, 'But the end of socialism, Stefan . . . They'll never destroy the Socialist Bloc. That'll *never* happen.'

'No, it will never happen. But, really, we could do without the bother.'

12

At the Lake

Potsdam, August 1980

The end of socialism troubled my mum all the way back to Tamworth. But when she got in, she reread Peter's letter and that made everything all right again. It was my mum's sticking plaster and it worked every time. Having Peter on her side meant the world would go on beyond midnight, that there was hope for life at the end of the day. We'd never lived with so few cataclysms and so much cope.

Which was good, because straight after our embassy meeting, Stefan sent the course paperwork to Saskia, and a fortnight later, her corrected version was back in Tamworth. She'd highlighted factual errors in the lectures, which my mum skimmed. 'Not errors. Nit-picking,' and she batted minor truths into the air and let them break on the living-room tiles.

The course programme had been tightened. The only Evening Off was now a cinema trip to see *The Way We Were*. 'We do admire Barbra Streisand,' Saskia wrote. 'It is a most principled performance. Is there anyone among the tutors who could offer a sound class analysis?' It went straight over my mum's head. She was already in the back row of the Filmtheater Charlott with her German Robert Redford and a bag of popcorn.

The end-of-course break had been turned from the Harz into Eisenhüttenstadt, 'a socialist model city and home to a world-famous steel works'. My mum didn't seem to mind. She'd climbed lots of mountains, and now she'd visit a foundry, which was more than the Mother Abbess could say.

And then Saskia dropped Don. It meant we were down one tutor and short of a lecture on sport. 'He was *never* a gangster,' my mum said. 'Peter liked him. Peter played cricket with him.' But if Saskia didn't want him, that was that. Finding a replacement wasn't so easy. It wasn't a big party. Martina had said once, 'Is it too much pressure to be a communist in a capitalist country? Does it make you strange? I mean the clothes that look as though many people of different sizes have worn them. The not standing up straight. The out-of-proportion of what they say.'

My mum found someone in the end who followed Cayton's tips in the *Star* and gave his winnings to the Fighting Fund. 'He'll more than do,' she said when she phoned Saskia.

'We are aware of the name and if that is the best you can manage . . . But next year, we will need some kind of expertise. There is far more interest in sport here than in Britain . . . but then we win far more medals.'

So my mum went to Collet's to gen up, but they only had something by Lenin on transport, so she bought a *Wisden* instead. We put *Grandstand* on the TODO and came close with Spot the Ball.

From the moment we arrived in Potsdam, my mum was a model of socialist industry, performing in the Eisenhüttenstadt way. She had to double output with a love-affair *and* a summer course to run. I'd never seen her so busy, and she did it without TODOs. She said she didn't have time to make lists. And there was a burn to her enthusiasm, a passion that spilled from Peter to the course and back again.

Not sleeping didn't matter. 'Who needs sleep?'

I did. And I'd been given my own room this year.

And now, standing in her doorway in the early hours of

6 August, her Hiroshima Day Peace Address still unwritten, I knew from the lack of oxygen she hadn't been alone. Her room was strewn with debris from some kind of party: charred remains in the ashtray, smoke I couldn't identify, a slew of cassettes we didn't own, beer bottles ringing the wastepaper basket that had caught the binned beginnings of her speech. 'You know theory . . .' she said.

'They'll like you more if you put some in.'

My mum's mouth thinned to an M-dash. Theory never was her thing. She always said: Capitalism's bad. War's bad. People matter. What else do you need?

I said, 'How about the Three Laws of Dialectics?'

'Did you get them from Ivan?'

They were part of the Essence of Everything, and they applied to the whole universe. For all time.

Except, it turned out, tonight.

My mum filled the gaps in her head with hummed peace songs: 'Blowing in the Wind', 'Where Have all the Flowers Gone?', 'We Shall Overcome'.

Then she tried to remember Stefan's speech to Tamworth CND. It was the first People-to-People event. He'd mentioned Ronald Reagan and *Bedtime for Bonzo*. Cruise and Pershing and SS20s as a necessary counter-measure, while raised eyebrows were tipped over warm Marston's Pedigree. Stefan had taken questions, though no one had any apart from Rosie, who had lots of short ones: 'Why don't the Russians disarm? Unilaterally? Now? Or at least start? What harm would it do?' She'd said both sides could destroy the world a hundred times over. What difference if you could only do it ten times, or only once? 'And think what a propaganda coup it'd be . . . if you're into propaganda. If you're into coups.'

Stefan had an answer, a long smooth one about wrong signals and signs of weakness. 'We have to constantly ask ourselves: Who is threatening whom?'

'That's splitting hairs. And infinitives,' Rosie had said. Which meant she'd taken against him. She only ever corrected the grammar of people she didn't like.

My mum and I fell into bunks when the first army trucks rattled the windows, and the piles of brown coal in the yard took on the pink of the dawn. My mum tossed about in her sleep, making the bedframe sway, and mumbled parts of her speech. Two hours later, the alarm went off. She got out of bed too blurred to judge distance, and when she walked into the mirror, she found she'd woken with the perfect face for Hiroshima Day. The Audimax was ashen, all the summer colours gone into the wash. My mum wore the black Crimplene skirt she'd bought for Sam, and took small steps to the lectern you could hear above the hush. She didn't need her notes. She recited her lines as she had last night in her dreams. Her voice was slow and deep with lack of sleep, her wrists too weak to whirr. The address wasn't long. In the end, we'd decided to forget Stefan and go for drama: paint pictures from Hiroshima of the dead and the dying. No theory. Mention history. A rousing ending about the 'unbreakable union of peace-loving peoples' – actually a rewrite of the first line of the Soviet anthem, but the Germans wouldn't know that in English.

Saskia caught us on the way out. She thanked my mum for her speech. 'It was . . .' She took time to settle on a description. 'Brief. And impressionistic. By which I mean it made a good impression.' She looked at my mum with her mineral-blue eyes, the kind sealed for safety in chemistry jars. 'And I think you said – correct me if I am wrong – that the Second World War ended with atom bombs on Hiroshima and Nagasaki.'

We nodded. We remembered writing that.

'I am sure you know that it did *not*. I am sure you know it ended with the Red Army victorious in the Battle for Berlin. The atom bombs were not the last act of the Second World War, but the first act of the Cold War. I am sorry to have to bring it up. But the facts of war and peace are too important for error.' Something had crept across Saskia's face. It could almost be mistaken for a smile. She rested a hand on my mum's shoulder, as if all that were friendliness, nothing but compliments, then slid off into the crowd.

My mum tracked the back of Saskia's head till it disappeared. 'She knew what I meant. She knows I know that the bombs didn't *end* the war. They were just *at* the end of the war. *Bloody words.*' As we shuffled down the steps, my mum mumbled on the back of people's necks, trying out 'end' in every combination she could think of: end *with*, end *at*, end *on*, end *up*, end *of story*. My mum shrugged. 'So I remade history on a global scale. You can't always get the Second World War right.' My mum swung her bloodshot eyes at me. 'Saskia's taken against me, and I don't know why. You should like people. Her own brother said so. Especially nice ones.'

I thought: Saskia didn't dislike people. She disliked people's happiness.

Even though everyone lived happily ever after in the GDR.

Three days after Hiroshima, on Nagasaki Day, Peter and Martina invited us to Schwielowsee. They wanted to give my mum a day off, let her be lazy. And now, she was laid out on a patio lounger, foot-lit by boxes of marigolds and shaded by arches of vines. 'You told me I'd like it, Jess, but under all that snow, I hadn't imagined *this* . . .' Trees dripped fruit. Flower beds had been seeded by the wind and tilted by the sun. Somewhere in the lawn, grasshoppers did maracas with their thighs. The garden was rambling and random, untamed and tended – the inside of their heads in earth and flowers.

Martina clacked back and forth in flip-flops, emptying welcome snacks onto plates, some of them hard to identify – salted and sugared pellets from their Armageddon chest. She had the radio on. Pop music drifted onto the patio, forty per cent of it from the East, sixty per cent from the West. By law. From time to time, she sang along in half-guessed English lyrics.

'I love it here. I love . . .' and my mum named everything in her line of sight from her dimpled thighs shiny with Alberna to the distant shimmer of a heavy goods train. Peter was bowling apples into the compost, practising top spin. He rocked plums from the trees and caught them in an apron pocket. Every so often, he stopped to breathe, stand stock-still, take time out from Time. He gardened around the trench in the middle of the lawn, the first few feet of a fallout shelter Martina had dug when the news broke about Cruise and Pershing – and abandoned because it was December, the depths of winter, and the earth had refused to give.

My mum drew herself into a curl. Soon her eyelids fluttered. Underneath, her eyeballs flicked to and fro. Her breathing was heavy and she wheezed in her dreams. A while later, she was roused by the smell of charcoal. I must have fallen asleep too, and lost half an hour, because suddenly Peter was tending already-browned sausages, turning them with foot-long pincers on a barbecue that was never set up. He handed my mum one of his bottles of wine.

'Your *summerhouse* wine?'

'Château Eden.'

Martina washed proper glasses and dried them. She put a paper bib on their feet. It was the kind of arrangement my mum knew she should sit up for. She struggled against the lounger that had already taken her shape. My mum blinked into the sun. 'I could do this for ever. Sheer bliss. I am lucky, lucky, lucky,' and she ticked each of us with her glass, releasing the smell of compost and Ribena.

'*Zum Wohl*,' Peter said, which was brief and very German.

By mid-afternoon, when they were anchored with sausages and adrift on innocence, Martina and I headed to the lake. She threw down the picnic bag and started to strip. I could tell another Mons Incident was coming on. She hummed 'Fairest Isle' as she undressed, pulling at her clothes as if unloading a washing machine: home-made denim hot-pants, T-shirt, orange knickers.

I dipped my head into the picnic bag and breathed in ripe flannel till I had no choice but to come up for air. Martina's skin wasn't two-tone. She didn't have swimming-costume lines, which meant she'd spent all her summers naked.

She pointed to my Speedo. 'You cannot be shy.'

'I'm English.'

'But think of the things you said for the glossary.'

But the words for things were different from the things for things. And Martina's things were slender, hairy in parts, muscular, menacing, unmissable. I felt hypnotised, giddy, and ever so slightly sick.

Then she needed a new word, and pointed under her dart-board breasts – the nipples hard, the rings brown. 'How do you call this mark in English?'

I could have said it was a mole. 'It's a beauty spot.'

Then she announced she had more, and as I flung my face back to the flannel, I saw a finger reach for the dark join of her buttocks. I wondered how on earth she knew. I pictured the logistics and decided it wasn't possible without breaking your neck. 'Did a doctor tell you?'

'That is one very good thing in our GDR. There is no lack of helpful boys.'

'Nor in Tamworth.' But I'd never fancied their assistance. Spit had ridden out on 'Tamworth' and landed on my leg. I circled the wet into what was left of a bruise. We had seasonal swarms of helpful boys: in the back row of the Palace in the winter; in the Pleasure Grounds in the summer.

Over our heads, dragonflies clung to each other, probing as they flew. A Red Admiral beat its wings in a slow kind of hand-clap. Martina said, 'A whole *town* of boys that are not nice?'

A whole West Midlands of them. A whole island. And, anyway, nice was not the point. The point was, there was no male in

Tamworth under the age of fifty who passed the Czechoslovakia Test.

'Perhaps you do not see that they like you. Do you know the signals?'

Of course I knew. The Soviets were either right to go in or they weren't. Prague '68: Good is a good sign. Prague '68: Bad is a bad sign.

Then Martina showed me how to transmit to them. 'You must stand very close and look somewhat angry.' She brought her face within an inch of mine and put her breath on my lips. The only person who'd ever done that was Ivan. But that was in a meeting when things weren't going his way, which meant it didn't count. On the other hand, Ivan did pass the Czechoslovakia Test. Once, my mum had asked me if he liked me.

'Of course he likes me.'

'I mean *likes* . . .' She didn't seem happy. This was my mum who liked liking. 'You spend a lot of time in Walsall. Has something changed by any chance?'

'I'm Assistant Secretary.'

'And he's married.' It was last December, in the gloom before Peter's letter, and the only time I'd ever seen her jealous.

Now I unfolded a towel, unfolded myself, closed my eyes, and sighed. I heard a bicycle bell and a stage-whisper, '*Etwas zu trinken! Bier! Wasser!*' I swung an arm for our water, but my hand landed instead on the biscuits. I worked my way down the packet. The sun soaked through my swimming costume, steaming off the possibility of effort, burning away the will to try. I thought: if I defected, I could do this all the time.

James had no regrets about defecting. He'd rung us soon after he'd arrived in the GDR. 'England already feels like a fiction. Money seems, frankly, pointless.' He'd sold his house at half-price to a newly qualified accountant, a sapped young man with long arms and uneven skin. He put his possessions in a

Party branch jumble sale, then got on the plane with a single suitcase and landed in Berlin. 'I just wanted to be shot of the whole damn fiasco.' He'd spoken over a crackling phone line from the English Department office. My mum said in the background she could hear the secretary, Alice Martin, chime, '*Ja*, shot of the thing. Shot.' Alice liked to echo odd words through dried red lipstick and a bobbing cigarette while she stabbed two hardened fingers into a typewriter.

Alice was someone else who'd defected. She'd fallen in love, across chicken wire, with a German POW held in a camp at the edge of her Welsh village. She'd passed him slices of bara brith wrapped in greaseproof paper. 'It is *genauso* like our stollen,' he'd said. He whittled hearts from the pine tree by the wash-block and handed them back through the fence. When Hans was released, they could have gone to live with Alice's parents in Sully, South Wales, or with his parents in Potsdam, so they emigrated to the Soviet sector, which turned out to be the GDR.

It would have been easy to defect right now. I was actually in the country. There were no border guards to threaten me with recipes. I gazed out across the water to where a canoeist was practising capsize disasters and surviving them. He rocked his boat and I rocked the word from side to side: de*fect*, *de*fect, de*fect*, *de*fect. Funny that. Completely different meanings, leaning left and right. I wanted to turn my boat over, vanish from my English life and appear right here, right now, on the edge of this lake on this sunny Nagasaki Day.

Martina reached for a biscuit and put the whole thing on her tongue as if it were the body of Jesus. 'It is a good place, our GDR.' It came out muffled, half-gagged. 'But you do not know everything, you know.'

I knew I didn't. Then I thought I didn't know what she meant.

'How many times have you been here? Three? For a month each time? What can you know in three *months*?'

But the rest of the time I lived in Tamworth as if it were the GDR. 'What don't I know? Give me a for-instance.'

'For instance the bad news.'

'What bad news?'

No answer. Martina cleared stones from the ground, undoing the landscape, making this small patch of Brandenburg look shot to pieces. She hummed a tune I vaguely knew – 'Unsere Heimat', possibly. Or maybe it was just something by the Carpenters.

I said, 'Just like your postcards.' The last one was from Rostock – a photo of a sailing boat with no sails. She'd written nothing and signed it *Rod Stewart*. 'I don't know why you bother. What's so hard about saying something?'

'I do, Jess, every time.' Then she shook her head and sighed, 'Aaah, *Jess* . . .' Which was what Stefan had said, but this time it didn't come out sounding like 'Aaah, *Bisto*.'

I didn't like the way she used my name to pat me on the head. 'You're not my big sister.'

'I know. I am only allowed to be fraternal. Which, you could say, is some of our bad news.'

I'd never seen the news. I'd seen a GDR telly – Martina had one – but it was usually covered in a crocheted blanket, never actually on. But I knew some of the bad news. There was a housing shortage. But then there was Marzahn. There was a long wait for a car. But it was a very small country. You could get everywhere for nothing on a bus. Not everyone had a phone. But who wanted a phone? I hated the phone. The fruit from Cuba didn't always arrive. But so what? If that counted as bad news, I wasn't put off.

Martina said, 'Would nothing put you off?'

I shrugged. Further round the lake, two old men undressed into carrier bags. Their dog was leashed to a tree. It lengthened its throat and mourned as they waded into the water and disappeared. 'If something happened to you, maybe.'

'But something *has* happened to me, *oder*? That is why I am here, not on the summer course.'

Martina had told me as soon as we'd arrived in Potsdam all about the Treptow fallout. When the tutors had gone back to England, she'd complained about being banned from the holiday, and Saskia had said, 'Choosing the funfair over the dead was an error.'

But Martina had had enough of death, more than her fair share.

'We all have unfair deaths.'

'But the Treptow dead are yours, not mine.'

And that was what had done it. It was Saskia's generation. They were all like that, she said. You don't disown their suffering. 'But I was born in peacetime, into ordinary life and eating ice cream and riding the Big Wheel.'

Saskia's voice came back to me. 'And so a friend becomes an enemy.'

'Not an enemy. Our GDR has enough enemies already. But do they really need to lose another friend?'

Now two middle-aged women drifted past us, heads poised above the water, perms safe, spectacles dry, batting the breeze to breaststroke. When they were out of earshot, 'Suppose Saskia had changed her mind . . .'

Martina shook her head. 'I would not have come on the course. Being banned and then un-banned is not the same as never being banned.'

Martina made me want to give up. She wanted it all ways, and all of them hers. She was right, though. Something *had* happened to her. She'd had to spend her summer here, on Schwielowsee, a local beauty spot – where the water was clear, the bottom sandy, beaches empty, sun shaded and refreshments served. And if it all got too much, she had a sailing boat moored just around the corner . . .

Martina said, 'You have learnt it already. That is exactly how you do it. You do not say something, and even so you say it.' Then she seemed to lose all strength and flopped onto her back.

She brushed sand from her towel-etched belly onto me, then silence.

In the silence, I watched a young woman stroke her boyfriend's back, running her fingertips across his skin as if the pimples might hold a message in Braille. A man fresh from bathing graffiti-ed his chest with deodorant.

In the end Martina said, 'It is easy for you, coming here whenever you want. But I want to see *your* little town. I want to eat some of your English food. I want to see *your* country.'

'It's not my country.' And it was a stupid idea. '*You* try living there.'

'I do not want to. That is the mistake they always make.' Then she rattled off a list from some tourist book: Houses of Parliament, Piccadilly Circus, Stratford-upon-Avon, Ben Nevis, The Old Curiosity Shop, Dirty Dicks.

'Ben Nevis isn't in England.' I picked up a pebble and skimmed it across the lake, but got the angle wrong and watched it slump into the water.

'I cannot wait till I have a pension to be allowed to go.' She nodded to one side, which was where West Berlin always was – just a nod away. 'I know about England from Charles Dickens. France from Emile Zola. I want to see how it is *actually*. This century.'

I told her to try more modern writers. *Love on the Dole. Kes. The Road to Wigan Pier.* They'd give her a better idea. But Martina didn't want to read those. She said the GDR probably didn't even have them. Her gaze stropped to the water. A red-faced chick with ginger tufts paddled past, looking like a lychee, or Uriah Heep. '*You* tell me about England, then.' She felt for a handful of dust, panned it in her palm and let it trickle through her fingers. 'At least you are this century.'

So I told Martina about Tamworth CND and our torchlit procession around the town with candles made by Rosie that were laced with human hair. They were meant to smell of the apocalypse. We'd invited Bruce Kent and Joan Ruddock to address the rally, but they both had prior engagements. What they meant was they'd never heard of Tamworth and couldn't even find it on the map. Instead, Ivan spoke – stood on the castle mound and threw his voice to the drunks in the Pleasure Grounds till we all got cold and drifted off for chips.

Then the Queen came to Tamworth in a lime-green suit and opened Ankerside shopping centre. The whole town went mad. There were Union Jacks in every window apart from ours. We put out a GDR flag and a red flag, and a policeman stood outside our house and tight-lipped reports into a walkie-talkie.

I told Martina how I came home from school, tore off the uniform, had porridge and paras for tea, dashed off the home-work, then ran to the Prince for a meeting. I did Hansard, then passed the humbug tin round for the room, and off to Hamlets to spar over half a pint of Strongbow. My mum had vouched for me so often they'd stopped asking me my age.

At first Martina listened. She asked if many English people were called 'Ivan' and if I'd really met the Queen. But gradually her attention slid and I had the feeling I was talking more and more to myself. Then she said, 'There is a chance my father will see London next year. He has been asked to give a confer-ence paper on Phillip Bonosky. The American communist writer.'

I didn't know there were any.

She said Peter wrote his PhD on him. The university was compiling a survey of leftist literature, working through the alphabet, and Bonosky was next on the list. Peter had applied for a visa, and now he was waiting while they thought about it.

I imagined the British Security Services considering his appli-cation. There was George Smiley in his office in Cambridge Circus, in his three-piece suit and shoes with leather soles. He reads Peter's case, his lips thread-thin, his too-large spectacles drifting up his face. Alec Guinness's brown-button eyes swivel towards the window as he mulls matters over. Outside, double-decker buses queue on Shaftesbury Avenue. Lights glow yellow in the music shops and bookshops on Charing Cross Road. They glow in the café on the corner of Manette Street, where we go when we're on a demonstration and my mum's feet hurt, and we drink sludgy coffee and eat caramel shortbread till it's time for Hyde Park and the speeches.

Would George Smiley allow communist Peter from the socialist GDR into England to talk about leftist Mr Bonosky? Probably not. I told Martina he'd hear soon. It wouldn't take them long to think about it.

'They will take as long as they possibly can. They will think till they are thinking about nothing, and still they will think.' Martina lobbed a twig off into the undergrowth and followed its fall, waiting for the sound of it hitting the ground, and turned back only when it never came.

I said *if* Peter got a visa, she might be allowed into the country with him – as his assistant. It was how I got into the GDR.

'Father *and* daughter? Never, *ever*. There must always be someone to miss.'

And then I thought she was probably right: you had to have someone to send a postcard to. And, anyway, Smiley would draw the line at two communists entering the UK at the same time. With both of them and the two of us, we'd have a Party branch.

'So we wait while they check, and then they check their checks. Who you know, contacts, background.'

That was us. We were contacts. But then the Circus had kept a file on the Mitchells since our first trip to the Brandenburg Gate. For the last two years, they'd steamed open our post, tapped the phone, taken cuttings from the *Herald*, and filed notes on our visits to the GDR embassy. They were probably at the meeting when Stefan came to Tamworth. There was someone new there, in a very bad hat.

Martina said, 'My father's visit to London is . . .' and she measured the chance between a thumb and an index finger that very nearly touched.

I told her how lucky we'd been with Stefan. He'd fixed all

our paperwork in minutes – fifteen people allowed into the country with ever-shorter strokes of his pen.

Martina didn't react. I thought she'd be glad the GDR was welcoming, that her country didn't have a George Smiley who took months to think about whether or not to let us all in. '*Stefan* helped us. You know Stefan, don't you.' It wasn't a question. Stefan was Saskia's brother.

'My father has had something to do with him.'

'You know Stefan came to Tamworth.'

Martina drew her knees to her chest, and planed with a fingernail between her wood-brown toes. 'And how did he like it?'

'He didn't see it. Just the train station and the Prince.' He'd said he was on duty. No hesitation, repetition or deviation.

'What, no castle? Mr Peel? No dyke? Is he not the perfect diplomat . . .' Martina turned her face to me, hard and blunt in a way I'd never seen it. She gave me a mock salute. '*Zu Befehl!*' Then she sprang to her feet and charged towards the lake. Her limbs worked the water to a froth. She surged forward, going deeper and deeper till she ran in slow motion, then the water tipped her off her feet. She tumbled under. The surface stilled. I watched the spot where she'd disappeared, and saw water turn from white to almost black.

Then Martina tore through the surface. Her body forced a way against the pull of the water, trying to break free of the lake. Instead, she landed back, sleek-haired and gasping, dressed in the ripple and flow of beauty-spot water, looking breathtaking, and utterly defeated.

13

The Travel Directive

Martina rigged up their boat, and she spent the rest of August cross-legged on the deck like some kind of naked sage. And because the deck was narrow, I always ended up at her feet like some kind of naked pupil.

In the end, I'd taken my Speedo off.

The summer had grown hotter – too hot to speak – and there were things now that we didn't want to talk about. So I filled the silence of August clinging to Peter's fishing rod, hope pinned to a hook, reciting in my head all the reasons I wanted to live here, why I couldn't go back to Tamworth.

The day we said goodbye, Martina announced we had to part on the boat. She didn't say why, and I didn't bother asking because I knew her answer would be in code. I clambered over the edge and waded back to shore. It took me ages on tiptoe, trying not to touch the bottom because of the broken bottles and the bodies that had never been found. I finally reached the bank, where my clothes were folded and stacked as if I'd faked my own disappearance, and when I glanced back, Martina had moved into the cabin. She had her hands on the wheel and was on her way to nowhere, a white sail hanging half-mast.

My mum sweated out the summer in the lecture theatre, and in love, and at the end of the course, in the Eisenhüttenstadt foundry. The works foreman presented her with a souvenir hard hat – bright yellow with an emblem of smokestacks releasing a dove. 'The sky is falling!' she said because her brain was fried in the thirty-eight degrees of the works *Kantine*, and *Chicken Little* was her favourite children's story, and they'd just had *Hähnchenbrust* for lunch.

The day we left for Tamworth, we got up extra early to sort out the van. My mum had somehow found time for shopping sprees and had stockpiled GDR-abilia while I'd been at the lake. She wanted to make 'a home from home for all of us', she said. She'd labelled the boxes as if we were moving house: *Bedroom-Fragile*; *Kitchen-Inedible*; *Bathroom-Hazard*; *Garden* – which made me worry because that meant gnomes.

I had to arrange the boxes because my mum said getting one face on a Rubik's cube meant I was good at three dimensions. She sat in the driver's seat and made sure of the gap for the rear-view mirror. As we drove away from the *Hochschule*, my mum steered with no eyes, her attention pinned behind her. A shrunken Peter came with us in reflection, till we turned at the barracks, and then he was gone till July.

My mum was quiet on the journey, which didn't worry me because I knew from last year it was just love and the left-hand drive. But something was different. When we idled at red lights, my mum didn't dream. Her distant look wasn't reliving the summer; it was imagining – moving pieces on the gameboard in her head, playing Snakes and Ladders with the future.

She had the runs on the ferry, which might have been the All You Can Eat Buffet, though she'd eaten so little it hadn't been worth it. And she couldn't sleep that night. She talked to herself in the pitch-black of the windowless cabin, 'If this . . . if that . . .' going round and round, and getting her no closer to happy.

The next morning, in the gloom of the car deck, when the side of the ferry hit the dock and we ground against Harwich making sounds from Hell, I told my mum it wouldn't be too long till we saw light again.

'April,' she said. Peter had told her about Bonosky and the

conference, and she'd convinced herself that his visa was as good as in the post. It didn't matter that Martina had rated his chances as more or less two fingers touching. Peter had measured them with his fingers too, and given them an inch, and from that my mum had taken a mile of Hope.

She went straight into planning their long weekend in London: a B&B run by the T&G that advertised in the *Star*. It was in the East End, five stops on the bus from the street where she grew up. My mum had no parents to introduce him to, so she'd show him their ghosts instead – tour Bermondsey and tell stories of the war and knitting to keep the Red Army warm. 'Then it'll all make sense,' she said. 'Not that it *doesn't* . . .' But still, this would be Eleanor: the Prequel. 'And I'll make arrangements for you.'

'I'll be sixteen. Old enough to marry.' I didn't need a fridge stocked with Smash and faggots and a welfare visit from Mr Howard.

It turned out what she meant was, would I do the *Star*?

The months rolled by, and there was no sign of Peter's visa, but my mum didn't stop believing. 'It's *Peter*. It's *Bonosky* . . .' as if no one could refuse them. It was only when April came, and there was still no news, that first doubts were raised about Bonosky. My mum had bought everything he'd written, but given up on it all. Then she blamed the *Hochschule* for the alphabet system. 'Why couldn't Peter have been allocated Jack London or Robert Tressell? They'd have got him a visa, no trouble.'

On the Thursday the conference started, my mum put on her Eisenhüttenstadt helmet and stayed in her pyjamas all day. They were bright yellow too – brushed cotton from the Exquisit store – and she dragged herself around the house looking like a gassed canary.

Now, two days later, my mum was still unwashed, her pyjamas less exquisite, on her bedroom floor, behind a barricade of

TODOs, and the telephone wouldn't stop ringing. I knew she wouldn't answer it. My mum wasn't currently on speaking terms with the outside world.

But whoever it was kept believing we were in and would be willing to say hello.

I took the receiver off the hook and let it hang from its cord. A miniaturised voice talked to the wallpaper until I heard something that sounded like 'Peter'.

When I picked up, he was swearing in German about English public phones. I'd caught him on his last coin. He had time to say he was making a day trip to Tamworth and to meet him at the station in half an hour. 'And give . . .'

But the pips cut the order short.

When I told my mum that Bonosky had delivered after all, she didn't bother looking up from her lists. She sat propped against her bed, in her hard yellow hat that meant there could only be bad news. Between splayed legs, pots of Marmite and honey, gummy lids off, and a pat of butter sitting in its own wet. Her TODOs lay in columns, sheets overlapping, like a giant game of patience. My mum refused to believe Peter was on his way until I asked where we kept the hoover.

Then she wanted to know exactly what Peter had said, word for word – which was easy because there hadn't been many.

'And what else? He must have said *something* else.'

'He said to give you his love.'

And she took her helmet off.

Then my mum leapt to her feet, sweeping her patience aside, and spinning lists off the top of her head. She gabbled sanitation orders. I was on House, she was on Self. But there was only time for tactical cleaning. I grabbed wads of toilet paper and smeared a shine onto line-of-sight surfaces. I found an aerosol and steeped the stairwell in vaporised violets, covering two days of fustiness with the fresh scent of the morgue.

My mum dashed into the bathroom in her yellow pyjamas and came out in a white nightie. Actually it was a dress from

Laura Ashley, bought especially for Peter's visit, and had cost a fortune. Now she darted about trying not to trip on the hem, looking like the Lady of Shalott with her orange hair and large, black pupils.

In the minivan, my mum reached for the toolbox, took out the tweezers and did her moustache in the mirror. She sprayed herself with her emergency perfume – cheap, honeyed, won in the school raffle and kept for days when it was back-to-back meetings. Then she turned to me for a once-over, with a look torn between tail-end pain and imminent delight.

Which meant there was no need for Bermondsey. That face was the story of her life.

We arrived at the station as Peter's train pulled in. My mum stood on the *STAND WELL BACK* that was painted inches from the edge of the platform. We watched arms reach out of windows and feel for the latch, then families lurched from the train with prams, bags of Saturday shopping and an outpouring of pink children who left a trail of bright sweets behind them.

And then Peter.

He was hard to recognise in a silvery suit, the trousers an inch too short, flashing white socks. He walked towards us in no hurry, shimmering under the April sun. In fact, he walked bow-legged, as if he'd just got off a horse, which was probably German height folded into British Rail seating.

My mum breathed, 'Kiss me as if it were the last time . . .' which was just another line from *Casablanca*. I thought it was overdone, but she needed steadying, so I took her hand – cold with excitement, her pulse fast in her wrist. Then she opened her chest for Peter's embrace and buried herself in his silver sheen. 'Am I dreaming?' she said. 'I daren't look in case I've made you up.' She held on, pressing her face to his lapel, and only came away when her cheek had been embossed with the SED.

It turned out Smiley had given Peter a visa after all. But

Martina had been right: he'd thought about it for months and months and months. The news had come through at the very last minute. On Thursday afternoon, when Peter was clearing his *Hochschule* blackboard of notes on the glottal stop, Saskia handed him an envelope, dismissed his class and told him to go immediately to Schönefeld. He'd grabbed his Bonosky papers, borrowed the silver suit from the caretaker – unworn since it went down the aisle at the end of the war – and had just enough time to leave a message for Martina that he'd be back for Sunday lunch. Everything he'd brought with him was in that briefcase. Which was why he'd been stopped at the border. The guard had checked the dates in his ticket and wanted to know where his luggage was. He'd led Peter into a back room and disappeared with the briefcase. Peter sat in the smell of an abandoned cup of instant coffee, under a flickering neon light, and waited. Three hours later, the guard had returned, bright and breezy. 'All in order, sir. Thank you for your patience. Welcome to England. It's St George's Day.'

'Also Shakespeare's birthday,' Peter said.

'Is it? I wouldn't know about that, sir. But do enjoy your stay.'

Today was the last day of the conference – the closing speeches, exchange of business cards, end of affairs – and Peter's only chance to visit. He was back in Potsdam in the morning. The GDR embassy had arranged everything, he said: a plane ticket and hotel reservation; sterling, a budget telling him how to spend it, and an envelope for receipts to prove he had; a time-table filling all free time. Last night he'd had dinner with Stefan. He'd wanted a report on the conference. 'Stefan finds Bonosky dull too. I made sure of that.' Also arranged by the embassy, a Travel Directive. Peter showed it to us. The form was grey and absorbent, and looked pulled from a paper towel dispenser. GDR handwriting filled the blanks and had leached into the form. As far as I could tell, Peter wasn't allowed past Watford

Gap, or to talk to anyone without a PhD. But he'd decided this morning to disobey orders.

I said I thought their connection was supposed to be discreet.

'True, it's not summer discretion,' my mum said. 'It's spring indiscretion. But you can't always get the season right.'

'And I wanted to *see* your little town.'

Which is exactly what Martina had said.

'Martina sends greetings, by the way.' Though she couldn't have. Peter hadn't spoken to her before he left. He'd made those up.

My mum said, 'You know her postcards stopped?'

'She is busy these days with . . .' He had no idea what. 'But when I see her, she seems happy.' He paused. 'Or maybe she is in love. Not the same thing. Or maybe it *is* the same thing. But happy, anyway. As far as I can tell.'

Which is not what I'd expected. Whenever I thought of Martina, I felt sad. Since last summer she hadn't written – the silence of last August had just stretched on and on. So now I reread her old postcards and tried to figure out what she'd been saying without saying it. My mum told me once, 'It's not *you* she's not bothering with. It's other things bothering *her*.' She said not to give up on Martina. 'A friend in need . . .'

'What does *she* need?'

'A mother?' my mum said.

But then a mother would.

Now she fell behind the minivan wheel and struck up 'Oh! Tamworth!' to the tune of 'Oh! Calcutta!'. She pushed back the curtains of her sleeves. 'So let's get this show on the road!'

Which was a bad idea. For one, it was Tamworth and there was nothing to see. Plus there was Peter's paper towel. And Smiley was out there too.

'We're in a car, Jess. Bright sunny day. No one can see in. Just reflections.'

'But the Mothers and Babysitters and Ferrets . . .' One time,

Ivan had said, 'They're all over us. We all have an SB marker. We're all flagged. *You're* flagged, Jess,' sounding proud. And there *had* been trouble with the phone – background noise, crossed lines – which just proved the Circus had been doing its home-work. And every so often, people rang us and got a recorded message asking for their name, address and phone number. Only we didn't have an answerphone.

We reversed out of the station car park, bumping the kerb and alarming a pack of Brownies. We cruised along Upper Gungate, past my school, where I booed, my mum booed, and Peter booed without knowing why. My mum shoved open her window. A rush of air blew hair in her face, making her gasp and even more Pre-Raphaelite. She squeezed her foot to the floor and the dial swung past legal. The engine hit a high note. Tamworth sped up.

Peter released his seat belt for an unconstrained view. 'Finally! I get to see your town!' He was sounding far too pleased.

'There you go, Jess. Peter has to *see* it. He's got to know what it's like if . . .' and let the rest of the sentence be taken by the wind.

'*Willkommen* to our open prison. Approximately 60,000 inmates, mostly docile. Only the occasional attempt to escape.'

We dropped down the western edge of town, farmed all the way to the trees of Hopwas Hill. 'England is so green,' he said.

'It's just first impressions.'

'On the way from London, there were open fields for miles and miles. It is a green and pleasant land, just like in the song. I had not expected that.'

It was unlike Peter to be disproportionate. 'Are you hungry?'

'No, no. I had your wonderful full English breakfast in Euston station.'

When actually we ate Coco Pops.

He put a finger to the window. 'I had expected Engels. *The Condition of the Working Class in England.* The Brixton Riots.'

'We have those. Just not viewable from here.'

'And, in fact, you have sleepy villages. You have sheep!'

'Sheep. Yes. We eat them.'

And my mum wasn't helping. She was bright with guiding. She was, for the first time ever, in love with Tamworth. I listened to her scatter enthusiasm on whatever was on the other side of the window. There was something about the swing to her voice that sounded straight from the Tourist Office: 'Once the capital of the ancient kingdom of Mercia, Tamworth has a unique place in the historical landscape of the country . . .' I think she'd secretly been rehearsing for a day like this. She pointed out the places of basic maintenance – the Health Centre, Marmion Motors – and told Peter which days the dustmen came. Then she wove round all the points of political interest: Middle Entry, the Prince, Hamlets. The Riverside flats, tower blocks that were perfect for leafleting. 'Lots of front doors and no garden paths.' Six ideal stacks of the working class.

Then my mum turned a corner and we crashed into the Middle Ages. Knights in bed-sheet tabards and metal-bucket helmets swiped blind at the air. Buttress-hipped women with lace-up fronts rolled cannonball breasts towards the crowds. 'Three cheers for England and St George!'

The crowd slurred back. They swigged cans of Bass and bottles of Babycham, and little girls who couldn't see past their fringe poked themselves in the face with Orange Maids.

'See, Peter? *This* is Tamworth.'

'People are so happy!'

'They're drunk.'

Then came the uniforms, amateur regiments in all the shades of dull, marching on each other's heels and skipping back into time. Peter pointed to a banner: *Unity, Loyalty, Comradeship, Patriotism.* 'Just like ours, no?'

The photographer from the *Herald* spotted our van and waved to my mum. He loved her for the action shots you didn't usually get on a local paper. The policeman gave her a *Dixon-of-Dock-Green* salute. It was the cross-eyed one whose strange green gaze curled over our written requests to stop Market Street traffic so we could march on the Town Hall to demand world peace.

'You are a celebrity here!' Peter said.

We were the village idiots. If they'd still had stocks, we'd have been in them. If they hadn't repealed the Witchcraft Act, we'd have been burned.

Peter stepped onto our *Willkommen!* doormat, then took off his shoes and put on slippers – giant, grey felt ones my mum had bought in Potsdam – the kind they issued to visitors at the New Palace to glide over Frederick the Great's marble floors. We slid over our B&Q tiles, keeping close to the walls so we could dust the house in transit.

My mum gave Peter a tour while I set up the *Kaffeestube*. We went to our GDR coffee shop whenever we were feeling wistful, or the summer was taking a long time to come, or on their *Ehren- und Gedenktage*. There was an occasion to mark at least once a week. Yesterday was the International Day for Youth and Students against Colonialism and for Peaceful Coexistence, and the washing-up was still in the sink.

I laid the table: a lace cloth and matching placemats embroidered with sugary sentiment; a *Kännchen* of Mona coffee kept just-below-warm-enough by the orange lick of a nightlight; Mitropa cups, chipped already from overuse; and in the sitting room, Brecht reciting his poems at thirty-three revolutions a minute.

From upstairs, I caught snatches of Peter's commentary. He recognised most of what we had. My mum loved her GDR bedding: a quilt instead of sheets and blanket, which meant she never had to make it, and square pillows she could truss behind her neck and drink her tea without dribbling. I thought I heard something like '*Your* side' but wasn't sure of the verb: could be, would be, is . . .

When they finally reappeared, my mum waved the white flag of her sleeve across the day, surrendering to its possibilities.

'I just want to live with you for . . .' Peter glanced at our clocks, then stopped.

'For international solidarity,' I said. 'So we know what time fraternal comrades are on.'

'What time *you're* on.' My mum had set Moscow to Berlin as soon as we'd got back from the summer course.

Peter had five hours before he had to leave, and he wanted to spend them as we usually would. To have our normal Saturday.

Normal, for us, was my mum polishing the knobs on our Cabinet and mouthing a wish as if it were a wardrobe and Narnia might be in there instead of political admin. Then the two of us beating quick-time on the Coronet and Olivetti because there weren't enough hours in the day. Today, my mum said, 'Welcome to the Ministry of Information. The Politburo Bureau,' and she folded back the Cabinet doors to present our political files: Communist Party; CND; Education; Anti-Nazi League; Unemployment; Other. She reached for an armful of grey folders and spread them across the floor. The peace movement lay lifeless like a catch on the deck of a ship. They were in priority order and she picked up an urgent dead fish and flapped it at us. It was the CND newsletter, for immediate release.

My mum dealt it out, 'One for you, one for me, one for you . . .' We spent the afternoon as if Admin were a parlour game, fun for all the family, except there were no aces, no trumps and little hope of winning, while through the wall Ron and Reg roared winners on in *Grandstand*.

I watched Peter copy the mailing list onto envelopes, his writing slowed by Staffordshire surnames, the shapes of his letters textbook GDR. I knew the postman would look twice and wonder: Tamworth frank, weird foreign hand. My mum talked about our contacts with the familiarity of friends. She knew everything about them, especially the disasters, because that's what they recited when they rang to say they wouldn't be at the meeting. She went down the list, retelling their life stories in alphabetical order, while in the sitting room Brecht said over and over because of the scratch, '*Ach, wir die wir den Boden . . .*'

The one person she didn't talk about was Rosie – our only actual friend. She'd just come back from a demo in Brussels convinced 'womyn' were going to save the world. She'd written a report for this newsletter. 'There is a clear connection between male violence and the arms race . . . We must nurture a caring opposition, starting with ourselves, families, friends and colleagues.'

'Balls! What utter balls!' my mum had said, but still she'd typed it word for word, thumping her Coronet and correcting the spelling.

At six o'clock, my mum phoned the Light Dragoons. 'The usual, please, but *twice*. I know, things *have* changed.'

Peter came with me to collect the order and get an idea of night-time Tamworth. I took him the long way round, through the churchyard, lingering at the graves that on a Saturday night doubled as a public toilet. Sodium lamps spilled orange over the abandoned town centre, wastebins overflowing with beer cans and flags of St George. A cat walked on tiptoe, sniffing through the wreckage.

'Is your normal normally like that?'

It was normal for us, if odd for the town. We were strugglers, and that's what we did.

Peter said he was used to struggling. Just life itself, that was a struggle. But also our kind – meetings, demonstrations, solidarity. Faraway countries tripped off his tongue. I'd seen his solidarity book, the monthly dues like Co-op stamps only prettier, as if one day he'd be able to collect divi on World Revolution. 'But in the GDR, our mass organisations arrange everything. All I have to do is turn up.'

The Light Dragoons had only just opened, but already a woman was waiting for her order, perched on a high stool by the counter. 'All right, bab.'

'All right.'

'All right,' she said to Peter.

'Yes, I am all right, thank you very much. How are you?'

The woman laughed. It snagged on her lungs. She tipped back her head, showing us a ring of gold. She had gold-rimmed glasses, gold studs in her ears and bronzed hair from a packet. 'Not from round here then. You sound foreign to us. Where you from?'

It was safe to say Australia.

'Germany.'

'Ooo, blimey. One a them, Raza.' She pointed with her ciga-rette at Peter, pursed her lips, and chimney-ed the smoke towards the ceiling. Raza gave Peter a nod, then tilted his face to the television screwed high on the wall and let his attention stay there.

Snooker was on.

'You're not a foreigner, are you, our Raza?' She didn't wait for an answer. 'Him's not a foreigner. Even though he might look it. Born in Small Heath, wasn't you.'

Raza didn't react. He left his gaze on the man in the waist-coat and bow tie, bent over a table, taking aim with a stick. Then the snap of the black into a pocket and a round of turned-down applause.

The woman cleared her throat, bringing on a cough, and she pressed it into the back of her hand. Her chest heaved, a sharp chest, the breastbone angling to get out. When she'd recovered, she fingered a necklace, soothing herself with the feel of the cross.

Then the kitchen bell rang. Raza steered his eyes from the snooker to the pearl-drop curtain without it landing on any of us.

'I'm a Tammie, me,' the woman said. 'If you could get a Tammie passport, I'd have one. I were born in Halford Street, went to school in Hospital Street, I live in Alfred Street and me daughter lives next door. Kids in and out each other's houses all day long. And guess what? We're happy. All on us. A nappy family.' At least, that's what it sounded like.

Then she leant in close. 'Was you on the parade? Weren't it su-*perb*?' Her words smelt of Silk Cut, her lips zigzagged in the kind of mess you made in First Year sewing. 'We got Heritage, we have. We got History.' She meant the words with a capital letter, but said them without an 'h'. 'Not that the town's what it used to be. Middle Entry. Church Street. Them had fifteenth-century houses, them did. All pulled down in the name of progress. If that Phil Dix had had his way, he'd have pulled the bloody castle down!' She rolled her eyes and swallowed a cough. 'He lived up the road from me brother. I never liked him. Me brother hated him.' She puffed on her cigarette, dismissing the smoke over her shoulder. 'I says it every time and I'll say it again: we're as good as that Stratford. Who wants any truck with that Shakespeare man anyway? We got *more* history. We was a royal borough in the eighth century.'

Peter whispered, 'Do all local people do this with the subject-verb agreement?'

My gaze drifted out of the window, to where two local people stood at the entrance to the Palace, backs turned, mid-disagreement. They smoked, sucking so hard their cheeks caved in and chucked the butts onto the pavement in sudden phuts of red.

'Sorry for Tamworth.'

Then a car cruised past, its stereo blaring 'Making Your Mind Up'. The song was everywhere. It was the anthem of the moment. Bucks Fizz had just won Britain the Eurovision Song Contest.

Peter didn't respond, but what I heard his silence say was: I think I could get used to it.

Then the kitchen curtain rattled. 'Chicken korma and chips.' Raza leant across the counter, a white plastic bag dangling from two fingers.

The woman took it without looking.

'That Dix did more damage to this town than bloody Hitler.'
Hitler didn't have an 'h' either. Then she looked at Peter and
put a hand on his arm. 'Excuse me French,' she said.

We ate our curry and drank a toast of campus shop *Korn*. 'To
socialism!' my mum said. 'And to us! To socialism and us! And
to us and socialism!' We emptied our glasses to all the permu-
tations. Then Peter did what we'd all been waiting for: checked
his watch and said he had to go. It was the moment that had
loomed all day from Havana, Berlin and Hanoi.

I knew my mum would try to delay him. She'd want to make
last-minute sandwiches that took forever because the butter
wouldn't spread from the fridge. She'd say 'foff, foff, foff, foff' to
the gas rings, lock the house, then have to go back and check.
She'd lose her car keys, find them, then get tangled up in the
One Way to the station. And if, even so, he made it to the train,
she'd want to wave till it'd disappeared, then wave to the sound
of it, then wave at the thought of the man who was on the train
till I tugged at her sleeve and told her he'd be in Rugby by now.

And Peter must have known because he was already putting
on his jacket and heading for the door.

'But you've been so . . . I've seen how . . .' On one tot my
mum couldn't have been drunk, but she was having trouble
finding words and finishing sentences. 'And you're *here* now,
and what if . . .' Her face folded with the unfinished question.
I hoped she wasn't about to cry. My mum raised an empty glass
to what none of us had mentioned and had filled the entire
day. And she put her glass back down.

Peter had to borrow the train fare back to London. My mum
tipped her purse into her lap and handed him all the fluff and
money she had. Then he held her to his chest, to the milky
smell of two-star hotel soap and mothballed suit.

When he let her go, my mum retreated to the dining room.
She slumped into his chair, soaking up his warmth before it
was lost. She laid her head on his placemat. *Bedenke das Ende*

crept in chain-stitch out of her ear. Her hands hung to the floor. Her face was twisted away, her neck at such an angle that for all I knew it might as well be broken.

I ran into the kitchen and found strawberry Angel Delight. It was for Martina. 'It's what England tastes of. She wanted to know. I hope she likes it.'

Actually, I hoped she didn't.

Peter promised to send a postcard as soon as he was home. 'And take care of your mother for me. Tell her she has to *believe* . . . And to *think* . . .'

Which was a problem because usually it was one or the other.

I stood on the top step and watched Peter head down Church Lane. He walked as if it was hard to hurry. His briefcase seemed heavier than when he'd brought it, which couldn't be just Angel Delight.

Then from the dining room, 'What if I . . .?' but my mum didn't finish.

I watched Peter get smaller and darker and then turn orange at the car park lights.

'What if he . . .?'

I watched him all the way to the bend in the road.

'What if we . . .'

And then Peter disappeared.

My mum was working her way through the personal pronouns. She didn't get to the 'What if they . . .' She didn't know there was a 'they', let alone what they might do.

But from here on, that was all that mattered.

Peter and Eleanor was now their affair.

14

Troubles Mount

Tamworth, April–June 1981

The night Peter left, my mum refused to go to bed in case he changed his mind and rewrote the ending. In her head, he didn't arrive at Heathrow in blinding fog, climb the steps of the plane, and take off to the roar of propellers and 'La Marseillaise'. In her version, he got to Tamworth station, looked back at the glow of the town on the underside of the clouds, heard the toll of St Editha's and knew it was now or never.

My mum sat in Peter's chair, keeping it warm and keeping herself awake by chain-sucking Fisherman's Friends. Every so often, she broke into song: 'The Times They Are a-Changin'', while watching the clocks that never seemed to turn; 'If I Had a Hammer', beating time with a spoon on her coffee cup. My mum only broke off her vigil to empty her bladder, or run to the front door when she heard the gate go, and say 'Hello?' to her imagination.

Then the first bus revved up in the garage, the driver rocking on his pedals, burning off the overnight cold, and Peter hadn't come back. My mum phoned Heathrow and asked a woman with a bright, clipped voice to check the morning's passenger lists. She spelled Peter's name and told her where Schönefeld was. While she waited, my mum checked her Laura Ashley nightie. She wanted to keep it pristine, and dabbed with a wet finger at what were only shadows. When the woman came back on the line, 'Because I'm concerned about him,' my mum said.

'Confidential? But not for relatives, surely? . . . I'm his *wife* . . . On the grounds of whether he should be on the flight at all. Whether it's a mistake to go.' Then Passenger Care said something careless. My mum rounded on the phone, putting her face so close, it caught her spit. 'It is *not* in trouble. And it has *not* just ended. It hasn't even *begun*,' and she banged the receiver down hard enough to make Smiley's people wince and left a hiss we never got rid of.

But Passenger Care had been right about trouble. All morning, my mum recited what the trouble was, pealing the problems at me, while in St Editha's, the pious swung from ropes, filling the town with off-kilter calls to prayer. 'I *want* Peter to stay, but I *don't* want him to stay. I do and I don't.' Which was the trouble with logic. 'Because if he stayed, he'd be a defector, strictly speaking, wouldn't he. Or that's what they'd say. He wouldn't be Peter. He'd be Solzhenitsyn.' Who we didn't read. 'He'd be just like the rest of them, seduced by the West. The *Herald* would have a field day. They'd camp at the gate waiting for shots of History-in-the-Making. MI5 would love it. Peter would never get back. And what about Martina? He couldn't just leave her there.'

I said, 'So let's sell up, pack a suitcase, and go to the GDR. It's what James did.'

'James did fifty years first. How long have *I* done? How long have *you*? If we went, just think what'd happen. No Party branch. No CND steering committee. Tamworth would lurch rightwards.'

My mum's eyes rolled rightwards, which was also eastwards – towards Schönefeld, where Peter would have landed by now, welcomed at border control by a stuffed Berlin bear. 'But if things stay as they are, I'll only ever have him long-distance.' She'd have one twelfth of Peter, a fraction of the life she wanted. My mum totted it up – she was good at twelves, having O-level imperial maths – and over a lifetime she and Peter wouldn't add up to much.

★

Over the next couple of weeks, more trouble brewed. Peter's postcard, the one he'd promised the night he left, was never delivered. Every morning, at the sound of the front gate, my mum skated to the door in her giant furry feet and plodded away with a handful of bills or give-away papers. We knew from James that Peter was safely home, but his card simply didn't arrive.

My mum reported it to the Post Office. She got a standard claim form back. Under *Details of Missing Item* she put: 'Unable to provide as item missing.' Under *Approximate Value*: 'Does everything have to have a price?', and she screwed the form up and threw it in the bin.

Then we went in person to speak to the Post Office manager. It took a while for him to appear, and when he did, turning the ends of his moustache and checking his fob watch, he said he was aware of The Purloined Postcard, and it was – 'alas' – beyond his powers to help.

But my mum knew it had been sent.

'May I ask if you have proof?'

'For a *card*?'

'I venture, then, that perhaps it wasn't.'

'*You* don't know the sender.'

He asked if we'd pursued the matter with the Reichspost.

'It's Deutsche Post der DDR. *East* Germany.'

'In which case, regrettably, we may deem the item irretrievably lost.'

You didn't meet them often, but Tamworth still had odd men like that, tucked away in browning offices, breathing Victorian air, filling out their grandfather's waistcoats, and using long words and commas to prop their unhelpfulness up.

My mum turned dogged after that. She went over the Post Office conversation, repeating the last line. I think it was the word 'lost' that did it. She monologued about losing things: the postcard, sleep, trains of thought, weight, regular bowels. Even my dad got a mention.

My mum wondered if she was losing faith about things working out with Peter. And that thought, and too many prunes, did something to her. It put her out of sorts. Mr Howard noticed, and wondered to me if we'd gone over to non-stick pans. He'd read about Teflon in the paper, which was much worse for you than butter. But my mum hadn't cooked for weeks. She'd just stuck harder at the politics, grafting at it all hours through gritted teeth and bellyache.

I supplied her with cups of tea and offered her the cosy. But she never took her helmet off. She said she was trying to have a revolution. 'It's the struggle, Jess, which means hard hats and overtime.'

Some nights, when the town was asleep and the only noise was St Editha, I heard her pounding on the keyboard. And when I came down for breakfast, my mum was still at the dining-room table, fingers numb because she'd typed all night.

She was going to make something break: the stalemate over Peter or the Coronet.

In the end, my mum went to the doctor and told him she couldn't sleep. She listed her commitments. The doctor didn't write them down. He said he knew all that already. He took the *Tamworth Herald*. He was also the butcher's nephew, which meant vivid weekly updates. The doctor looked like his uncle too, the same glassy, wide-spaced eyes, only the spring lamb version, and trimmed of fat. 'So what's going wrong?'

'Nothing to put me to sleep.'

'Is anything in particular worrying you?'

'Not sleeping.'

'You say you're too busy . . .'

'I *am* too busy.'

'So what would happen if you *weren't* busy?'

'Wouldn't sleep.'

The doctor pondered her. He was fresh-faced in his pressed white coat. He wasn't yet thirty, newly qualified, and still doing things by the book. Which was the trouble with young doctors, my mum said. They wanted to help instead of hand you the pills.

'Is this being busy instead of something? Is anything missing?'

'No . . . Yes . . . Time. And pills.'

He turned over her notes, looking for next of kin. Since Passenger Care, Peter had become her husband. My mum told the doctor she didn't live with her next of kin. He wasn't even next door. Or in the same town. Or even the same country. In fact, they lived on opposite sides of the Iron Curtain.

'But, Mrs Mitchell, you *choose* this life.'

That made my mum furious. 'I do not choose not to sleep. And I did not choose to be born on the wrong side of the bloody Cold War.'

The doctor winced at 'bloody'.

He swivelled round to his books: formularies, therapies, anatomies, anomalies. He raised his eyebrows at some thought in his head, then wrote out the prescription, quick and illegible. 'I'm sorry I'm not qualified to issue plane tickets,' he said and pushed the docket for Valium across the desk.

When Rosie found out about the sleepers, she started calling round more often, always with a thermos of home-made soup. She lied that it was leftovers and best not to waste it. I didn't know what she put in it, and maybe it was just the effects of a warm meal, but afterwards my mum was always weighted down and calmer.

Then, one time, Rosie said, 'If it goes on like this, Eleanor, you know it'll all end badly.'

'No. It all started badly. It's going to get better.'

'You're in trouble. You aren't eating properly.'

Local schools had contracted their catering to the cheapest bidder in anything orange: fish fingers, pizza, beans, ravioli. There'd been letters in the *Herald* about what it would do to the town's IQ. My mum gave Rosie her thermos back. It was carrot, which meant it was orange too. 'You won't solve the world's problems with home-made soup, you know.'

'I haven't made it for the UN.'

'Ours neither.'

Rosie put her hands up as if to surrender. At close range you still caught the citronella. The oil had got into her nails. Rosie smelt permanently of the Peter vigil. When she turned to go, 'We'll miss you, Eleanor, but you'll be surprised how well we manage without you. *Please* . . . just go and have your affair . . .'

'It's *not* an affair.'

My mum had banned the word since Peter became her husband. She'd said to me: 'Affairs don't last and someone's always been cheated. And that is *not* the case.'

But we both knew something was wrong the next time we saw Stefan. He didn't come down to embassy reception. There was no arm to tiller my mum anywhere – just a message for her to go to Visas and for me to come up to his office.

Stefan took the papers I'd brought, and leafed through them, saying too little, considering. At the end of the last YCL meeting, I'd lifted the entire END file – dipped into the cabinet while behind me Ivan was on the phone to his wife, arguing about whose turn it was to put their daughter to bed. Then I heard, 'When you file, Jess, you put things *in* the cabinet. You don't take them out. You might have keys, but these are *my* filing cabinets. This is *my* information. And I don't want it going anywhere I don't know about.'

Stefan opened a drawer, tucking END away, and announced it was time for a talk. Actually it was a quiz. I expected questions on my specialist subject: The History of the British Peace Movement 1978–81. But somehow, the cards had been mixed up and instead I'd got: Things on Stefan's Plate.

He addressed me from his *Mastermind* chair in a quick-fire, even voice, and he must have known I was going to get the answers wrong, because he gave me them without bothering to wait: Thatcher, Reagan, Poland-on-our-doorstep, Cruise, END, the so-called Independent Peace Movement, The Bloody Church.

It was the first time I'd heard Stefan swear. But it didn't work. Bloody didn't sound like bloody in a German accent.

'Hostile-negative forces. Dissidents. Antisocial elements . . .' Which made me think of Martina. She'd said she wasn't one, but I wondered if by now she might be. She'd been antisocial to me: still no word from her, and no thanks for the Angel Delight.

Stefan had a long list of hostile-negative forces: hippies, hitch-hikers, journeymen, blues freaks, loafers, fools, romantics, people who should know better. He batted them aside, leaving his hand somehow pointing at me. 'People who forget this is a war. People who should know that sometimes politics and discipline come before personal feelings, do you not think so, Jess?'

I didn't know what to think except Stefan seemed angry.

'Angry? With them. Yes. Very. With you? No.'

'Only, it sounded as though you were telling me off.'

Stefan thought about it. 'Perhaps.' Then he smiled to himself and let his face soften. 'I believe you have an English expression: "Do not rock the boat." Well, the boat *has* been rocked. And when that happens, no one stays entirely dry.'

Then Stefan went over to his drinks cabinet and held bottles up to me. 'Whisky? Vodka? Calvados? Not gin. Armagnac? Armagnac.' He held big-hipped glasses up to the light, digestif glasses, the kind used to soften endings. He poured exactly equal measures and gave me mine, then took his in his palm, coaxing it into eddies. 'So tell me, how *was* Peter?'

'Peter?'

'Is he keeping well?'

'Last I heard.'

'And did he like Tamworth?'

'I don't know what you mean.'

Stefan stopped spinning his drink and waited for it to settle.

He ran the glass under his nose, inhaled, and all the while the grey mirror of his eyes soaked me in. 'Very good, Jess. First class, I would say.' He showed me the label. 'Domaine d'Espérance, 1961. Rather expensive. Use with care.' But the bottle Stefan held was almost empty.

Not long after that, there was more fallout from Peter's visit. I think I'd sensed something was coming because I hadn't been sleeping well. Usually, when I couldn't go off, I had warm milk and counted sheep, but tonight they wouldn't jump over the fence. I'd asked my mum once for a Valium, but she said that'd mean pushing drugs and going short herself. And, anyway, tonight she was in London and had taken all her sleepers with her.

I heard St Editha's strike one. Downstairs, on Havana time, it was still yesterday. It was eight o'clock in the evening. Fidel Castro had just finished dinner and was smoking a Romeo y Julieta. The jazz clubs were opening, and swaying crowds headed in the salt breeze and fairy lights of the Malecón to the heat and sweat of a dance. The night hadn't even begun. No one thought about not sleeping. In Havana, no one really wanted to sleep.

I wrestled with the duvet and bundled it onto the floor. In the heat, my thighs had stuck together. I reached for my T-shirt and stuffed it between my legs. I knew, in the morning, it'd smell of the unwashed ladies with moustaches and furry boots who sat out their days in the easy chairs in the library between shelves of Popular Fiction.

My bedroom curtains were closed, but a glow from the street fell under them, spilling onto my GDR shrine. It lit in orange the plug-in, revolving TV Tower, which I unplugged at night because of the hum. My eyes slid over the map on the wall. According to that, Britain was a speck in the sea. This town didn't exist. I wasn't here. But I wasn't in the GDR either. Emigration was looking as far away as ever.

My mum and I had talked about it, over and over. I'd told her the GDR was short of people and we'd be boosting the population. They even gave away flats in exchange for children. We'd be socialist heroes, which made her say yes, then no, then yes, then no again. No matter what I said, she just couldn't find the heart to go. 'What would people think of me?'

'Like who?'

'Like Stefan, Saskia, the Ministry, Ivan, you, me . . .'

'What would *you* think of *you*?'

'What *would* I think of me?' And my mum did a line from 'Man's dearest possession'. 'I don't want to be seared with the shame of a cowardly and trivial future. And if I went, I'd be doing it just for me.'

'And me. And Peter. And Martina.'

'But Jess . . .' and she picked up a fistful of *Herald*s – a fistful because this Friday our photo was in it. 'I know what I'm doing here. The town knows what I'm doing here. I know who I am. If I went, I wouldn't be able to live with whoever-I-was. I wouldn't be able to sleep.'

As if she slept here.

And tonight, I was sure my mum wasn't sleeping – not on Cynthia's sofa, rolling towards the join, TODOs and Peter troubles turning in her mind. I imagined her in her yellow pyjamas, the soft cotton stiff with the spills of weeks. She'd draw her eked-out body into the position of sleep and wait for the Valium to work. She'd try to convince herself she wasn't in a council flat in Streatham and the racket through the wall wasn't Cynthia's snoring. She'd soothe herself with the thought she was at Ostkreuz station, listening to the rumble of passing goods trains, the sound of socialist industry in motion.

St Editha's struck two. Downstairs, on Hanoi time, it was eight o'clock in the morning. Their night was over, their sleeping done. The sun was up. Farmers were in the fields. They were knee-deep in mud, tiptoeing between leftover landmines. Markets were full of the roar of motorbikes and the slap of dying fish.

Old men in black pyjamas sipped noodle soup through white beards and missing teeth.

I was hungry and thirsty and I ached.

I reached for more paracetamol. It didn't matter that the water glass was empty. I'd trained myself to swallow them straight from the packet. I tossed onto my belly and waited. But the mattress springs dug into my face and my lungs were squeezed too hard to breathe. I tossed onto my side and waited. But my arms were in the wrong place. My heart thumped loud in the pillow. I didn't know how it kept going, why it kept beating, why I couldn't will it to stop.

Then I heard the doorbell. It happened sometimes on hot summer nights. When the pubs shut, the winos headed to the bandstand in the Castle Pleasure Grounds where they passed round bottles for as long as they liked and threw up in the beds of pansies. Then they staggered through town and sometimes ended up here, in this street, and opened the first gate without a sticky latch.

I swung an arm out and reached under the bed for the clock, scraping it with my fingertips and pushing time further away.

Then another ring, a finger held against the bell, which made me think it wasn't a wino after all. Drunks gave up sooner, or lost track of what they were doing.

If my mum had been here, she'd have got up in case it was Peter. Since his day trip to Tamworth, she'd believed anything was possible. She'd round a corner and there he was. Or he'd turn up on our doorstep and ring the bell, just like this.

I pulled on my T-shirt and felt around for tracksuit trousers. Downstairs, the living room was thick with the Dragoons, the containers scabbed in brown. The clocks said it was just before 10 p.m., 4 a.m. and 9 a.m., which meant it was nearly three.

The doorbell rang again, quick, sharp stabs this time, pressing out SOS in Morse. Which made me think it might be my mum, given up on Cynthia's sofa, and driven back early and couldn't find her keys.

I went into the sitting room and turned on the light. I squinted against the brawling colours and nag of the wallpaper, which is what you got with showroom seconds and Co-op end-of-line. I put a hand on the key in the door. 'Who is it?'

'Guess.' A man's voice.

'Not *Peter*?'

'Yes, Peter. It's Peter.'

It wasn't Peter. That wasn't how he spoke. So it *was* some drunk who'd lost his way and thought he'd made it home.

'Will you let me in?'

'You don't live here.'

'Anyway?'

I switched out the light and turned to go back to bed. 'Just bugger off. And don't piss on our doorstep.' My mum said they pissed in her tubs, which was why nothing ever grew. Actually she forgot to water them, and piss might have helped.

'Where's your mam gone to, Jess?' The sound of my name stopped me in my tracks. My eyes flicked to the chain. Last night, I'd forgotten to put it across. I'd seen what happens next on the telly: the letterbox opens, a slow lift against a strong spring. A black glove comes through, and swift fingers groping for the key.

'Is your mam in trouble?' He pitched his voice to mimic a woman. 'The trouble *is* . . .' Then he said what I'd heard before: 'Time for a talk, Jess. How's Peter?'

'Peter who?'

'Your Peter. Our Peter.'

'I don't know any Peter.'

'And that's the question. Is he yours or ours?'

And there they were again, the pronouns. Possessive this time.

Whoever they were, it was one of them. *They* were at our door.

15

Berlin Wall Day

I sat by the front door with a claw hammer and six-pack of Club biscuits till I heard the minivan in the lane. I'd phoned Cynthia and my mum had answered. She hadn't been to sleep and said she knew I was going to call. We went straight to the police station. The man on duty stroked the short, white pelt of his hair, then reached under the desk for a ledger. He had trouble forming the letters, his biro fixed to the desk with a too-short piece of string. Then he clawed at the counter, filing his nails on the grain. He glanced at his watch. 'What's six in the morning in foreign o'clock?' A new regulation had just come in to use the twenty-four-hour system. The policeman took our name and address, hooking his lower jaw at us, showing us his bite. I nudged my mum. That kind of look meant he'd heard of us. But she didn't notice. She was breathless reciting the events of the night as if they'd happened to her, only worse – because in her head, a hand *had* come through the door and found the key and . . .

'And what *crime* do you say has been committed, Mrs Mitchell?'

'Harassment. Intimidation.'

He worked his jowls at that.

'Breach of the peace. Breaking and entering.'

'Did someone actually enter the property then?'

'Their *voice* did. Their *threats* did.'

He didn't write those down either.

Then my mum lost patience. 'I don't care what name you give it. No one's coming round while I'm away to scare my daughter. You're not going to bully us out of here.'

A week later, an officer came to the house to take a report. He had to borrow a pen to fill in his form. He said what we described was typical of Saturday-night drunkenness and it was one of the downsides of living in the centre of town.

'You've left it too late for fingerprints,' my mum said.

'We don't take prints for drinking. Having one too many isn't a crime. You're lucky to be living in a free country.'

Then my mum found a solicitor and drew up a will. She left everything to me if we died separately, to Peter if we died at the same time, and to GDR solidarity if all three went together. 'And G-D-R stands for?' the solicitor said.

My mum put locks on the windows and changed all the keys to the house. She had a new night-time routine. When I was in bed, I sometimes heard her: 'locked, locked; locked, locked; locked.' Just like the detritus check. She said it in her meeting voice if she needed to convince herself, and did it all twice if she still wasn't sure. Then she had a catch fixed to the letterbox, and put it across at night to stop anything coming through – threats, dog shit, fire-bombs – and a bucket of water on the doormat in case they did. But it meant setting the alarm even earlier and getting up before the postman so she could take the catch off before he arrived. It was a matter of principle to wait for the postcard from Peter.

My mum observed the ritual of dashing down to release the catch and returning empty-handed till I came down one morning and found a man on his hands and knees paying close attention to the skirting. I thought it was BT checking for a tap on the line. Actually it was an estate agent come to value the house. My mum was finally selling up.

The agent stood up, brushing the dust from his palms, and said he'd get a quicker sale if we 'disposed of the trinkets'. What he meant was: take the flag down, turn Honecker to the wall, and have one clock set to Tamworth time. But he must have guessed my mum wouldn't put the GDR away, so in his ad he wrote: *In the heart of historic Tamworth, a property offering classic local charm: a red-brick terrace, fireplace and chimney in working order, coal shed in the garden. See past the current use as an East European curio, and you have a quaint Staffordshire cottage asking for a family to call it home.*

Once the house was in the estate agent's window and *For Sale* had been hammered into the yard, a calm descended. My mum's troubles were over.

Somehow, Ivan got wind of her plans, and he rang to instruct her not to go. He said she'd kill the branch, when in fact the branch was almost extinct already. Like all species in a hostile environment, there were no longer any viable pairs. There'd been three more funerals, and my mum had done the oration at all of them, each time 'Man's dearest possession'.

Ivan said, 'And what good do you think you'll do over there?'

I'd searched my YCL homework for something my mum could do in the GDR that wasn't cowardly or trivial. 'I'm going to wither away the state. They'll need plenty of help with that.'

When my mum told Rosie, she said she'd step into the breach and do her best with CND. It'd be different methods, but same result: peace, love and universal happiness.

Which worried my mum.

That was code for sex, drugs and rock and roll. It meant circles and feelings when what you needed was rows of hard seats and a Chair. But still, Rosie was better than nothing. My mum photocopied the CND file to take with her to the GDR.

'Is this remote control, Eleanor?'

'It's solidarity.'

Then my mum rang James and announced we were going 'to live in the GDR *forever*'. He said there was a good chance of that, what with the saunas, the cures and the solid regular meals. James loved regimens. He said he'd never felt so good. He had a woman there now. She'd left her husband in Bitterfeld and moved into his flat, and they planned to marry as soon as her divorce came through. Angela was a stout but still hourglass teacher with a fondness for baking and English proverbs. 'A stitch in time saves nine!' she liked to say as she smoothed a crocheted doily onto the coffee table. 'Have your cake and eat it!' and she passed round the pastries. James said he was so smooth-faced he looked decades younger than in England, which might have been socialism, but maybe just lard.

When my mum told Saskia we were emigrating to the GDR and wondered if there might be a job at the *Hochschule*, there was silence at the other end of the line. She took so long to respond, my mum thought she'd been cut off. She listened to the Passenger Care hiss, till finally she heard, 'I am so glad your stays with us have made you feel welcome, made you feel well. *Alles zum Wohl des Volkes*, as you know. But you realise there would be implications.'

My mum knew she'd have to give up the summer course.

'Not only for the course.'

And that I'd have to finish school in the GDR. 'But she doesn't mind that, do you, Jess?'

Who could mind going to the Einstein-Gymnasium?

Saskia paused. 'I would urge you to take time to think it over, Eleanor. Think of what you are already to the GDR.'

My mum did think. But only briefly. She'd been wrestling with it for weeks and was sure this was the best decision. We'd make a life with Peter and Martina and do what everyone did in the GDR: live happily ever after.

My mum got Cynthia to drive to Potsdam and courier the stuff for the *Morning Star* bazaar. Marmion Motors had failed the minivan. My mum didn't want to smuggle an illegal vehicle out of the country. And she didn't want to risk a breakdown in West Germany, or to cut the engine at border control, then be push-started into defection.

So we flew to Schönefeld. My mum had bought tickets in Business Class because changing sides was a serious business, she said – though it turned out we didn't have the legs for all the room. My mum read the cocktail menu and ordered the Grüne Wiese because it was greener where we were going. She watched her old life being taken from her at 900 kilometres an hour, then the hostess brought her a phial of bitter potion, which put her instantly to sleep. My mum woke up when we touched the runway. She looked out of the window, at the bent grass and snapping windsocks. 'I can't quite believe that I'm going to spend the rest of my life here,' and she listed all the things she'd do in the GDR, ending with 'Die and be scattered here. Shall I be scattered, Jess?' And all the while, her new life circled the airfield waiting for a gate. When the plane finally came to a stop, 'Thus ends a tale of woe,' she said.

Though it didn't. We had return tickets. In a month, we'd be flying back to tie up the ends of our Tamworth life. My mum had papered her bedroom with TODOs. She had to hand in her notice and work her last term; sell the house subject to contract then have it fall through because of the chain and start all over again. 'Roll on Marzahn,' she said. Then there were all the goodbyes. She planned to let the whole town know where she was going, and had allowed weeks for that.

My mum was first out of the plane. She stood on the top step and waved at the terminal building because Peter had said he'd come to meet us. Then we ran to immigration. The stuffed Berlin bear was still there, looking more tired, sawdust showing at the seams. The same border guard was there too. My mum was sure it was him from the slow-motion way he did the paperwork. She didn't chat, just tapped an impatient foot to the leisurely folk dance that turned in the speakers, then whisked her documents from under his fingers and dashed into Arrivals.

My mum and Peter clung to each other, exchanging sweat and superlatives, and by the sound of it, saliva – though I was trying not to look. Across tannoy announcements for missing passengers, my mum muttered love-things, which I tried to blank out. Peter muttered them in German, which I tried to work out because exams were still in my brain. '*Hätte ich länger warten müssen . . .*' If I would have had to have waited longer . . . Which was the trouble with O-level German. Like *Star Trek*, it took you into dangerous time warps.

I hugged Martina and found ribs in my hands instead of shoulders. Since last summer, she'd got Business Class legs. I wondered what it was like being so tall you lived at the top of a tower block. She had to crane to scoop me in her arms. Like a mascot. A cuddly toy. Then came calls for a flight to Bulgaria, which made me feel like a Womble.

We chatted all the way to Potsdam, swigging apple juice from their garden. It was cloudy, musty, almost cider. We passed it round, turning the bottle so the dead flies stuck to the glass. Peter put the Beatles on, bought duty free with my mum's extra sterling as he'd dashed through Departures, late for his plane. We all sang along to 'Please Mister Postman'. It turned out my mum's letters hadn't arrived either – not even the ones she'd sent from London, addressed like a child just learning to write. We listened to the Beatles till we got to Stahnsdorf and 'Yellow Submarine'. Then Martina reached for the knob and switched it off. 'I do not want to spoil the mood. At first I thought it was a happy song. I liked it. But then I thought it was about living in the GDR.'

I'd heard nothing from Martina, nor she from me. My Bee Gees cassette had gone missing, and my *Don't do it, Di!* badge. My mum had put it down to the Royal Mail. Underpaid staff. Lack of morale. I didn't know where our post was. But somewhere along the Cold War front, all our offerings had been taken apart, X-rayed, decoded – when all there was was an offering.

Martina and I sat at the back of the van, her legs reaching down the aisle. Apart from those, she was just as I'd left her last summer. And then I noticed the new armpits. I thought she'd marry whoever he was if she'd started shaving those. And then she brought out the sunglasses, a present from Heathrow – big round brown lenses which made you wonder where her guide dog was. 'My world is tinted the colour of England,' she said.

Which was true. The colour of HP sauce, Tetley tea, Brain's faggots. 'And what did you think of the Angel Delight?'

'I did not even have to chew. I sucked the taste of England through my teeth.' Then she sucked on a cheek. 'But still no England. Lake Balaton instead.' Martina was going to spend the rest of the summer pressing a beach into buckets and turning out palaces of sand. It was an FDJ trip to Hungary. In the Socialist Bloc, it was what they did for foreign holidays – went round each other's countries. She shrugged. 'Our pleasures are sometimes enforced.' She said Lake Balaton would be like Schwielowsee, only even further away. And it was still just a lake, a big paddling pool, so the same range of possibilities.

And then she said that this time next year, she'd be gone. Which made it sound like a vanishing act, when in fact she'd be at the Humboldt University, an hour's train ride from Potsdam. 'We will not spend another summer together.'

I took a swig of apple juice, watching her down the length of the bottle and catching a fly. Of course we'd do it again. My mum and I had come to live here.

But Martina was serious. She'd looked at me as she'd said it as if those English-tinted lenses had let her see into the future.

Martina was in Hungary by the time of our first family outing. It was 13 August, Berlin Wall Day, and the course programme had an Afternoon Off. Peter, my mum and I – and Martina symbolically – lay on the lawn rim of Leninplatz in the smell of mown grass and hot tarmac. She'd written as soon as she'd arrived, and it was the kind of cryptic message that was starting to make me yawn. She'd bought a blank postcard and drawn a capital 'I'. On the back: *My last letter. Please take it with you when you go.*

We ate cornets of yellow and orange ice cream. They'd melted too much for maracas, so my mum awarded them to us instead: Here. Happy Life. Banana and mango flavour. The ship must have arrived from Cuba. She'd bought four, one for Martina, which I ate for her. Martina hadn't put on any weight, even though she was taller, which meant she was less dense than last summer. She had gaps that would buoy her. She'd float on Lake Balaton. She might even be able to walk on water.

Around Leninplatz, families lined up to face the sun. Dogs closed their eyes and spilled their tongue into the grass. Silent babies lay knocked out by the heat. Children doodled in chalk on the pavement: flowers, planes, stick-soldiers. My mum leant her cheek on a hand and looked at Peter across the puffed white heads of clover. He licked a handkerchief and dissolved the crust of her yellow moustache. Such was the chemistry of love.

This was how they celebrated twenty years of the Anti-Fascist Protection Barrier: with a family day in the sun. I had no idea what they were doing on the other side of it. Acting like fascists, probably, dressed in black, sour-faced because the sun shouldn't shine on a day like this. We had no right to the weather on our side.

Twenty years ago, it was hotter still, Peter said. He was at the Baltic, on the island of Hiddensee, in his first ever Trade Union holiday home. He had his own room, but it was too hot to use. He slept instead on the beach, in a breeze that had come straight across from Middlesbrough. It was the kind of heat you couldn't escape from, and everyone was restless. And then one morning, the restlessness speeded up. Instead of staggering to the seafront with bags and children, people were dashing to check out, still packing as they handed in their keys. It didn't make sense: they couldn't wait to get away from the subsidised, two-week holiday they'd waited a working life for.

There was no hard information, just rumours coursing through the building that something disastrous was unfolding in Berlin: Russians, Martians, World War Three. The queues for the ferry were longer than the pier. Some people made it to the mainland. Others were stranded on their holiday. Peter decided to stay. He'd have a sea view of the End of the World. As it turned out, the Berlin Wall just meant more room on the beach.

'There might be a wall,' my mum said, reaching out for Peter's hand, patting the lawn and failing to find it. 'But at least now we're on the same side of it.' Then she pressed her palm to the grass and frowned. 'I just felt the earth move.'

I fingered the mud and felt it too: the kind of buzz you get from whisking up Angel Delight. A cloud of ravens blew over us, cawing so hard they could have been retching. Peter checked his watch. 'That will be the tanks.'

We dashed towards Karl-Marx-Allee, past faces and flags dangling from windows and slogans as long as tower blocks. We ran past horse and carts that had rolled in from the countryside laden with red carnations. At least, I ran. My mum half-trotted and half-strolled, saying 'How fast do tanks go?' Peter was in no hurry. He'd seen tanks before. He took his time browsing the flowers and choosing the best carnations. 'Please think of them as roses', as he gave them to my mum.

The crowd was so dense I had to pogo for glimpses of the parade. Peter offered me a piggyback. It was like scrambling up a wall, which was the trouble with men – no angles, no hips, nothing to grab on to. Then I saw the Official Stand, three tiers of important people, pearled with honours and tied with a ribbon, like a celebration cake. 'Which one's Honecker?'

'White hair and glasses.'

But they all had white hair and glasses.

My mum wanted me to say hello. Instead, I said, 'The tanks are coming, mum! Hundreds of them!'

'Big ones? Are they big?' and she lifted herself onto tiptoe and tottered around up there, the way you would if you once hoped to be a ballerina.

The tanks came three abreast, khaki green on fat black wheels, pressing down Karl-Marx-Allee in a haze of heat and rubber, smelling of Marmion Motors. Out of the top, identikit men in earmuffs, under orders not to blink, looking straight from an Airfix packet.

Behind them, the *Kampfgruppen*, the ones who'd built the Wall in the first place. My mum yelled, 'Hello, Wall-builders!', and raised an imaginary glass to the raggle-taggle army that tripped by in a uniform a size too big. They stumbled over each other in a jumble of red flags, and tossed carnations into the crowd. My mum made a swipe for them, even though she hadn't got a chance here at the back, and already had her hands full of flowers.

Then the OAPs went by, armoured for the end with Zimmer frames, wheelchairs, hearing aids, oxygen. They were covered in blankets and medals, their cheeks purple, eyes dim, chins up. 'The Old Guard, now, Mum.' I just made that up. I had no idea who they were.

'That's me, Jess, in the future! That's your mum in thirty years' time.' She loved the thought of being one of the Old Guard, of a medal for services to Actually Existing Socialism and shuffling down Karl-Marx-Allee with a stick and bad knees. Thirty years from now, my mum would be a GDR pensioner. She'd be in a Lunch Club and fed *Kasslerbraten* and *Klöpse* that'd snag on her false German teeth. After the meal, they'd sit in the lounge in armchairs pressed against the walls and my mum would teach them songs from her days in the YCL, making up the lines that'd slipped her mind. Every so often, she'd get an OAP visa and make a day trip *drüben* to stock up on digestive biscuits and English tea. If she could bear to go over. If she still had any kind of taste for England.

My mum couldn't resist the Old Guard. She circled her shoulders, schmoozing through the crowd. She stood at the barrier and raised a clenched fist, and some of them, the ones whose eyesight was good enough to notice, raised a clenched fist back.

Now, underneath me, I felt Peter sway. I thought it was the music. 'The Internationale' had just struck up in the speakers. He rocked from side to side, only not in march-time, and when I looked, I saw a hand on Peter's arm. Someone was jostling him. A man was pulling him aside.

I slid down Peter's back, passing close to the stranger's face – one eye hooded, the slash of black brows, the collar of his mac turned up, the only person here dressed for a change in the weather. He said something into Peter's ear, then turned, and with a shoulder sliced a path through the crowd.

I tried to keep track of Peter, catching glimpses of his head till I wasn't sure if that was him or shadows I was seeing. I half-expected the man in the mac to turn and say, 'Just one last thing . . .' like they did on the telly. Instead, Peter's face scanned for me. His mouth moved. I couldn't see enough to lip-read. But he raised a finger and jabbed at the ground, and I knew I was to wait.

I waited till the parade had thinned, till at the end, the marchers didn't bother marching any more. They lifted a leg over the barrier and disappeared into the U-Bahn. I watched the sky grey over Alexanderplatz and people retreat from their balconies. The speakers on the lamp posts exhausted all their songs and now played feedback.

When my mum returned she was flushed and anxious and empty-handed. She'd given all her carnations away. 'I thought I'd lost you . . .' She'd been navigating by the banners and they'd all been taken in. She waved an arm up and down Karl-Marx-Allee. 'I went miles. It's like the M1. Do you think they built it for the tanks?' Then my mum registered my face. 'Where's Peter?'

I shrugged. 'He said to wait here.'

My mum glanced round. Here, on Strausberger Platz, the

fountain was back on, scattered by the wind. An iron sky lay over the TV Tower and the Hotel Stadt Berlin. Ornamental cats sat on windowsills like unhappy ceramics, eyes glazed over. My mum closed her eyes and lifted her face, sunbathing beyond the clouds. When she opened them again, she looked hopeful. Behind her eyelids, Peter had come back.

She checked the faces at the pavement café in case he was there, but found strangers sipping drinks and toying with their sunglasses. She glanced at her watch. '*How* long did he say he'd be?'

But he didn't.

My mum shuddered. 'It's getting late. Getting cold. Aren't you cold?'

'It's August.'

'I'm suddenly freezing.' But she didn't go in to get warm. She kept watch. Teenage boys who knocked about a football thought she was keeping an eye on them. They waved at her and got no response. She probably didn't even see them. She flicked her head left, then right, then left again, repeating the Green Cross Code for a street she didn't cross.

Then she wanted me to repeat exactly what had happened, and as I told her, and she only half-listened because she was too busy scanning faces, Peter appeared on the far side of the road. He was in someone else's suit again – charcoal grey this time, with a white shirt – the kind of clothes Jehovah's wear to pass themselves off as harmless, and when you spot them round the curtain, you know not to open the door.

We didn't run to meet him. We watched Peter cross Karl-Marx-Allee in shoes that seemed to hurt. And he walked slowly, as if his pace were set by a hearse. He stopped an arm's length away. 'I have just been released from a meeting.'

He looked like he'd come from the morgue.

My mum was relieved, though. Meetings were all right. She went to hug him, and he let her. But it was just that – let her – his arms stiff at his side.

He said he had some news about his solidarity work. 'I have to intensify my efforts. I have to train English teachers.'

'But you do that already.'

'In Vientiane. Laos.' The words didn't make sense. You couldn't even tell which language they were in. 'Eleanor, they are sending me away.' He said they'd tell Martina when she got back from Hungary. She was to stay in the GDR. Her grandmother would care for her. They'd moved quickly. Arranged it all. Taken care of everything.

'But you're here for the summer course.'

'I am leaving now.' He had a one-way ticket. They'd post out the return when the time came. 'I must do things by the book.' It sounded as though Peter had been given another paper towel, only much thicker this time. 'And if I do, then we see each other in two years' time.'

My mum made herself wide. 'Jess, don't let him go!' and the two of us stood primed for a break, as if Strausberger Platz were a playing field, and this was British Bulldog, and Peter might run for it, even in those shoes. In the stand-off, my mum told Peter it wasn't true. She refused to believe he was going. She'd lived her whole life as if conviction itself could turn things around. 'And we're *here* now . . . *We're* here.' Then my mum reached out, building a wall two arms wide, her face made of breeze-blocks and wet mortar.

Peter didn't look. He turned the stillest face to me. The last time he'd left us, he said: tell your mother to believe, and to think. This time he said, 'Do not let Eleanor think too much.' Over his shoulder, small in the distance, the cleaners were out, sweeping what was left of the day into the back of a truck. Peter stood in abandoned flags and the first dark spots of summer rain, his feet wreathed in crushed carnations.

16

Our People

Peter had been right. They'd moved fast and taken care of everything, because the very next morning, Saskia introduced his replacement. It turned out to be the woman who'd sat in the back row with me all that week, smiling from time to time, as if wanting to make friends, repelling me with the force field of her perfume. It was acid and metallic, more Eveready than roses. I'd noticed the way she'd taken notes, but out of sync with everyone else. And the SED badge on her dress wasn't a brooch. It was a frank from the Authorities, a mark of despatch. I'd put her down as some kind of Quality Control. In fact, all week, I'd been sitting next to Peter's understudy.

Frau Dr Blech stood at the front of the lecture theatre and effused about the honour of her new post. She said how demanding, exacting and nagging it would be. Synonyms rolled off her tongue. After a while, I noticed they were in alphabetical order. She'd memorised her thesaurus. She asked for communication, dissemination, intelligence and intercourse. No one had felt able to tell her about her word choice. Which was the downside of being an official. Unofficially, people thought things they didn't like to say.

Frau Dr Blech didn't have a first name. The man she was replacing was Herr Dr Roth, but still she only ever called him 'Peter'. She said how hard it would be to step into his shoes, when actually she'd have fitted several times over. She propped herself on stubs for feet. Her square-cut, polka-dot dress made her look like a pocket transistor, the round dial of her face gleaming under a thin film of sweat. It turned out she never stopped broadcasting. Even when I raised what had happened to Peter, her voice simply went fuzzy and crackled, as if losing reception, then settled back into a stable frequency and went on transmitting as if I'd never spoken.

I didn't think my mum would warm to Peter's replacement, but in fact she was grateful for the permanent burble. Silence made her uneasy. It gave unwanted thoughts the chance to sound. And my mum was under instruction: Peter had said, 'Do not let Eleanor think too much,' and she'd decided not to think at all. She'd gone to the fuse box in her head, flicked the trip switch, and that was it. All circuits down: thinking, remembering, registering, reacting . . . She was going through the course on autopilot.

On the other hand, it meant she slept better than she had for months. She hardly ever took pills. My mum was still vague – as if she *had* taken pills – but she lived in a dream instead of a fug. She didn't look forward and didn't look back, drifting from event to event with a permanent look of mild surprise. Apart, that is, from once – exactly a week after Peter was sent away. I woke in the middle of the night to the call of wolves, then realised it was coming through the wall. My mum was howling. Not crying. It came from deeper down than that. She was at her window, neck taut, and making animal sounds at the moon. Except there was no moon that night – just low damp clouds and a false dawn over Eiche-Golm. The army was already up. I didn't go in with tea. You couldn't comfort with tea so thin it tasted more of kettle. And I didn't want to sit with her till sunrise, chewing on black bread spread with puréed heart. Mother pâté. Here: have some. But mostly I didn't go in because I wanted my mum to howl. Because even if her head wasn't thinking, her gut was. And it was outraged.

★

There was a holiday, as usual, at the end of the summer course. We were going to the countryside. Last year, when my mum had requested something rural, she'd got Eisenhüttenstadt. So the Spreewald was a gesture: Peter for gherkins. We made one visit to a pickling factory, and apart from that it was all nature. The area was a network of canals, and punting the main means of getting about. All the tutors were issued with a life jacket, insurance, a canoe and a map. My mum was a geographer, but kept getting lost. She'd turn a corner and say, 'Oh look, it's shit creek again, Jess.' The waterways were lined with trees in leaf, which meant a week of dark-green gloom, of paddling up and down the Styx. Frau Dr Blech said, 'Do you not relish the calm, hush, lull, repose, the truce, Eleanor?'

She much preferred the foundry.

She couldn't wait to go home.

My mum left the gifts from the holiday in her *Hochschule* room. The students could do what they wanted with *The Illustrated Gherkin*, the bucket of gherkins and the gherkin liqueur. The only thing she couldn't leave behind were the calluses, and she picked at those for weeks. We flew Business Class home. My mum locked herself inside the Interflug headphones and poked stiff fingers at the channels. It didn't matter what came out. It just had to be loud enough to drown out thought. Then she ordered cocktails: a Bloody Mary and a Whisky Sour this time, and when we touched down at Heathrow, she was sick into the paper bag.

When we got back to Tamworth, she announced that every thirteenth of the month she'd buy herself a red carnation. It would be a reminder of the day, 'but a good reminder. A happy one.' On the Oxfam calendar, she went through the months ringing the date. In total, there'd be twenty-four thirteenths before Peter came back. Three of them would be Fridays. Swollen bellies and darkened eyes loomed from around the world over our own personal disaster.

'Pinch punch thirteenth of the month, no returns whatsoever.'

'But he *will* come back, won't he, Jess?'

My mum was such a literalist.

Over the autumn, instead of leaving, we settled back into Tamworth life. My mum took the house off the market and folded away her emigration TODOs. 'Paradise isn't off the agenda. It's just deferred to the next meeting,' she said to anyone who asked. Then we tried to track Peter down. We asked Saskia for his address, which she said she'd forward once Peter was settled, but then she never got back. Stefan knew less than his sister. We tried to contact Martina – sent a postcard to Zwickau and to Potsdam, a GDR slogan card, which my mum said fitted the bill: *Mit unserer Tat für unseren sozialistischen Friedensstaat!* With our deed for our socialist peace state! Because that was the version of events she'd settled on. Think that and you didn't have to think any further: Peter wasn't in exile doing time. He was in fraternal Laos doing a Good Deed.

No response to the postcards.

Then my mum tried the Britain-Laos Friendship Society, and they were sure they'd be able to locate him. They were used to finding people who'd gone to ground, they said. So my mum took out a two-year subscription to the Society, and waited. This was going to be her new thing: sitting under our three clocks that were set to Havana, Berlin and what she now called Vientiane time, doing two years' solidarity with Peter doing solidarity. And then their newsletter arrived. It turned out they were all Laos exiles, anti-communists who'd fled the country. And when they got back about Peter, they'd found no trace of him.

And then a letter came, and amid all the junk and freebie papers, my mum almost missed it. She very nearly binned the reused envelope with the scrawled address and the stamp stuck on askew. But an airmail letter fell out, and a note ripped from a pad: *BEEN ASKED TO GIVE YOU THIS.*

My mum skimmed the wafer-thin letter with a frown that

deepened as she read. She re-checked the start and end. It didn't say 'Dear Eleanor', or 'Love Peter'. Without a wave hello or goodbye, it wasn't really a letter. She handed it to me:

Vientiane is the quietest city in the world. In the marketplace, you can hear the sound of scissors on silk. Old men offer you finest teak and rosewood, but will not say a word. In temple compounds, bell towers rise to the sky, but do not ring. Dogs have given up on barking. Babies have forgotten how to cry.

On the road out of town, farmers walk in single file, sandals dragging dust. Their fields lie just east of the city. To the west flows the Mekong. Across the river is Thailand. On the other bank, young women wash their clothes and bathe. Their laughter does not quite reach across the water. The Mekong must be the only river that can be heard above the sounds of a capital city. I imagine it murmurs the entire length of Laos.

At first, I thought it was a silent city. Now I think it is a silenced one. My clothes match the colours of the wash on the walls. All over the walls are geckos. I see faces in the faces. Names come easily to mind.

Tonight, I will lie in bed, under the new stars of this upturned sky, and make sounds against the silence. I will listen to the chafe of this pen, to the age-old flight of skin, and to the give and take of air, which is life in all languages, a word when there are no words left.

I held the letter up to the light, looking for a message in lemon juice. I read it in the mirror. I copied the start and end of every sentence, but nothing was spelled out – not in English or German. I read it in a *Jackanory* voice, listening for escape plans between the lines. I was going to tell my mum it was a letter from exile, but I knew she'd just hold it to my face, so close I couldn't see anything, and say, 'And where exactly does it say *that*?'

My mum said, 'Peter doesn't like it if it's too quiet either.'

Then she smoothed the letter with the flat of her hand and skimmed it again. 'But listen to that: silk, teak, rosewood. When he gets back, there'll be plenty of nice souvenirs.'

In November, it was CND conference and the annual gathering of the communist clan. Ivan had been busy preparing for weeks, and I'd had to help him – partly with the admin, but as much with his domestic arrangements. I'd spent more and more time in Walsall as Ivan's PA, his shopper, cleaner, his babysitter – lying to his wife about where he was and why he couldn't get back for *Postman Pat*. My mum gave me extra money for all the bus fares. She said how lucky I was to have a mentor, 'especially one who's good at the theory'. Sometimes, she came into my bedroom and gazed in awe at the formulas Ivan had given me to stick on the wall and memorise. He had the science to prove what my mum could only feel. She thought it was all good. But then, she wasn't really thinking.

This year, CND conference was at Queen Mary College and Cynthia's flat had been turned into HQ for the weekend. We were all there, massing our forces in defence of the Soviet Union. It was an unofficial Party Congress, a chance to compare notes on struggles with the Euros and the Ultras, with black-listing and incurable disease. On the Friday evening, Cynthia gave us a briefing on how to look inconspicuous, what to say to the neighbours, and on evacuation procedures. It was always a risk, she said, bringing so many comrades together in one place, and should there be an incident, the order of exit was rank-and-responsibility.

Which meant that I was dead.

Ivan had arrived at Cynthia's way before everyone else. He'd stripped the sofa of its cushions and installed himself in what he called 'the Mess'. The kitchen door had a bolt, so if he wanted, Ivan had monopoly access to the fridge, the phone, the kettle. Cynthia had allowed the takeover, which was most unlike her, and made me think it was subject to some Higher Command.

It took ages for people to go through their bedtime rituals: pills, plugs, and coded nods in the direction of Gods we knew didn't exist. My mum took a sleeper and went straight out. I lay awake, listening to the throb of a High Road nightclub and the turmoil of displaced dreams.

I was just about to drift off, when I felt a hand rocking my shoulder. Ivan was standing over me, a finger to his lips. I followed him into the kitchen, and into the smell of hot chocolate and buttered toast. My stomach rumbled loud enough for him to hear. I stood in my tracksuit, bare feet curling from the freezing floor, while Ivan bit into his toast and watched me watch. When he finished, he licked the plate.

Then he recited an address at me. 'Be there at one.'

I glanced at the kitchen clock. It said just after two, and for a moment I thought I'd missed it.

'On the dot,' Ivan said. 'Our People are never late.'

'*Our* People?'

'You heard me.'

Our People were just a rumour. They were so secret, no one knew who they were. *They* didn't even know who they were. And now I was going to meet them. I hadn't thought to pack a balaclava.

'What about my mum?'

'Is she standing here?'

Actually, I was relieved. I didn't know what Our People did, but with Ivan in charge, it wouldn't be maracas and singing. He prodded my chest, fingering Lurpak on my Life Saving badge. 'I want to be clear you understand the status of this information. Not even your mum. And tell me why.'

'Need to Know.'

'And does she?'

'If you say not.'

'Well then.'

I didn't go back to sleep after that. I sat up and studied the corpses humped on Cynthia's floor. She'd padded the lino with

214

leftover *Stars*, and the room was thick with the smell of news-print and meals boiled in the bag. I wondered if any of these people were secretly Our People. There was my mum in her cotton pyjamas and alpaca bedsocks, clinging to the scarf she'd rolled into a comforter, and mumbling through her Valium, spilling the beans in her sleep. In her pyjama pocket, a red carnation. Today was Friday the 13th.

Saturday lunchtime, I slipped out of conference early to get to Our People on the dot. It meant I got there too early and had to dilly-dally, trying not to look suspicious. So I read the notices on the lamp posts about littering and dog mess. Hackney had more rules than Tamworth. I walked up one side of the street and down the other, tiptoeing to avoid the jinx. But Hackney had more cracks in the pavement too.

I'd expected the secret cell to meet somewhere secret – across an abandoned industrial estate and round the back of an empty warehouse. That I'd have to answer a personal question that only I, and somehow they, knew the answer to. That I'd be frisked and hooded and led blind into an unheated garage. Instead, I stood outside a red-brick terrace with nets in the bay and a garden of stringy grass – the kind that sews sand dunes together and keeps England the shape it is.

I checked the time. It was one minute to one, which was close enough to the dot. The street was empty. No other Our People seemed to be coming.

I rang the bell and the door buzzed off the latch. A dark figure stood at the top of the stairs. 'Lesson One: In operations, early is no better than late.' His voice wasn't loud, but he projected it in the way actors do to reach the gods, when all he had to do was reach the doormat. I wondered if it was the voice of the Higher Command.

In the sitting room, I found a row of hard seats and a Chair, one at the end untaken. I might have been one minute early, but I still seemed to be late. Everyone else was settled in. And the Chair was actually a three-seater sofa, and Ivan was taking up all of it. He didn't acknowledge me. None of them did. It was just faces to the front and silence while Ivan talked.

'Resolution 92. Hull END.'

Papers turned without making a sound.

I didn't have any papers. Ivan hadn't mentioned those. He read the resolution out: 'Cetera, cetera, cetera, blah, blah, blah . . . "support those struggling against repression in the Eastern Bloc and in particular the Solidarity movement in Poland." This is the one we're going to kill stone cold dead.' Ivan had changed since last night. He'd put on a ribbed navy jumper and black combat trousers, and looked military, in a Millets kind of way. Our People seemed unremarkable, which I supposed was the point for undercover. They could have been Probation Officers, patrolling convention in their low-rise shoes, nameable haircuts and grey clothes from a catalogue. I'd come as a pirate. Actually, I was a New Romantic. Apart from a change of knickers, it was the only kit I'd brought to London. I'd thought I'd fit in, it being the capital and 1981.

Ivan reached to the corners of the sofa where stacks of papers had taken the place of cushions. 'These are going to take out Resolution 92.' We were going to attack Hull END with Ivan's speeches. He'd written one for each of us, and we went in turn to collect. Ivan wasn't far enough to get upright between chair and sofa, and we reached for our speech as if taking a blow to the belly. I crept across for mine: *As a young person, concerned for my future and the future of all young people, East and West, I wish to oppose Resolution 92 . . .*

More papers.

Ivan said, 'Plan of the auditorium. We're going to monopolise the microphones. Get the truth out and shut the opposition up. Six mics. Twelve of you. Which one you're to cover is at the bottom of your speech. Get to the auditorium early. Watch what's going on like a hawk. Be ready to move fast.

This resolution will be popular. Queues. Argy-bargy. Just stand your ground.'

I was on microphone three. I glanced at the papers on the lap beside me and tried to see which mic my neighbour was on, but he clocked my look and curled his papers away.

Then a map of the college, the toilets marked 'X'. Every couple of hours, we had to check the middle cubicle. Under the cistern lid. Ivan didn't say what for: bacteria, dead pigeons, a broken ballcock.

'But don't all turn up on the hour. *Obviously*.'

There would have been laughter, except for the Rule of Silence.

'Questions?'

Of course there'd be no questions.

Ivan checked his watch. He said we had thirty minutes to make a good job of our speech and get back to conference. He didn't wish us luck, or give us any idea how to memorise five paragraphs in less than a single period. When we'd done *Macbeth*, we had a whole week to get 'tomorrow and tomorrow and tomorrow' down pat, while breathing so it still made sense.

Then Ivan said we'd disperse by the usual means. I was halfway out of my seat when I saw no one else had moved. He nodded at a woman and then at the street and pointed in the direction I'd come from. She slipped her papers into her handbag, fingering the clasp so it didn't click. I stared hard at her, willing her to look at me, the way I could make my mum feel my eyes and turn. But she stayed blinkered all the way to the door and left without a goodbye. It was like theatre, a modern play with no lines but plenty of meaning. If only you knew what it meant.

Two minutes later, Ivan picked out a man and pointed in the opposite direction. He dropped his papers into a briefcase and stepped out of the room. Everyone waited their turn, memorising their assault on conference. No one came up with a question for Ivan, not even with time to think about it. It was just one departure every two minutes. Leave the house to the left, then right, left, right. That was the usual means.

The room cleared, and in the end there were just the two of us. Ivan made himself comfy, settling in for something when it was actually my turn to go. He asked what I thought of the meeting. I wanted to say: so this is what you've got lined up for me. I've been admitted to Junior Our People. Intermediates get to arrive at the start of the meeting. Advanced Our People see the face of Higher Command. Instead I said, 'I thought it went like clockwork.' Wasn't that Lesson One? Our People are on the dot.

Ivan approved of that, giving me a tick with his head. Then he turned to the urn on the sideboard. 'Where's my tea?' The urn had been sighing all meeting, keeping itself just under the boil. I made him a cup. I'd done it thousands of times: teabag till liverspots, squeezed dry between two spoons. Cream of the milk. Three sugars, heaped. I gave Ivan the mug and a garibaldi because I knew he'd dunk and wouldn't want to fish for a corpse.

Ivan was happy with his tea, and happy with his biscuit.

And that was Lesson Two: Our People keep Ivan happy.

Which I'd done. Two out of two. 'Can I go now, Ivan?'

'And the rest.' Which meant give him the tin. I knew from the way his eyes cruised the biscuits that it wasn't a matter of which, but order. He settled on a bourbon and prised the top off with his teeth.

Then he said, 'Who's your mum's East German friend?'

My heart sank. This was going to be another: 'Time to talk about Peter.' And this could be a long one. Ivan had settled in for the duration of the tin.

I shook my head.

'Why the shyness, Jess?'

'Why the interest, Ivan?'

Ivan felt his fists. He had hands as big as gloves. Just the right size for punching people. And those fists were Lesson Three:

Our People don't answer back. Then he said, 'Friendships like that don't come cheap. What do you have to do to be in with the embassy?'

My eyes slid over Ivan's face. There was no sign of bluffing, or double bluffing, or however many bluffs a single face could make. The East German friend he meant was Stefan.

I said, 'Friendships like that come at a price.' And I thought: you know all about prices, Ivan. Exchange value. Use value. Rate of exploitation. You gave me the formulas for them. They darken my bedroom wall. 'And you quickly get into debt. There are hidden costs.' Peter, for instance.

'I want a name. And I'm not letting you out of this room till I get one.'

'But, Ivan. *Need to Know.*'

Something like a smile hit him in the face then vanished. He got out of the sofa and moved to the door. He turned to me with a look that was sour, brown, squeezed dry of all kindness, and he turned the key in the lock.

I spent the afternoon in a corner of the room. It must have been the quietest corner in the world. Next door, restless dogs paced themselves to stillness. Babies had already cried too much to cry. In the yard, children shot each other over the privet, their death throes not quite reaching through the glass. The silence was only broken when Ivan shifted on the sofa or when he said, 'Got a name yet?'

No answer.

'So learn your speech.'

Each time, I held up his sheet and let my eyes hover over it without touching. And maybe it was no food, or no air, but instead of Ivan's words, other words spooled in my head in a code I was a breath from breaking.

The sky darkened, and he must have lost patience, or needed the loo, because he suddenly said, 'Just shut it, Jess.'

'I didn't say anything.'

'You breathed. I don't want to hear you breathe.'

And breath was life in all languages. Peter had said: I see faces in the faces. Names come easily to mind.

'Peter.'

'What did you say?'

I turned to face Ivan. I said it again, louder this time. I said it because it was a name, the one that was on my mind, the one that mattered. Because it was over. Because I was never going to dress like a Probation Officer, or live by Lessons One to Three, or fight the enemy on our side to elbow my way to a mic and give voice to Ivan.

Ivan sighed. He swung himself upright from the sofa and brushed crumbs from his front to the floor. His mouth crept into a shape that on a different face might have been a smile. 'Peter. Now did I need to know that?'

'No.'

'So should you have told me?'

And that was Lesson Four.

Ivan said to get back to conference sharp. I could still make myself useful. He sent me to the right out of the house. He hadn't lost track of the usual means.

I turned left.

Outside, Hackney screamed. The cold air burned. And it tasted of curry and fish and chips and litter and dog mess. I swallowed large gulps of Hackney. I filled my lungs with it. Then I walked, and kept walking. It was the only thing I could do – keep moving, not looking back. Soon I lost all sense of direction. I walked long streets lit in orange that beaconed into the distance, streets that rolled out Time, years and years of it, so much Time that parallel lines met. I tracked endless rows of houses where people weren't on a mission, or whose only mission was to get through the day. Houses where normal things happened on this normal Saturday: watching telly, paying bills, unpacking shopping, and where people wondered what the point of it was – but not for very long, only as long as it took to unjam the drawer and stuff the carrier bags away.

I ended up in a park. I sat on a bench by the lake, and fingered the gouged-out messages of love and hate. The clicks and pips and tic-tac of bird code had gone quiet. Geese rested their U-bend necks against their breasts and slept as if the world were not at war and there were no sides. I thought: I had no idea it was so easy to switch sides, what a fine line – a broken line – it was between Us and Them. I thought of Peter and Martina and how sides could be switched for you, whether you wanted it or not, sometimes without you even knowing.

I took Ivan's speech from my pocket, five dark paragraphs meant for microphone three. *As a young person, concerned for my future and the future of all young people, East and West . . .* I folded it into a paper aeroplane, sharpening the edges with a nail. I stood at the edge of the lake and aimed for the other side. The plane charged upwards, forcing a way against the pull of the earth, stopped, somersaulted, and fell on its back. Then Ivan's words, his weapons, turned wet. His speech surrendered to the water. The page sank. It went from white, through all the shades of grey, to black.

Then I heard heels on the path and a low song, 'The Sound of Silence', the words ebbing from notes they couldn't quite reach, the kind of singing my mum did to the washing-up. Then the voice stopped and a flashlight swiped my face. 'No home to go to? Better get a move on. Park closed at dusk.'

'Are you the keeper?'

'Of the flame, of the faith, of the grail, of the oath, of the peace, of the zoo.'

'Which way's Streatham?'

'You don't want to go to Streatham, love. Your exit's this way,' and he shone his light ahead of us. He walked me out of the park and into the roar of a main road. I listened to the keeper whisper to his song as he wrapped a chain round and round the gate, tying up its iron flowers.

17

A Useful Evening

London, November 1981

It took hours to find Streatham. Everyone I asked had heard
of it, but was vague on how to get there. In the end, I made
it via Croydon. When I arrived at Cynthia's flat, there was no
sign of Ivan. Everyone else was back, though, soaking sore feet
in the buckets they'd used for donations, and settling down for
an early night. My mum had found the local Light Dragoons
and polished off the usual. She was already in her sleeping bag,
worrying at her teeth with a cocktail stick and 'just beginning
to get anxious, Jess'.

At half-five, an alarm went off, and after that, it was mayhem.
Figures fell over each other in the darkness. The urgencies of
ageing bodies tripped into action: thirst, urination, pontification.
People lined up outside the bathroom, arguing about the tonnage
of nuclear weapons before they'd even put in their teeth.

I didn't bother waiting. I wanted to get out early anyway.
Stefan was at CND conference and I had to intercept him.
There was something I needed to ask. When he'd told my mum
he'd be an Official Observer, she couldn't believe it. 'But they're
so anti-Sov. How did you manage that?'

'It is my job to manage things like that,' he'd said.

I got to Queen Mary just as the sky was lightening. Knots
of shadowy figures had already gathered on the frozen lawn.
There were no leafleters or newspaper sellers yet, just the pinched
faces and hungry looks of the insomniacs and schemers. I knew

Stefan wouldn't be long. He had his work cut out at an event like this.

And now, here he was.

Stefan walked briskly, looking all set for business in his fine wool overcoat, briefcase and umbrella, and his hands in leather gloves. I noticed people give him a second glance. I gave him a wave. A query crossed Stefan's face as if he couldn't quite place me. I put it down to the frilly shirt and naval jacket. So, I waved again, semaphoring this time. And before I had a chance to speak, 'It can wait,' he said.

I told him it couldn't. I had something for him, something confidential. He just looked bored by confidential. In the background, drivers on the Mile End Road had a set-to with their horns. Then, 'Does it concern my work?'

'*Our* work.'

'And Eleanor?'

I shook my head.

Stefan suddenly seemed to feel the weight of his briefcase and swapped hands with the umbrella. He gave me a nod. 'But not here and not now. When all this is over,' and he jutted his chin in the direction of the schemers. He said to go to the Van Hoa, Kingsland Road, six o'clock sharp.

'Where's the Kingsland Road?

'On every map of London.'

'Why do we have to go there?'

Stefan checked his watch. In his head, he was probably saying: because I'm a very busy man, an embassy official, a peace secretary in a time of war. Because there's an arms race out of control, and it'll bankrupt my country if we're not careful, and if nuclear war doesn't get us first.

'Because I like the food,' he said.

Stefan held his menu like a book and read it as I'd seen him read everything else: fast, attentive, faintly pleased, as if the contents were just a reminder of something he already knew.

On the cover, *Welcome to Dalston's Dreamboat* and a man in a coolie hat stood in a canoe and paddled into a sunset. We'd never been this close. Here, at this table for two, I had to be careful where I put my feet. Lovers would have asked for a table like this – to breathe each other's breath, look into each other's eyes and know they know what the other is thinking. They would have set aside the vase with the plastic orchid and clasped hands, fingering each other's fingers, remembering the shape of each other's bones. I glanced at Stefan's hands. 'Is that a ring? I didn't know you were married.'

'All diplomats are married,' said without looking up.

When did that happen? Did she come with his posting, in the diplomatic bag? Where had he been keeping her? 'How long have you had a wife?'

He replied to the menu. 'For as long as I have needed one.'

Stefan reached the ice-cream desserts and pinned the menu open under his folded arms. 'You know, I have been in England several years and still I have no taste for your favourite foreign foods. Your Indian food with the hot towels and After Eight mints. Your Chinese food with the orange glue. But I *do* like Vietnamese.' He motioned at the restaurant: the tourist-office posters of Halong Bay with green knuckles doubled in the sea. The potted palms dotted with nylon butterflies. The golden cat on the counter, its paw raised like a clenched fist, defying friction, waving forever against the laws of physics. 'Vietnam, I know. Here, I feel like at home.' And he looked at home, settled and spread into the scoop of his rattan chair. And then he added, 'Though, of course, the Vietnamese at home are invited. International solidarity. They are fraternal guests. These people jumped ship.'

I pictured our waiter leaving Vietnam, pressed in a hurry into a night-time boat. His wife stumbles after him and tells him to send a message as soon as he gets to wherever he's going. She waves at the sound of oars in water, listening to it get smaller and waterier till there is only the water, and it'll be months and months till she's heard of a place called Dalston.

I became aware of Stefan's gaze on me. I met his look. 'Your eyes can change colour.'

'Have you only just noticed?'

'According to what?'

'East–West relations, my tie, how interesting the exchange . . . So you have something for me.' He held open a palm so that I could put whatever it was I'd come with, this thing that couldn't wait, into his waiting hand.

'I have a question.'

Stefan sighed. He leant back in his chair and signalled to the waiter.

He came over, hands clasped behind his back. 'Wasn't it Pho Bo, sir, and a beer?'

'And she takes the same as me. But no beer.'

The waiter nodded and backed away.

I said, 'Do you come here often?'

'Regularly. But not frequently. Many times a change of personnel. They move on. But this man, I happen to know.' Stefan didn't look as though he knew him. He'd stared straight through him when he gave the order. 'It is the problem with these people. They should try to forget more.' He made an elaborate fold of his hands in his lap. 'So that was your question. What else do you have for me?'

'Another question. Why did they send Peter away?'

Something unbidden registered in his eyes – surprise or irritation – and then vanished. Stefan went quiet. I watched the slow rise and fall of his white shirt, perfectly ironed, his maroon tie, clipped.

'It's important, Stefan.'

'Oh, *Jess*. Is this really why I am here?' The restaurant was hot. We were beside a radiator, but he didn't loosen his tie. Instead, he straightened it, smoothing it out like a tongue.

'Peter was taken away by a man in a mac.'

Stefan laughed at that.

'Do you know a man in a mac?'

'Many. *I* have a mac. You know Peter volunteered.'

'He said: "They're sending me away." Who are *they*, Stefan?'

'There is no *they*.' And that was that. Fact announced. Then silence till the waiter approached with a pint. Stefan's eyes followed it onto the table. He put his hands around the glass, feeling the cold, letting it sink through to his bones. 'I know you wanted to live in the GDR. But would it have worked, really? Is it not better this way? *This* is your country.' He cast a hand at the restaurant, at this little outpost of Vietnam. 'It would have been such a loss if you had gone. Things are moving here. Last month, more than a quarter of a million on the streets of London. Unheard of. But the peace movement needs direction. It needs good people. We have seventeen million in the GDR. It is not enough, that is clear. But two more English teachers will not help. If you really want to be of use to us, stay in England.' He presented his glass as if for a toast, but I didn't have a drink. '*Zum Wohl*,' said to my empty hand. I watched his top lip foam with beer. Then he pressed a finger across his mouth. It was the old infant school sign for quiet. In the quiet, the Police sang 'Every Little Thing She Does Is Magic'.

'And Martina? We wrote to their Potsdam flat and didn't get a reply.'

'That, I imagine, is because she did not write one. You know Martina's grown up now. Going her own way.' And the way he said it, so flat and ready-made, I thought that must be the official line on Martina. I was about to ask if he had any news when he said, 'I have a vital job to do. I am trying to prevent nuclear war. I do not have time to check on the status of teenage friendships.'

The waiter brought two bowls. It looked like our washing-up, pale meat and dead leaves milling on the surface. Stefan tipped his chopsticks from the wrapper and prised them apart in a perfect break. He rubbed the tips together as if trying to make fire. He saw my look. 'Against splitters.' He made a show of sanding his cutlery.

227

'Is that what they do in Vietnam? Or Laos?'

'I do not know. I have never been. To either country. But I *imagine*' – he made a point of the word – 'Laos to be rather like this restaurant: palm trees and heat, butterflies and orchids, freshly cooked food. All in all, not *so* bad.'

He inspected the table before putting his chopsticks down. In the lip, a scattering of ancient rice had dried on a bed of dust. A white heat-ring and the permanent stains of cheap red wine. He rested the chopsticks on top of his bowl.

'But if they needed someone for solidarity, why *Peter*?'

'Because he is trusted, I imagine.' Stefan knew that wasn't true. I looked at his untroubled face, the unruffled smile. The word 'imagine' allowed him that expression. He could lie all he liked and still not be called a liar. Stefan saw my look. But he didn't backtrack. He just imagined harder. 'He is a trusted Party member with an important job to do.'

Stefan exhausted me. I looked up and away from him. Over my head, a wall-light shone through the fronds of a palm, casting a giant jungle onto the ceiling. Something upstairs had leaked. A brown stain sat in the leaves like a piece of poisonous fruit.

'You know, you surprise me.' But Stefan didn't seem surprised so much as disappointed. 'I had you down as a tough one. I had not expected you to pursue this. That this so concerns you. Eleanor is not sentimental.'

'She's very sentimental. She just has different sentiments. And, anyway, I am not my mother.'

'No. I have observed this. In some ways, you are not at all like your mother.'

And that was the thing about diplomatic faces: whatever you said, they wouldn't react. The complete opposite of my mum whose face burst with everything she felt, and everything everyone else felt too.

'It is war, Jess. You know it is. We have the Federal Republic on one side. Fraternal Poland going off the rails on the other. West Berlin right in the middle of us. There.' Bang. That was a fist on the table. He raised his hand and swung it towards the soya sauce and ketchup. I thought he might lay out the political map of Europe with the condiments. Instead, he picked up his glass and studied what was left. 'And now we have to deal with . . .' He paused to choose the phrase. '. . . internal turbulence. Up and down the country, hostile-negative forces go to church every Sunday to pray for peace and the end of socialism.'

For the first time, I noticed the way Stefan said 'peace'. He pronounced it 'peas'. I pictured the services: the pastor in black robes, bat wings flung across the pulpit and rows of the faithful mumbling into their fingers for peas: garden peace. Processed peace. Frozen peace. Mushy peace.

'They get stronger, braver, make themselves felt. Welcomed by END and, I have to say, by CND.' He threw me a look as if CND were my fault and I could have stopped them if I'd tried harder. 'Yesterday, you passed a resolution supporting people, "struggling against repression in the Eastern Bloc".' He clawed the air for quote marks. 'You are about to send a delegation to Berlin, an official movement-to-movement visit. And you would not believe how keen people are to put hostile-negative forces on the itinerary, and how busy it keeps me trying to stop them.'

Stefan glanced at his watch as if to check just how busy he'd been. It was black-faced with squared-off numbers, the minute hand an arrowhead, all clunk and urgency. I pictured Stefan going to bed in the early hours. He places his watch beside his stack of reading. On one side of him, his mysterious wife who frets in her dreams and talks to herself in German. On the other, his watch, the mechanism amplified on the bedside table, the time left to stop hostile-negative forces ticking away.

'They fool people on our side too. People we once trusted. People who think you can make peace by losing the war. And that we cannot have. We need all our warriors, Jess. Do not be fooled. Do not be a fool.'

'And *Peter?*'

Stefan raised his glass as if to toast him. A yellow ring had settled at the bottom. He tipped it back, waiting for the trickle. 'Such a nice man. But I might say, he had a tendency to be *too* nice.'

Stefan had used the past tense. Peter sounded over and done with, sent to history as well as Laos. 'Is *that* why? Because he's nice? What's wrong with being nice?'

'There's nothing *wrong* with being nice. It can be most *useful* to be nice. But one must think to *whom*. And *when*. And *why*. Indiscriminate niceness is not only a waste, it is also dangerous. You give too much to the other side.'

'Like my mum.'

'Come now, Jess . . .'

'She just *likes* people. She doesn't ask all those questions.' My mum just gave her niceness to anyone who came her way.

Stefan paused. 'Eleanor is lovely, of course. But will lovely help us win? I do not think so. Is that her main contribution? No. Is that why we value her? No. It is her work. Her commitment. She never stops.'

'Who do you mean, *we*?'

'Really, Jess. I have been good enough to give you my time. I do not expect a grammar class. Sentence analysis. Also it is not helpful to make everything so personal. Faces do not sit well on principles. They look ugly. Like heads on spikes.' Stefan signalled for another beer. 'We are at war. And in war there are casualties. The careless go first. Then the trusting, the innocent, the nice.'

'And who's left?'

'The winners.' He didn't want to smile at that, but something like one broke out anyway. 'There is one choice only: you are with us or you are against us.'

'But it's too complicated for *that*.'

'It is so complicated there *is* only that. Us or them. It has shaped our entire century. It has deformed it, you might even say. But that is how it is. No escaping it.'

Then the waiter approached with the beer, and as he lowered

it onto the table, the light caught the shape of his face. The whole luggage of his life was laid out there – the folds, the bags, the knock of cheekbones. When he'd got out of the boat, empty-handed, had he written to his wife: *London is the noisiest city in the world*? Had he told her about the restless dogs, the crying children, the all-day wail of police cars? Did his letter ever arrive, or was his wife still waiting, and hoping every day for the post?

And then I felt Stefan's eyes on me. 'I see more and more that you are not like your mother. I see someone else to take account of.'

'And be nice to?'

'Sometimes. More often than most.'

'Is that meant as a compliment?'

'It is meant as a fact.'

'But why, Stefan? What *use* would that be? Why be nice to *me*?'

Stefan pushed his bowl aside to give himself more room. The waiter took it as his cue we'd finished and came over to clear the dishes. The soup was cold now, the meat and green leaves sunk, the surface marbled yellow. Neither of us had touched it.

'You seem unhappy, Jess. What would cheer you up? Some dessert?' He retrieved the menu from the bottles of sauce. 'How about an ice cream? Mango flavour. I know you like it.'

'Not any more.' It was what we'd had on Leninplatz the day Peter was sent away. I wondered if he'd gone off it too, if you could even get ice cream in Laos. Probably not. I thought babies who'd forgotten how to cry would never have learnt how to eat ice cream.

'What will it be? Mango or coconut?'

'Are *you* responsible, Stefan?'

'We are *all* responsible. For all our actions. Nothing we do is without consequences. We must simply try to intend them.'

By which he meant Peter for saying yes against the odds, for being sure even when it was all so unsure. He meant Martina for being Martina. He meant my mum for her innocence, and me for my doubt.

Stefan ordered mango ice cream. It was chemical yellow in a glass shaped like a trophy. He nudged it towards me, trying to make it mine. 'Oh, *Jess*,' tilting his face as if to coax a child, as if he couldn't take this sulk seriously. 'What would make you happy?' He put his forearms on the table. For a moment, I thought he would reach for my hands.

'Getting Peter back.'

He picked up the spoon, and watched me, holding it over the ice cream like a doctor with a surgical instrument about to make the first incision, the most important cut. 'I might be able to help, you know. Get a message to Peter at least.'

He waited for a reaction.

I refused to give him one.

'Or even a visit. I do not see why not.'

'But I want Peter home.' And I wanted to go back to where we'd all left off, as if none of this had happened.

'Very much harder, obviously. But in principle, there is no harm asking.'

'And who would have the answer?'

'The relevant authorities. An approach would have to be made.'

He'd used the passive and named no names.

'And, depending, of course . . .'

And that was the thing. On what? In exchange for what, exactly? And still the spoon hung there. The only thing I had to trade was Ivan's filing cabinets, and yesterday I'd forfeited the keys.

'*Ach!* The filing cabinets!' Stefan batted them aside as if they'd never held anything. I could have been bringing him comics. Then he cut into the ice cream. I watched how he turned the glass, taking from where it was softest. It was all so precise, so operational.

'How old are you, Jess? Sixteen? In a couple of years, you

will go to university. You will meet interesting people. Important people. Move in new circles.' I could tell he'd sketched it out already. He'd seen the summary of my future, held it in his hands, and read it as he read everything – fast, attentive, faintly pleased. 'What will you study? Russian? That was always on your plan. German?'

I needed air. It was too hot in here.

'Which university? Let me guess . . .'

'That's enough.'

The tone of my voice pulled him up. 'Of course, Jess, of course.' He sat back and smoothed his tie. 'Plenty of time.'

I stood up. My thighs hit the table. I struggled to get out, caught between the palm and the wall. Stefan dabbed his mouth with a napkin, then felt for his briefcase and rose to his feet. He tried to hurry without hurrying. The waiter saw us move. He picked Stefan's overcoat from the stand and held it open, then slipped it onto his shoulders. He brought the bill. Stefan didn't even read it. He fished a note from his wallet and told him to keep the change.

'Sorry, sir, too much . . .' The waiter tried to give the note back.

'Just *keep* it,' because I was already at the door.

When someone buys you dinner, usually you say, 'Thank you.' But the word refused to come. Sometimes, people say: it's been nice. A nice evening. Nice to chat. But none of that was true. I could have said: it's been a useful evening. Useful to spend time with you. Instead, I said, 'Stefan.' What I meant was: *so that was you*, Stefan.

He nodded. 'Jess.' Though, actually, it might have been a question. What he might have said was, 'Jess?'

I offered Stefan my hand.

He took it, but not firmly. He took it, but only just.

The waiter held open the door. I turned to him. I wanted to take his hand. Actually, I wanted to hug him. I wanted to do what my mum would have done: spill her guts. Tell him I

233

was sorry. Sorry for his left-behind wife. Sorry for the letters that didn't arrive. Sorry for the longing. Sorry for Vietnam. Very sorry for Dalston.

I stared at the waiter, hoping he could read my face.

He shuddered.

'Cold,' he said. It was November. It was night-time. The air was damp. He was on the Kingsland Road in a thin cotton shirt and shivering.

18

The Wait

Tamworth, 1981–3

On cold evenings, my mum toasted her shins on our gas fire, imagining British Gas gave out tropical heat. She'd pinned a map of Laos over the mantelpiece and liked to read out names, sounding like a kung fu film. Sometimes she just burbled to it: 'There's the Mekong, look, murmuring. That's Vientiane where the bells don't ring.' She knew Peter's letter off by heart and repeated phrases, always dreamily, as though it bore good news. On New Year's Eve 1981, at midnight Vientiane time, we set the compass for south-east, raised a glass of Rotkäppchen, and called out 'Happy New Year!', clinking glasses with a phantom Peter.

Then once – it must have been the next summer because my mum stood a long time in front of the fire and you couldn't do that if it was on – she turned away from the map and said to me, 'You know, I find it harder and harder to picture him.' Even though she had a picture of Peter right there on the mantelpiece, one taken at the summerhouse, in his shorts and apron, the time we first tasted Château Eden. She picked the photo up. 'Does he look faded to you? Is it too hot by the fire? Is it making the colours go?' On New Year's Eve 1982, my mum got out the Rotkäppchen, raised her glass generally east, and said 'Happy New Year' aloud, but not loudly – the way people do when they stand at a grave because they know the dead can hear them.

Every couple of months of that two-year wait, an invitation came for a meeting at Belgrave Square. It was on an embassy letterhead and always addressed to Eleanor and Jessica. Despite the Van Hoa, Stefan hadn't given up. Each time, my mum wondered if I was coming, and every time, I said, 'You know I'm not. And I don't want you two talking about me. *I'll* talk to Stefan if I want to talk about me.'

'I *know*.' Though in fact my mum had no idea at all. She put it down to teenage. In all this time, she'd put nothing down to teenage, and now, when it was nearly over, she blamed my 'm*ooooo*d'. She said, 'It's just not *yooooou*, Jess,' reduced to making farmyard sounds by a daughter she couldn't fathom.

So my mum went to the embassy alone, and when she came back, she always said, 'Stefan's such a nice man.'

'And did you mention me?'

'We talked politics.'

Which didn't answer the question. But whatever they talked about, my mum always returned from Belgrave Square 'primed, clear, ready for action'. Stefan encouraged her to stand for CND District Committee, which she got onto, then for National Committee, which she didn't. She dreaded telling Stefan she hadn't made it. But he didn't seem to mind. He said she'd put her name forward. That was the main thing. 'It gives me a measure of where we are at,' as if my mum were his plumb line – lower her overboard and see how far she sinks.

She and Stefan kept People-to-People going. They arranged exchanges CND-to-Friedensrat of handshakes, business cards and compliments – most of them unmeant. Their big event was Easter 1983 when my mum led a delegation to Berlin. There were to be mass protests against Reagan who'd just announced his plans for SDI. My mum was interviewed for *Neues Deutschland* and got a five-minute slot on GDR telly. Then on the last day of the trip, one of her group went AWOL. The only German speaker wanted 'spontaneous contact people to people' and got himself arrested. My mum went to identify him and signed his release form. She wrote an apology to the GDR state and an even longer one to Stefan. 'I was tempted to leave the bugger locked up,' she said. My mum had invited me on the trip. She said the Easter demo would be a chance to get my German back. I hadn't seen the GDR for nearly two years. 'A nice break. Free too.' But I didn't want to be a chorus-girl in a stage-show against Star Wars. I wanted to stay at home and watch the video. I hadn't seen it when it was on at the Palace, being too busy at the time and the film too anti-Sov.

And then, in the autumn of 1983, my mum came back from Belgrave Square with sweat rings under her arms and panting, which made me uneasy. Breathlessness in my mum always did that. She said she had news. Stefan was about to be posted to Washington. Routine rotation of embassy staff, he'd claimed. 'But it *can't* be. Stefan's on his way up. It's *America* . . .'

America had always been the place we'd never wanted to go to. The place we *couldn't* go to if we told the truth on the: 'Are you now, or have you ever been . . .?' form. It was the land of imperialist running dogs. But I supposed if you were a diplomat, it was the pinnacle of your career. There was nowhere to go after America. Just oblivion, or banking.

Stefan had said to my mum, 'Time for a change all round, perhaps.' He knew she wanted to live in the GDR and he'd heard of an opening at the Humboldt. They needed a part-time English teacher and the job would come with a Berlin flat. He'd said my mum had made a lifetime's contribution already, and now might be the moment to retire. 'But a bit early, isn't it?' she said to me. 'I'm not *that* old. I don't look that old, do I? I didn't know how to take it. What's your take, Jess?'

I thought Stefan had done with my mum and got whatever he'd wanted. That she probably wasn't much use to whoever replaced him, which was why she was free to go.

'Stefan said I was kind to everyone except myself. "Is it not time to be nice to *you*, Eleanor?"'

My mum took it as an instruction. She started a Nice-to-Self

TODO, a weekly ration of minor pleasures. On Saturdays, she was going to treat herself to a bag of fudge from the market; on Sundays, press Snooze when the alarm went off. She wanted to know what I thought.

I thought fudge wasn't the point. After the Van Hoa, I'd decided 'nice' was too short a word for the scope it had to cover. There weren't enough letters for all the complications. A bit like 'love'. Stefan had been right about niceness. It *was* all a matter of why, and of what you wanted in return. And there was my mum, ever willing, endlessly amenable. She couldn't stop being nice.

She didn't dare.

She needed too much to be liked.

That was the point.

Stefan was going to recognise my mum's outstanding services to the GDR with a certificate. It would be an honour, he said, to make it his last diplomatic act in the UK. My mum invited me to the awards ceremony at the embassy. By then I'd already moved to London. She said I was only down the road – it wouldn't take up too much of my time. But Stefan had been right about giving too much to the other side. All my mum would get for two years of indiscriminate niceness to him was a token piece of paper. And instead of applauding it, I lay under my duvet, reading *Will the Soviet Union Survive until 1984?*, while Frankie Goes to Hollywood clamoured from headphones, and my mum soaked up Stefan's compliments, then was clapped out of the room.

At the end of November, my mum did her last ever *Morning Star* sale. She went to the paper shop and cancelled the order. 'I don't agree with a word you say,' the newsagent told her, 'but I have to say you've kept on saying it. You haven't given up. I admire you for that.' Then my mum felt guilty. And unadmired. He saw her face. 'I can keep the order going if you like. If you pay me in advance.'

'But what about the papers?'

'Don't you worry about them. I'll put them in the bin for you.'

Then my mum composed a notice for the *Morning Star*, announcing her departure from England. She rang me up to check. 'I'm about to send it off. I'm saying that *I'm* leaving for the GDR. Just me. Is that right? You know you can always change your mind about London. I'm sure you'd get a place at the Humboldt. I've got connections there now.' There was a pause, a rustle of paper. 'I'm licking the envelope right now.' She spoke with her tongue stuck out. 'I'm sticking it down now. I'll stick it down now then, shall I?' My mum thumped the envelope shut.

Then she put a notice in the *Tamworth Herald*: *Eleanor Mitchell will shortly be leaving for the German Democratic Republic and wishes all her comrades and friends in Tamworth the very best in their struggle for peace and justice.*

Strictly speaking, 'all' her comrades should have read 'both'. There was only Mr and Mrs Bell left now, and their house full of cats. When Ivan found out she was going, he rang her up, just like last time, to ask what the hell was going on. He told her it was betrayal and acts like that killed the movement.

'I think you'll find, Ivan, the Tamworth branch is already dead. I'm merely unplugging the life-support machine.' And then she hung up.

Mr Howard cut the notice out of the *Herald* and came round with it in both hands. 'If it'll make you happy, Mrs Mitchell, it don't matter where it is.' He said there'd never been so much life in this little street since we moved in. Nor in this little town.

Rosie hugged my mum a very long time the day they said goodbye. 'I can't imagine you over there. I can't imagine over there.' She looked across my mum's shoulder to the space where the Laos map used to be. My mum had taken it down. According to Stefan, Peter was back now. He'd done his two years and was home. 'You know, I don't think I can come and visit you. Not behind the Iron Curtain.'

'It's not really an Iron Curtain. More a Veil of Misunderstanding.'

'Even so. Just. Come. Back. Soon.'

Then my mum packed up. She took Peter's photo out of its frame, slipped the picture into her diary and used it as a bookmark. She took the last red carnation out of the vase. All along, she'd kept up with the red carnations, but in the end, she'd stopped seeing them, the way you don't see the flower in cafés beside the menu and the salt. Where the map had hung, she papered the wall with TODOs. She made piles of stuff all over the floors. Then she rang me. She'd found the box with my GDR shrine, and what should she do with it? Which pile should it go in: Store, or Give to Oxfam? The Throw Away pile wasn't an option. And my Black Book. She'd found that under my bed. She'd hoovered under there. It was the first time since we'd moved into the house. There was enough dust under the bed to make another me, she said. My mum had started talking about cleaning, which meant she didn't want to put the phone down – anything to hear my voice. 'It's quiet without you, Jess.'

Which it might have been. But I think what she really meant was: it was quiet without the clocks. She'd taken those down too. She'd set them all to Berlin time. Then she'd changed her mind and set all three to noon and taken out the batteries. She said it was like taking the heartbeat out of the house.

Then my mum sold up and emigrated.

She defected to the GDR.

Without me.

The day she went – 'for *good*. For ever, Jess. This time, for *ever*' – she slipped an inch of string into my hand. It was her leaving token. We had one end each. She said no matter where I was, if I ever needed her, all I had to do was tug. She might be going away, but actually she was at the end of that piece of string. It was like tin-can telephones. This was my mum's make-believe version of that, her fairy-tale hotline to her daughter. Our actual hotline was a bad connection between her departmental office and the porter's lodge in my halls of residence. That first Christmas, 1983, the stand-in holiday porter spent his shifts smoking roll-ups in a party hat and efficiently fielding incoming calls provided you gave him a tip. Food would do. I offered him stollen. My mum had sent a tin – a drawing of Dresden on the lid, pre-bombing and under snow. The porter knew stollen because his father had been in the forces. He said it was the taste of Paderborn. And he'd been to Berlin a couple of times too, 'For the illegality and the parties . . .'

When my mum's call came through, the porter picked up. 'Good morning, Berlin. How's your hangover?' There was a pause. He turned his face to the desk and sighed through smoke. 'I said: "Handing you over",' and he gave me the phone.

'Jess? Is that Jess Mitchell?' She spoke with an echo.

'Hello, Mum.'

'Only I thought I had a crossed line. I thought a man was talking to me.'

'He was. But it's me now.'

'So I can speak, can I? Can I begin?'

'Merry Christmas, Mum.'

'Yes, Merry Christmas.' She didn't sound convinced. 'Only it doesn't sound like you.'

'How's life in the Evil Empire?'

She perked up at that. 'Oh, Jess, I'm having a *whale* of a time!' and she told me about the nice people in her department, and her nice students, and her nice neighbours, and how everything was . . .

I cut her off. 'And Peter?' I expected to hear what I heard every call: Still No News. He was officially back at the *Hochschule*, but no one had actually seen him. His office was locked and desk cleared. But this time my mum said, 'Actually, I had a visit. A welcome visit. My Head of Department. The *Hausmeister* for my flat. Some man I didn't know.' My mum was given a booklet.

241

The Dos and Don'ts for Foreigners in the GDR – roughly translated. There were notes at the back – personalised ones with phone, post and visiting regulations for family and friends.

'For *family*? There are rules for speaking to me? This phone call's allowed, is it? You're allowed to speak to your daughter, are you?'

My tone didn't make it down the echoey line. She took the question straight. '*We* can speak. Course we can!'

'And *Frohe Weihnachten* to whoever's listening in.'

My mum turned her head aside and repeated the greeting. Then she came back to the mouthpiece. 'Frau Pohl says Happy Christmas to you too.' Whoever she was.

'And Peter? What are the rules for him?'

'I'm not supposed to try and contact him. Or Martina. By any means at all.'

'But you *have*.'

But she hadn't. I didn't know what to say. I listened to the crackle and whoop of electronic silence.

'You there, Jess?'

I wanted to shout down the line: Just break the rules for once. Disobey. Displease someone. Risk being disliked, even.

My mum answered as if, across the silence, she'd heard every word. 'That's what *you* would do. But I'm not you. I'm a peacemaker. It's what I'm good at.' She sighed – deep and loud – filling the miles between us with the sound of surrender. 'And I don't mind. They need to know what's going on. I've got nothing to hide. I don't care what they know about who I know.' My mum paused. 'And with Peter it's something medical. He's not been well, apparently. No one's to disturb him.'

And then the line went dead.

19

Visiting Eleanor

East Berlin, December 1984

The Dos and Don'ts for Foreigners had capitalised the most important nouns. It said to leave 'ample Time for all Necessaries when seeking Permission for named Contact'. My mum applied in June for me to visit in December. The approval came through four months later and she sent me confirmation on an early Christmas card – a GDR one with 'peace' in all the languages known to the Socialist Bloc. 'May this card be the first of many, many, many!' she wrote. Which made me worry. My mum was already sounding breathless.

An East German Christmas had seemed quite do-able back in the summer. Now, as the S-Bahn coughed its way into Friedrichstraße station, it seemed like Day One of Seven. The train jerked to a stop and hands reached out for luggage – duffel bags, laundry bags, holdalls – insubstantial baggage, it seemed to me, for a journey from West to East, from one world to another. I was about to haul my rucksack onto my back when I saw that no one else had moved. All these people who'd done this before knew we weren't there yet. They stayed wedged together in their fat winter coats, their thick-soled boots pooling Berlin snow onto the floor. I looked at the row of puffy, puckered faces – balloons from a celebration long since gone. They breathed glazed-over thoughts onto the windows, where they turned to water and rilled onto the sill. Through the glass, damp posters for next summer's holiday and a hazy advert for international friendship.

Our train rolled the last few feet to the buffers of Berlin. The carriage doors clacked open. I heard gasps from the cooling train and the bark of voices that volleyed from the high curved roof: '*Aussteigen! Aussteigen!*' There was no '*bitte*'. We were ordered to get off. Soldiers kept watch as the train emptied, a rifle over a shoulder. Sniffer dogs ran their face along the carriages, gums pink and tongue steaming. No one seemed worried by the soldiers or the dogs, and no one was in any kind of hurry. A few young men hunched away from the crowd, pulling carrier bags from pockets and making for the Intershop. Men who looked just like them were standing on the other platform, their carrier bags so full they had to hug them or they'd break. They came to Friedrichstraße for the cut-price booze and fags. Everyone else wanted to cross the border.

I followed back-lit, grubby signs for *Einreise in die DDR*. I joined a queue for Citizens of Other States and stood nose to nape in the smell of wet sheep. I watched the other lines shorten. Citizens from West Berlin were processed so fast the line was an ongoing shuffle. Old women were nodded through, their shopping trolleys snagging on the closing door. It took a long time for Other Citizens to reach their booth. When I did, I found the border guard a foot higher than he should have been, installed behind his counter on some kind of plinth. He checked my photo then he checked me. It might just have been the angle, but I read it as disdain. I tried to disdain him back, which was hard looking upwards and when the reflection I saw in his glasses was flattened and green. He reached for something across his desk. I thought it would be the stamp, but his hand came back with a telephone. He made a call too short and muffled to hear. A colleague appeared. He showed him my documents. They talked about me as if I wasn't there. It all ended in grunts. Then the thud of approval and the buzz that unlocked the door. It was as heavy as they could make it. Citizens of Other States had to shoulder their way through to the other side.

I stepped into the GDR and onto the end of another queue. The line for the *Wechselstube* wound the length of the corridor. Sounds multiplied on the mustard tiles and concrete: the scuff of tired feet, the click of cigarette lighters, the swap of raking coughs. I skipped the exchange and found the sign for the exit.

And that was it.

I was through.

Two guards lounged feet from the final door, watching passengers with a lazy kind of interest. I walked straight past. Then I heard a voice: 'Come this way, please, Miss,' and wondered who else here spoke English. I thought how odd courtesy sounded when it came from a man with a gun. '*Bitte*, you, Miss,' louder this time. Then I felt a hand on my arm and before I could react, I was shown through a door that was already open, and the door clicked shut.

Two officials stood behind a table. I didn't know what they were: police, soldiers, border guards, customs – I couldn't tell one uniform from another. There was nothing else in the room, just two men and a table, which meant there'd be questions, but probably not many if there weren't any chairs. 'Where is your passport?' one of them said in English.

I reached into my jeans. He tested the cover with a nail and ran the thickness of the paper through his fingertips. He held the photo up to eye-level, scanning the flatness of the page.

'You did not change money. You have Ostmarks?'

I fiddled in a rucksack pocket.

He counted them onto the table. Four blue 100-Mark notes: Karl Marx, Karl Marx, Karl Marx and Karl Marx.

I dug about in my wallet. There. One Friedrich Engels. One Clara Zetkin.

'Where did you get them?'

They were left over from last time, three years ago, the summer of 1981 – the time Peter was sent away. Usually, we spent as much as we could in the Delikat and Meissen shops and gave leftover cash to solidarity at the border. But I didn't want souvenirs of that particular summer, and the last thing I would have done, in the circumstances, was give any more to solidarity.

'This is unauthorised money. It is not permitted to export the currency of the German Democratic Republic. This money is illegal.'

The word 'illegal' worried me.

But that was all he had to say. He gave up on money and moved on to my luggage. He pulled on white cotton gloves, opened my bag and drew out the contents. He reached right to the bottom till he was up to his shoulder in rucksack. There I was, dissected on that shiny Formica top: Jess Mitchell, student, age nineteen. He went through every item, flipping it one way and flipping it back. He shook out the clothing. He probably thought all that black meant something – anarchism, mourning or Art. He held books by the spine, fanning through the pages, letting strips of paper drift to the floor. He tried to read the titles and mangled the sounds: *The Savage Mind, Coming of Age in Samoa, The Elementary Structures of Kinship*. He removed the dust jackets and compared the titles. He turned the books sideways and squinted at my scribbled notes. Then he unzipped my washbag and placed the soap under his nose. He unscrewed the toothpaste, pressed a sample onto a strip of card and spread it with a spatula. He lost interest in my washbag when he got to the tampons. Then he held up the parcels wrapped in Santa Claus paper.

'What is that?'

'Presents.'

'What presents?'

'Christmas presents.'

But then he knew that. He took them in his white-gloved palms and toyed with them like a magician who'd just conjured them up. Then he opened the door and disappeared.

I waited in the smell of mint and lemon zest for my presents to come back. I glanced at his colleague who I'd almost overlooked – being silent, motionless and his shirt the colour of the wall. I wanted to say: I know I'm down in your files as Dodgy and Antisocial, but my mum got permission for this visit. For one week, I'm state-approved.

But he could feel my protest coming on, and when I opened my mouth, he stopped me with: '*Ich spreche kein Englisch.*'

So I began again in German and he interrupted in German: '*Auch kein Deutsch.*'

And that was that.

So we waited. From next door came the sounds of another interview, sieved through the porous wall. They were more vocal in there, snapping back and forth about the wrong kind of money, or the wrong luggage, or being the wrong kind of person – whatever the problem was. After a while, my guard had heard enough. He covered it up with the sound of fingers on his bunch of keys, beating time in his pocket: TAP-tap-tap-tap, TAP-tap-tap-tap. In my head, Number One in the charts – Band Aid's 'Do They Know It's Christmas?'.

Finally, his colleague came back. He delivered my presents into my hands, gifting them to me. They were still wrapped, the sticky tape intact. They'd come back ever so slightly warmed. I felt grateful just to have them. Which was probably what he wanted. I had to bite my tongue to stop myself from thanking him.

I walked into an ice-cold block of air. A crowd jostled at the barrier for a view of this new face. Then I heard: 'As we come marching, marching, in the beauty of the day . . .' I hadn't heard that song in ages. It was 'Bread and Roses'. My mum was singing again. And she'd brought roses with her, two big bunches of them. She leant right over the barrier and did maracas at me, shaking so hard the petals fell.

As we walked to the tram stop, my mum gabbled about how wonderful this Christmas was going to be. 'We'll have *Schaumwein* in the Palast der Republik and toast Us. *Us*, Jess!' She put an arm round me and squeezed Us together. I looked at my mum for the first time in over a year and saw a familiar stranger. And she was, now I looked again, stranger than I'd expected: East European already, with that astrakhan coat and those ruddy cheeks, like a woman raised from birth on thin borscht and firm belief. 'And we'll see *Mutter Courage*. And you know what Brecht said about love and war . . .' Which I didn't, but my mum did, and in German too. 'And I'll take you to the *Kantine* of the Berliner Ensemble. Round the back. Cheap, but so delicious. You wouldn't believe.'

I couldn't believe how quickly my mum had forgotten English.

'And the journey OK? And *alles* OK at the border?'

I wasn't going to tell her the details. It would have started a discussion. She'd have wanted to explain *why* they had to do that, why, in the circumstances, it was all perfectly reasonable.

'And S not U to Friedrichstraße?' She approved of that. There was something wrong, she said, about crossing the border in a tunnel, entering the GDR through its guts, then sliding out again. Which made it sound like defecation. 'And how is *drüben*?'

'They spray graffiti on their side of the wall.'

'You *saw* it?'

'I saw the postcards at the airport.'

My mum was appalled. 'They can't do *that*. It's a national border.' Though it wasn't on their side. Over there, it was a blank canvas, an open invitation. 'What *else* do they do over there?'

'Hard to say. The train windows were steamed up.'

'But general impression.'

'Cold. Snowy. Bit like over here.'

My mum tinkered with the key to her *Haus* with an ear to the mechanism as if trying to break in. She leant against the door, bending the footplate with her boot, and apologised. 'Fairy stories are never easy to get into . . .' But she had the knack. The lock gave and the door heaved open on hinges the size of a hand. In the darkness, she dabbed fingertips against the wall, then high in the vaulted ceiling a broken chandelier scattered into life: headless cherubs, alabaster peacocks, a rococo mirror reflecting its own rust. On the marble floor, pools of snow-water formed a chain of glinting lakes.

My mum paused at the rack of rusting mailboxes. 'These are my neighbours.' Each one had been prised open at some point and hammered back into place. She recited her Season's Greetings Scores – only five last year, but fifty this – measuring how liked she was in Christmas cards. She took out her key and checked the mailbox again, always did, she said, just in case. 'That's nice, look. You've got one,' and she handed me an envelope.

'Who knows I'm here?'

'Everyone does. The Department. The *Haus*. I've told everyone.'

I turned the envelope over: brown, typed, taped shut. It didn't look like a Christmas card. I tried to read the postmark, and through the smudge thought it might say Marzahn.

My mum led me upstairs, issuing a roll-call of her *Haus*, floor by floor, *Links*, *Mitte*, *Rechts*. She knew everything about her neighbours: births, marriages, deaths, gluts, shortages, swaps of this for that. Which was not surprising, because on every door, whole conversations in drawing-pinned notes. My mum paused to catch up on other people's news.

'Now *this* . . .' and she pointed to a corner cupboard and made sure I paid attention to the drum roll in her voice. '. . . is the *Prunkstück*! Our toilet!' She opened the door and flicked on the light. A bare bulb glowed weakly over rolls of grey toilet paper threaded onto string. A stash of *Neues Deutschland* on the cistern. Bottles of chemical hazard and cloths crisp with the cold. Through the wall, someone was singing 'The Song of the Volga Boatmen'. It was Rolf, my mum said, who wrestled for the GDR. She watered his plants when he was off felling men for his country. 'Actually, you've got a Christmas present from him.'

'But we've never met. He has no idea who I am.'

'You're my daughter.'

Which was the worst possible reason for giving me a present. My mum saw my face, but didn't comment. But I knew what was going through her head: it's what people are like here. They're kind. They give each other things. All the time.

'We share *everything*.' She showed me the cleaning rota on the back of the door. My mum adored this loo, I could tell. There was no private property in this toilet. There was no privacy. And she loved scrubbing at her neighbours' traces. It meant there was little they didn't know about each other. She took a deep breath, drinking in bleach and damp and intimacy.

My mum threw open her front door. The draught caught the Christmas cards that criss-crossed her ceiling, flags that fluttered every time she came home. She led me into the brown-coal smell of the summer course. Her heating stove was the size of our old political cabinet and tiled in the same colour too, only you shovelled in grit instead of minutes. In German, it was called a *Kachelofen*, my mum said – easy to remember because it sounded like 'cackle often'. That made her almost as happy as the toilet. Then she disappeared. I fell back into the sofa and let my eyes slide over a room of second-hand homeliness. It looked put together from donations made a decade ago: an orange lamp, brown table, beige armchair, brown-and-orange rug, beige-and-orange sofa. My mum called from the kitchen as if she'd read my thoughts: 'Didn't have to buy a thing! The Department had it all set up for me.' Even down to the display cabinet with its goblets and tankards – mementoes of other people's achievements and memberships – which she could share now, which just by the fact of living here were more or less hers.

Her own *Urkunde* hung on the wall. It was gilt-edged and embossed with the emblem of the GDR. But the clerk at the embassy had been unsure of the foreign name and it'd come out in a primary-school kind of hand. From here, it could have been a certificate for winning the three-legged race:

For special achievements and invaluable co-operation
in the areas of peace and education
the Embassy of the German Democratic Republic
in London
confers upon

Eleanor Mitchell

THE BADGE OF HONOUR

Beside it hung a gilt-framed photo of the awards ceremony. There was Stefan, his eyes red this time, caught by the flash. He looked into the camera and took possession of the picture, as if the occasion were all about him.

And next to that, a black-framed photo of James − black because he'd died this summer. His heart had given out while he was face down on a nudist beach, his long-wave radio broadcasting cricket into an ear that at some point had stopped hearing. Everyone thought he was snoozing till the sun went down and still he hadn't moved. He died nose in the sand, his body turning red as it hardened, while all around him, naked East Germans played volleyball and grilled pepper steaks.

'Such a shame,' my mum had said when she told me the news. 'He only saw five years of the GDR. And such a good soul too.'

I wondered if it was his wife's cakes that had done for him. Angela was, apparently, heartbroken. When finally she was able to talk about it, 'I suppose that is the way the cookie crumbles,' she'd said. Which was the trouble with idioms.

Along a shelf, my mum's display of postcards. The Soviet leaders were there − all solemnity, medals and seasick green − and dead, dead, dead and nearly dead. But most of her postcards were from me. Apparently, *The Dos and Don'ts* were letting my cards through. I was keeping a check, working my way through the National Gallery: Avercamp, Botticelli, Caravaggio, Degas . . .

I wrote to my mum, metaphorically, about the weather. Though quite often I wrote literally about the weather because it was a way of filling a card without talking about anything else. Which was fine. For both of us. The main thing was, postcards arrived from England, which meant I hadn't abandoned her. I hadn't given up.

Her old Coronet electric sat on the table, paper in the carriage. My mum was partway through a handout for the English Club. She'd already introduced the Humboldt to Burns' Night and Strip the Willow, to cream teas and tiddlywinks. This was a Christmas carol. She was going to teach them 'In the Bleak Midwinter'.

Out of the window, small, hard flakes blew at a horizontal in a snow-globe kind of glitter. I thought how strange it was that every single one of those flakes was different. I was going to say it to my mum, but I knew she'd just pull a face. She wouldn't believe it. She'd say *not* every single flake falling past that window. *Not* every flake that's ever fallen on Berlin, or fallen in the entire history of snow. She'd say there weren't enough ways of being a snowflake. Not enough angles in maths. That some scientist had made that up. A scientist in the wrong job, who should have been a poet.

On the other side of the street, the houses were still unlit. I forgot, with these winter dusks, how early it was – only mid-afternoon – and no one was home from work. I looked at the sooty, sulky, beat-up tenement blocks, regiments of faces unchanged since the war. I always said everything was too black and white. There was never any room for shades of grey. And here on this failing December afternoon, there were only shades of grey.

I wanted to laugh.

I wanted to cackle.

I thought I might repeat it to my mum. But I knew what'd happen. The laugh would dry on her lips, she'd fall quiet for a while – for hours, till tomorrow even – and then her response would come bursting out: 'It's not true! And you *know* it. It's Just. Not. True.' And she'd throw open her wardrobe full of GDR clothes and her kitchen cupboards full of GDR packets and say: 'There. Colour. Colour. Colour!'

And she'd be right about that.

Now I heard my mum's voice from the kitchen. She'd left the door ajar. If I let my ears wander, the words dissolved and she sounded like a household appliance, a washing machine that churned in a corner. I caught odd phrases through the warming kettle about the miners' strike, Greenham, Gorbachev. '. . . much of the visit?'

'Can't hear you.'

'. . . like the look of him.'

'Pork pie hat.'

Margaret Thatcher liked Mr Gorbachev too. She said they could do business together. Whatever that meant. But my mum didn't know that yet. Her *Morning Stars* were delivered two weeks late. *Neues Deutschland* was barely covering the trip. And my mum had no telly to tune in to West German news.

'How's it going? What kind of reception?'

'No good. Can't hear.'

And then she gave up.

My mum slid in with the tea. She'd changed into slippers. They were bored with holes from her trigger toes. She wore a housecoat, a blue nylon one with pink-and-brown roses and bows tied at the waist. She didn't introduce it, which meant she'd had it long enough to forget it looked peculiar. She offered me *Lebkuchen* and a cup of tea, acid-brown and mother-of-pearled because she'd chatted too long in the kitchen.

My mum balanced on the edge of the sofa. Behind her head, the photo of me. She'd asked for one as a birthday present, 'But one that looks like the you I *know*.' The photo I'd sent was not an easy picture, but a truthful one. Viewed from here, my mum's face and mine hung side by side, both expressions wistful, watchful, hopeful, on the brink of being hurt. She reached into her housecoat pocket and pulled out her end of our hotline. She held it up. I think she was hoping I'd reach into a pocket for mine. And then she sighed, blowing her breath across the gap between us. It was a sound I took to mean that life was a gust away from perfect. The only thing that was missing now was me.

Me. Not Peter.

I looked at the portraits of the men she'd chosen for company: Lenin, Brezhnev, Andropov, Chernenko, James, Stefan. I said, 'Is the picture of Peter in your bedroom?'

My mum shook her head.

'Not still in your diary?'

'I put him away, Jess.'

It was an odd phrase. 'Put away' made me think of jail. It made me think of 'childish things'. I said, 'And Martina?'

She shrugged. 'It's hard when parents get ill. Especially if you like them. And I half-heard – because it was only a rumour – that Martina got herself pregnant.'

'For a flat?'

'For a baby. And I heard she didn't get into the Humboldt. I think she's taken things badly. Personally, I mean.'

Under us, a door slammed, loud enough to feel in the floor-boards. A light went on. It cast a glow up to the window, to the black trace of a creeper that next summer, somehow, would find a way back to life.

'Only I was thinking of looking her up.'

'You know I'm not supposed to have contact, Jess. And I don't want to . . .' But she didn't finish the thought. 'And we've only got a week, and there's all of Christmas, and . . .' She motioned to the Advent candles, which should have been lit but weren't for Health and Safety. And to the Christmas tree – now that she was in the GDR, a normal, apolitical tree with baubles and chocolates. 'And with Peter, it's like I told you. No one's to disturb him. He got ill in Laos with something serious. Something contagious.' She shuffled her teacup in the saucer till it found the lip. It was odd, that clear ring of china – the note of formality, the sound that filled front rooms in the wake of bad news.

My mum hadn't seen Peter for over three years. Longer than she'd known him. Long enough to wonder if it'd really ever happened.

'I put him away because I'd lost him.' My mum nodded towards her *Urkunde*. 'When he gave it to me, Stefan said, "I am sorry for your loss." I didn't know what he meant at first. But the more I thought about it, the more I was sure he meant Peter, didn't he? "I am sorry for your loss." As if he'd died.'

My mum turned her face to her cup, and spent a while taking a sip. But she came back brightened. 'But I'm all right, Jess. I'm not alone.' She raised her cup to toast me, and then she toasted the invisible company that filled her room. There she was on the brink of her sofa, sipping lukewarm tea in a nylon housecoat, friends with her neighbours, her colleagues, the entire Socialist Bloc, and I remembered what it was like to love her for things like that.

Then my mum sighed, a different one from earlier, a last breath before going under, a long, slow emptying of the chest. It made the roses on her housecoat flutter.

'What *is* that thing you're wearing?'

'What, *this*?' and she fingered an inch of it. 'Mrs Jacobi's. Second floor, *Mitte*. Died a couple of years ago.'

Here we were, just the two of us. Me in my late-teenage mourning, my mum in her late East German neighbour's housecoat, in the middle of Berlin, in the middle of winter, at who-knew-where in this long Cold War.

★

The letter for me in my mum's postbox was from Martina:

Welcome to Berlin. Welcome to our winter. I hope you are wearing enough. I heard word-of-mouth that you come this Christmas and I wanted you to know that although I disappeared, I am not gone.

They did not allow me into the Humboldt to study English. They said I could take Russian, but anyway I got pregnant even before my Abitur. And how could I learn Russian and motherhood? So instead I study survival. How to make life – which, Jess, I tell you is easy, too easy when what you make can be so hard.

My baby was called Peter, of course, until my father came back. After that, she was called Petra. She is two now. We live in Marzahn (did I not tell you?) at the top of a tower block. She can name all the birds. She is nearer to the birds than the other children. Here on the twenty-first floor, we are almost flying. I got your postcard, thankyou. I keep it as a reminder: I am a mother who does nothing for the motherland.

My father came back sick from Laos. He got the plague and he very nearly died. His health has never been the same after. His colour is all wrong. He got back his job at the Hochschule, but he was at the same time retired – the way things are done here. He could stay on in our old flat, but he is never there. So my father also studies survival.

I have not given you my address. Please do not try to find it out. And even if you do, please do not write, never visit. Everything is noted. This letter will have been read by more than just you and me. Do not bring us the war. We are above it. We are peaceful here.

★

On the summerhouse patio, the marigolds were rounded with snow like giant tubs of ice cream. Martina's trench in the middle of the lawn had been levelled by the weather. No lights were on, and I knew I'd get no answer, but still I reached a fist to the door and knocked. I went to the window. Icicles had made a jaw of the sill. I breathed warmth on the ice-flowers and brushed away the melt. I could make out the sunlounger, folded; a sleeping bag, hanging; empty bottles of Château Eden skittled in the sink.

I followed the track down the side of the house and headed towards the lake. I found the glade where Martina had told me she didn't tell me the bad news, where she'd let Schwielowsee sand run between her fingers, where she'd vanished into the water, when it was still water. Now it was bright with ice. Trees that had drunk here in the summer were trapped until the thaw. Locked in the lake, red leaves from the autumn and last-gasp bubbles from the moment winter came. I reached out a boot and scraped snow from the edge. Vertical faces hung like veils far across the ice.

It was even colder out here than in the city, so cold my eyes smarted, the tears freezing as they formed. I'd borrowed winter clothes from my mum: an army coat, leather boots, her Russian soldier's hat. The scarf across my mouth warmed me on my own breath. It was scented with peaches, which I didn't mind at first, but then I thought it was the smell of old ladies, and I wondered if this scarf too had come from Mrs Jacobi. I walked to keep warm, but the snow was deep, the surface untouched, each step an effort. Sounds were over-sharp: the rasp of sleeves, my breath in the scarf. But sharpest was the last conversation I'd had with Stefan. I replayed it over and over. We were in the Van Hoa, the ice-cream chalice between us, and I'd asked myself, *depending on what? In exchange for what, exactly?* At that point, Peter had only just arrived in Laos. I thought: if only I'd seen Peter's face across the table . . . If it hadn't been so hot in there . . . If I'd taken the spoon and eaten . . .

My teeth broke into chatter. I pulled air through my nostrils and felt the pinch in the corner of my eyes. I squeezed them shut, and when I opened them, there it was: the white cusp of their sailing boat. A figure sat in the cabin, a silhouette pressed back in the seat. I knew it was him. I knew that shape. I recognised that amount of man. And I knew it was Peter because after all that had happened, this was exactly where he would be: on a boat going nowhere, arrested by the water, frozen into the heart of the lake.

Nothing we do is without consequences. We must simply try to intend them. I placed a foot on the ice, leant forward, added weight, and the ice held. I did it again. And still it held. It was snowing in flakes too light to fall. The stir of the air lifted them across the lake. I wanted to lose my weight and be taken with them. Instead, I took another step. The lake gave. Fault lines shattered the surface and fired across the ice.

'Peter!'

He turned to where the shot had come from and held up a face too far and dark to read. He moved slowly, unsurprised, as if he'd waited all along for this moment, for someone to catch up with him – even here – for this figure of defeat, this soldier from a distant war.

Acknowledgements

Motherland is a collective effort, born of the generosity of many people. My first thanks are to my mother, Isobel McMillan, for giving me the story and for trusting my intentions throughout the writing of the book. None of this would have been possible without Guy Batey, the kindest of men and my partner in all that matters. From the first mention in the Coach and Horses to the Rotkäppchen toast in Kohlenquelle, he never doubted this was a story worth telling and that I could tell it. I dedicate this book, with love, to him.

A very special thank you to Sophie Lambert, life-changer and agent extraordinaire who, when Jess and Eleanor turned up unannounced, decided to say 'yes'. Many thanks too to Jake Smith-Bosanquet for taking *Motherland* home to Germany, and to everyone at Conville & Walsh for their fantastic support. I'm very lucky to have the backing of Roland Philipps, Becky Walsh and Rosie Gailer at John Murray. My thanks to them and the whole team for the energy, enthusiasm and expertise that brought this book into being. A big thank you too to Andrew Wille and the Writers' Workshop whose advice turned a promising manuscript in the present tense into a publishable one in the past.

Motherland would not have been written without the generous support of Arts Council England and the National Lottery, whose Grants for the Arts individual literature award funded my initial research. The quote from John Brunner's song 'The H-Bomb's Thunder' is reproduced by kind permission of the Brunner estate. I would like to thank Progress Publishers, Moscow, for the extract from the English translation of Ostrovsky's *How the Steel was Tempered*. I am also grateful for the lines from 'To Those Born Later', originally published in German in 1939 as '*An die Nachgeborenen*'. Copyright 1939, © 1961 by Bertolt-Brecht-Erben/Suhrkamp Verlag, from *Collected Poems of Bertolt Brecht* by Bertolt Brecht, translated by Thomas Mark Kuhn and David J. Constantine. Used by permission of Liveright Publishing Corporation.

Some years ago, I was one of the Mary Ward travel writers. Many thanks to Jon Lorie and everyone in the group for a sense of place and for early encouragement – especially Nick Pretzlik, who believed till the day he suddenly died, and is still missed.

In Berlin, a big thank you to the Wildangel gang for the warmest welcome, in particular to Steffen Wagner, *Edelfeder* and first port of call on matters linguistic. I'd also like to thank Frauke Krahnert for Eleanor's flat, and the *Kantine* of the BVVG and the real Van Hoa for fuelling the writing of this book.

My dearest thanks to Professor Delia Davin. When my first life had come to an end and I was stranded in China, she made a decision that brought me back to England and allowed me to start again. I am forever indebted to Nan Capper who – though she never knew it – afforded me the time to write. She breathes in every line.

Motherland is many people's story. My thanks to everyone, living or dead, whose spectre haunts this book.